LONE WOLF

ISBN-13: 9781636960890
ISBN-10: 1636960898

Cover design by: Damonza
Printed in the United States of America

DAVID ARCHER

LONE WOLF

A NOAH WOLF THRILLER

RIGHT HOUSE

NOAH WOLF THRILLERS

"Throw me to the wolves and I'll return leading the pack ."

PROLOGUE

I n the course of protecting the security of a nation, governments must often make choices that are best kept away from public notice. Society being what it is, people want to believe that everyone has some innate good within them, and that when necessary, they will do the "right thing."

Those who choose public service, however, whether it be through law enforcement or political office, soon learn the truth: that even the finest examples of men and women are capable of horrific acts under the right circumstances, while the worst examples view those acts as nothing more than taking care of business. Such people are often beyond redemption, and in many cases they are far enough ahead of the rest of society that they avoid being detected, exposed and caught. While it may be obvious to some of us that they are evil, the vast majority of society never sees it, and so would never sanction the kind of action that is necessary to eliminate such evil.

For this reason, such actions are carried out by shadows, people who do not exist as far as society is concerned. Every nation has had such people, including the supposedly civilized Western nations. Over the years, the United States of America has publicly denied the existence of assassins within the ranks of the CIA and FBI, which it can do because the Alphabet Soup Groups that are known to the American people honestly do not engage in such things, or at least, only when there is absolutely no other alternative at the moment when such action must be taken.

Instead, there is a special organization that is so secret that even most of the government knows nothing more about it than that it does exist, including some of those Alphabet Soup Groups. Whenever one of those organizations comes upon an individual whose departure from the world would leave it a notably better place, a request must be filed through a highly secure computer network. The request must include as much information about the person or persons to be eliminated as possible, an explanation in great detail as to why the requesting organization believes it necessary to resort to elimination, and a projection of the benefits to society if the request is granted.

That request will be delivered to a single person who has demonstrated a capacity for common sense and a willingness to accept responsibility. She alone will determine whether the request will be granted or denied, and if it is granted, she will assign the mission to eliminate the target or targets to one of several teams that work for her. These teams specialize in doing just that— eliminating those persons whose presence in the world can no longer be tolerated.

Her name is Allison Peterson, and she runs a nearly invisible department known as E & E, which stands for *Elimination and Eradication*. This department was established under a secret order from the president of the United States, and given absolute autonomy. Allison alone can grant or deny requests for elimination, and no one, not even the president, can order her to approve one.

The missions she assigns are carried out by teams that normally consist of only four people. One, the team leader, is the assassin. He or she is aided in missions by three support specialists: transportation, intelligence and muscle. Each team is named after something from mythology, which has led to her department getting the nickname of Neverland.

Noah Wolf is Allison's star pupil, recruited because of something that most people would consider a character flaw, but which she saw as potentially the greatest strength any assassin could have.

When he was only a child, Noah Foster was present when his father murdered his mother, and then committed suicide. Something inside the seven-year-old boy broke, and from that day on, he had been completely without emotion—or conscience—of any kind. He would probably have found himself in an institution not long after that tragedy, but for the help of a genius friend who he met in foster care. Her name was Molly, and she was one of those rare children with an IQ so high that it was almost impossible to measure. While she lived at the foster home with Noah and other children, she was taking high school and even some college classes in a special education program, and one of those classes was psychology. It didn't take her long to figure Noah out, and to realize that if he continued to act so differently from everyone else, he would soon find himself locked away.

Molly convinced him to use his own surprisingly

intelligent mind to study the actions and mannerisms of people around him, and mimic them in order to conceal his emotional state. She compared him to Mister Spock from *Star Trek*, the famous Vulcan, because Noah had instinctively turned to logic. He naturally examined all sides of any given situation before attempting to react to it, and by the time he was ten years old, he could arrive at a conclusion so quickly that his reactions seemed natural and brilliant.

As he grew older, he continued to mimic others, keeping his logical nature as secret as he could. He was considered an asset to any task he undertook, because he would simply examine the problem, decide what needed to be done and then do it. He was never selfish, never lazy and always willing to do whatever it took to ensure the success of any project he was involved in, for himself as well as for others who worked with him.

A combination of circumstances led him to join the Army when he was only seventeen, and he found it to be exactly the kind of environment he needed. The rules, structure and discipline fit perfectly into his concept of how the world should be, and he excelled as a soldier. He rose to the rank of Staff Sergeant, served three tours of duty in Afghanistan and Iraq, and had more than a dozen different commendations in his file.

None of that did him any good, however, when his platoon leader, Lieutenant Daniel Gibson, one day decided to engage in sport with some Iraqi civilian girls that the platoon had stumbled across on a patrol. The girls, of course, objected to being raped, and so he ordered them killed. Noah had been assigned to sniper cover that day, and was unaware of what was going on until he was called down from his position. Only one of the girls was still alive, and Gibson offered Noah the chance to take advantage of her before she met her own fate.

Noah assessed the situation, and concluded that his commanding officer had committed and condoned the rape and murder of Iraqi civilians, which could be considered an act of war against Iraq by forces of the United States. He refused to participate, and demanded the situation stop, but Lieutenant Gibson told him to shut up and then shot the one surviving girl through the head.

Noah's computer-like brain saw that the situation was completely out of control, and took what he considered to be logical action. He shot and killed his platoon leader, and then attempted to place the rest of the platoon under arrest. The other men fought, and he was forced to kill several of them before the remainder surrendered.

Unfortunately, when they returned to their base, it was his word against theirs. When it turned out that Lieutenant Gibson was the son of Congressman Gibson, the up-and-coming presidential hopeful, the political pressure came down from Washington and Noah was arrested for multiple counts of murder. He was railroaded through court-martial and sentenced to die.

That was where Allison found him, sitting on death row at Leavenworth. She visited him there in disguise, explaining that if he was willing to put his talents and abilities to work for her, she could arrange for him to have a second chance. Of course, it would mean never having any contact with anyone from his past, since the official story would include that he committed suicide in his prison cell.

Noah made the logical choice, and agreed. Days later, he was taken out of his cell in the middle of the night and transported to the department's training compound in Colorado. The morning news carried the story that the renegade soldier who had murdered the son of Congressman Gibson had killed himself in his cell. His unclaimed body was interred in the prison cemetery only two days later.

Noah Foster became Noah Wolf, and his training as a professional assassin began.

His codename was Camelot.

ONE

Nouakchott was the capital of the Northwest African nation of Mauritania, and its economic and political center. As such, it was also the center of international interest in the country, housing embassies and diplomatic missions from many other nations, including the United States of America.

The US Embassy there was one of the busiest in that entire part of the world, with constant meetings between the Ambassador, Dwight Henry Morgenstern, and the country's president, Mouhammed Bamba Habib, and Prime Minister, Saleh Ndiaye. A meeting with President Habib was scheduled for that particular morning, and Ambassador Morgenstern was in his office early, briefing the two men who would be accompanying him to the appointment.

"Mister Colson," he said, addressing the tall, blonde man, "I'm fully aware of the sensitivity of your mission, but you need to understand that I cannot be certain that President Habib will give you any information at all. While he may be the leader of a moderately powerful African nation, he's also a father, and I'm afraid he's putting the welfare of his daughter ahead of anything else at this moment."

Colson smiled. "I'm going to suggest, Mister Morgenstern, that you leave that to me. All I need you to do is get me in the room with him, and then leave us alone for a few moments. I've been provided with certain credentials that we believe will convince him to cooperate. Besides, my whole purpose in being here is to try to find out just what we can do to help. I can't do him any good if he doesn't give me something to work with. Once he understands that, I believe he'll jump at the chance to tell me whatever he knows, no matter how little it may be."

Morgenstern simply stared at the young man for a moment, then looked at the much taller, thin youth that accompanied him. "Mister Starling, I don't know that they'll let you in at all. President Habib has tightened security all around the palace, and one of the measures he's put into place is a limitation on how many people can be in his presence at any given time. You may be required to wait outside the office."

"Seriously? And I was so looking forward to meeting the man." He smiled charmingly. "That's not really a worry. I just go where they send me, and I sit and wait wherever I'm told to sit and wait."

Morgenstern turned back to Colson. "Then I guess we're as ready as we're going to be," he said. "Shall we, gentlemen?"

Colson and Starling got to their feet, and were joined a second later by Morgenstern. The ambassador led the way out of his office, down the elevator and out the front door, past a pair of Marine guards. A BMW limousine was waiting for them, and another Marine opened the rear door for them to enter. Morgenstern climbed in first, followed by Starling, who took one of the two jump seats in the front of the compartment. Colson slid into the rear seat to sit beside the ambassador.

The drive to the presidential palace took only a few minutes, but because the weather was so hot, walking was simply not feasible. The three men rode without talking, looking out the windows at the modern structures that rolled by. The city, which had originally been built to house only fifteen thousand people, had experienced phenomenal growth due to droughts that had caused millions of native nomads to forsake their traditional lifestyles and pitch their tents in urban areas. Over only a couple of decades, the vast majority of those tents had been replaced by modern brick and concrete buildings, though there were still areas with tents, shanty-towns that were occupied by people who lived far below any reasonable poverty level.

The chauffeur pulled the car up to the diplomatic entrance of the palace, and immediately got out to open the driver side rear door. The men followed the same order in exiting the vehicle that they had used in entering it, and were immediately ushered inside by palace security officers.

Once inside, the three of them walked through the same type of security scanners used at many airports, devices that use backscatter radiation to show an x-ray-like image on a monitor. A technician watched the monitor for any sign of weapons or bombs. Mister Starling's computer was thoroughly examined, as well, subjected to x-rays to be certain that it did not contain a weapon or explosive device.

"*Ils sont propres,*" said the technician. Because Mauritania was formerly under French dominion, it was a common language in the country, although the official

9

language was modern Arabic.

"Ambassador Morgenstern," said a young man who waited just past the security station. "I have temporary credentials for your associates, if you would follow me?"

Without waiting, the young man walked away. Morgenstern, Colson and Starling followed him through a hallway and to an elevator. Before they could enter, the young man turned and handed Colson and Starling each a lanyard with a temporary pass, motioning for them to put them around their necks. Both of the men did so, and then their escort pushed the button to open the elevator.

"I apologize for the security measures," the young man said. "The situation here is very tense at the moment, as I'm sure you can imagine."

"We understand completely, Mahmoud," Morgenstern said.

The man known as Colson took note that he was not introduced to the president's aide, but said nothing. He trusted the ambassador to know the correct protocols for the situation and assumed that there was a reason for this omission. The rest of the ride in the elevator was in silence, until the doors opened. Once again, Mahmoud, the president's aide, led the way down the long hallway and motioned for them to stop just outside an ornately carved door.

He stepped inside and closed the door behind him, but it opened again almost instantly. Mahmoud stepped out and motioned for all three men to enter. He pulled the door closed once again after them.

"Mister Morgenstern," said a young woman in perfect, London-accented English. Mauritania was less restrictive than many Muslim nations on the roles of women in business and government, though the standard of dress for women was still somewhat extreme. The president's secretary wore a long-sleeved dress that came to just above her ankles, and a scarf that covered her hair. Her face, however, was unveiled and visible. "The president is ready to receive you and your guest." She looked at the two men with him. "I'm afraid only one of you can go in with the ambassador."

The tall, skinny kid smiled. "That's not a problem," he said. "If you don't mind, I'll wait out here with you."

The woman smiled, and indicated a chair against one wall, next to a window. "Certainly," she said. "You may sit there."

"Thank you, I'll just sit over here and play games on my computer." He smiled at Colson and Morgenstern, then went to sit down in the chair, opening the small laptop that he was carrying with him.

Morgenstern hooked his head at Colson, then opened the door beside the secretary's desk. The two men passed through it, and then it closed behind them. The young man called Starling smiled and gave a finger wave to the secretary, then began paying attention to the screen on his computer. A moment later, the sounds of a video game could be heard. "Oops, sorry," he said. "I forgot to turn down the sound." A second later, the sounds were muted.

On the screen, the display showed what appeared to be the controls of a spaceship, with a couple of alien crewmembers visible at the edges of the screen. In the center of the screen was what looked like a view port, showing some sort of battle taking place with other ships, but Starling's eyes were focused on a smaller frame just below that one. Text that looked like it was written in an alien language was scrolling up, but this was a font of his own design, one that the tall young man could read as easily as any other. Tapping the keys silently as he watched the text scroll by, he was scanning all of the wireless networks in the building, and a moment later he found a vulnerability in the system that allowed him to log on. Suddenly, he had access to every computer in the presidential palace, and lists of files began appearing in that same, alien script.

"Aha!" Starling said in a loud whisper. "I have you now, Commander Zodo!"

The secretary glanced up at him, amused, and Starling looked sheepish. "Sorry," he said. "Sometimes I really get into the game."

"It's all right," she said. "I have a brother who is the same way." She returned her attention to her own computer.

Inside the office, President Habib rose from behind his desk and came forward to shake Morgenstern's hand. "Ambassador Morgenstern," he said, "I cannot tell you how much it means to me that your country is willing to help in this terrible situation." He released the ambassador's hand and extended his own to Colson.

"President Habib," Morgenstern said, "may I present Mister Alexander Colson. Mister Colson is one of my country's most trusted agents, and a specialist in the elimination of threats. He has been sent here specifically to try to locate and rescue your daughter, and make sure that those responsible are brought to justice."

Habib nodded. "Then let us sit, gentlemen, and discuss what must be done." He started walking toward the conference area, where several overstuffed chairs surrounded a low table.

"Mister President, would it be acceptable to you for us to discuss these matters alone? It is quite possible that Ambassador Morgenstern might overhear information that could leave him in a compromised position if it is ever necessary to deny my involvement."

Habib stopped and looked at both men, then nodded brusquely. "Ambassador, if you would excuse us?"

Morgenstern bowed his head for a split second. "Of course, Mister President." He turned and walked out the same door he had entered through.

Habib eyed Colson coolly. "A specialist in the elimination of threats," he repeated, a slight question mark in his voice. "May I speak frankly?"

Colson smiled as he shook the president's hand. "Please do, Mister President."

The president hesitated for only a second. "Mister Colson, the only justice that will suffice in this matter is if those responsible are removed from the world. Is that within the parameters of your mission?"

Colson inclined his head toward the president. "Mister President, that is specifically within the parameters of my mission. My orders are to locate and retrieve your daughter safely, and to destroy those who have threatened her and yourself."

Habib and Colson sat down in chairs facing one another, and the president motioned for the blonde man to continue.

Colson reached into an inside pocket of his jacket and withdrew a small leather case, then passed it without a word to President Habib, who opened it cautiously. The president's eyes scanned the cards inside the case, and his eyebrows lifted by a quarter inch. He closed the little folder and passed it back.

"That is an interesting proposition," Habib said. "And one that I am most willing to accept, if you can deliver on your country's promises."

Colson smiled. "At this point, Mister President, all I can tell you is that I will do everything in my power to find your daughter and get her home to you safely, and as you just saw, I'm authorized to commandeer any resources my country has to offer."

Habib licked his lips. "Ambassador Morgenstern tells me that if anyone can do this, it will be you. What do you need from me?"

"If you can tell me what you know about your daughter's disappearance, I can begin developing my plans. I understand that you only learned about the situation two weeks ago?"

Habib nodded again. "Yes. My daughter's name is Selah, and she is seventeen years old. She left our home two weeks ago, to go on a shopping holiday with some of her friends. She was to meet them at the Women's Bazaar, but did not arrive there when she was supposed to. I did not know this at the time, of course, but late that afternoon I received a telephone call. A man who had represented himself to the palace switchboard as an associate of the Syrian embassy informed me that my daughter had been taken as a hostage, and that in order to see her returned, I must convince the Prime Minister to enter into an alliance with the Russian and Syrian governments. Russia has been trying to entice us into this alliance for many years, but we have always been an ally of the United States. For this reason, we have consistently refused any cooperation with Russia, other than in the areas of trade. Now, suddenly, the Russian ambassador has informed me that I must either accept the alliance, or face what he terms to be dire consequences. He has made threats about economic sanctions, and possibly even military action against my country, but I do not believe that any of these threats are real. It is my opinion, after consulting with my advisers, that the only true threat I face is the one made against my daughter's life. The rest, I believe, only exist to suggest a public reason for our agreement to the alliance."

He fell silent, and Colson leaned forward. "Mister President, did the caller give you any information that might suggest where she is being held? Or anything that might indicate who is specifically behind this?"

Habib shrugged. "He told me that Selah has been taken out of the country, and that I can have her back in one of two ways: either intact and alive, or in pieces and dead. He also told me that I have only until our next summit meeting with Syria and Russia on the twenty-third day of this month to agree to the alliance. I asked him for a way to contact him, so that we might possibly negotiate, but he refused. He said the only way to contact him was by notifying Russia's ambassador of our agreement. If the alliance is not in place by the twenty-third, then I will begin receiving pieces of my daughter in the mail." He rubbed a hand across his eyes, and then looked at Colson again. "I have discussed the matter with the Prime Minister, and he is in agreement with me. If the situation is not resolved by the twenty-second, he will notify the Russian ambassador that we agree to their terms, and we will make a public announcement during the summit."

"The twenty-second?" Colson asked. "That only gives us sixteen days." He looked at the president for a moment. "Let's concentrate on the caller for a moment. Did he have a specific accent?"

Habib nodded. "Yes, that was something I noticed. His accent seemed to be American, perhaps from the southern part of your country. He initially spoke to me in Arabic, but his accent made him difficult to understand. I suggested French, but he changed to English. That made his accent even more identifiable."

Colson steepled his fingers at his chin, his eyes half closed in thought. "Interesting," he said. "Of course, it could be a ruse, an attempt to throw you off, but there are certainly a lot of Americans involved in international crime, espionage and such." He opened his eyes and looked at the president again. "Were there any background noises, any sounds you could hear through the phone that stuck in your memory?"

Habib leaned back in the chair and closed his own eyes as he thought about his answer. "There was a roaring sound in the background, not close, but some distance away. It got louder at times, then seemed to fade away before it came back again." He held up a hand to indicate that Colson should wait, that there was more. "There was also someone speaking not far from the caller, someone standing nearby. I could not make out exactly what he was saying, but I caught a few words that I'm sure were in English. I would say that his accent seemed to be British, or perhaps Welsh." He opened his eyes and looked at Colson. "That is all I can remember."

"That's excellent, Mister President. The second person you mentioned, the one who was speaking in the background, did it sound like he was speaking to the caller?"

"No, no, I don't think he had anything to do with the

caller. He seemed to be speaking to someone else, perhaps a child. There was a scolding tone to his voice."

"How did the caller convince you that he was telling the truth? That he really had your daughter?"

Habib let his eyes fall to the floor, and when he spoke, it was softly. "We are a Muslim people," he said. "As such, it is important to us that our women are modest. Unlike the women in your country, our women do not ever display certain parts of their bodies. For this reason, when the caller described to me in great detail a specific mark on Selah's skin, a birthmark on the back of her thigh that no one would ever see, I believed him to be telling me the truth."

"Have you heard anything more from the caller since then?"

Habib hesitated. "I—I have. I did not tell the ambassador, but someone has sent me emails, with photos of my daughter. They show her wearing what appears to be some sort of coverall, in a room with only a bed, a chair and a television."

"May I see the photos?" Colson asked.

Habib smiled, and reached into his own inner pocket. He withdrew a manila envelope and passed it to Colson. "I printed these to carry with me. You may have them. I can print myself more of them. Perhaps they will help."

Colson opened the envelope and looked through the fourteen photos inside. Selah was a pretty girl, with long, dark hair. She appeared to be upset in a few of the pictures, and seemed to be praying in others. Colson scanned them, but did not see anything specific that he considered a clue to where she was being held.

"Thank you, Mister President," he said, as he slipped the envelope into his own pocket. "Is there anything else you can tell me? Please, I don't mean to be pushy, but if my time is that limited, I need to get started."

Habib gave a sigh. "The caller did tell me that he was not an agent of the Russian government, but only an independent contractor who had been hired to secure our cooperation. He alluded to successes that he had in similar assignments in the past, but gave me no details." The man seemed defeated, and Colson reached across the intervening space to lay a hand on his arm.

"Mister President, I'm going to take this and put it to work." He reached into a pocket and produced a small card, which he passed to the president. "This is a special number that comes directly to me. If you call it, I will either answer or I will return your call within a short time. If you think of anything or learn anything that may help me to find your daughter, call me as soon as you can. The phone is scrambled, and cannot be tapped." He rose to his feet. "There is one other thing," he said. "I've been cautioned that there is absolutely no way for us to know who in your government might be involved in this or compromised in some way. I'm going to ask that what we have spoken of today remains between us. Our ambassador only knows that I was sent here to investigate this case from our end, but he will not know any details. I'd like you to keep your people completely in the dark about me, as well."

Habib nodded. "I understand. I will tell no one, not even the Prime Minister, unless your mission fails or I run out of time."

Noah extended a hand, and the president took it. "Thank you for taking the time to meet with me. I'll leave now and get started, and send word to Morgenstern when I have something to report. All he will do is suggest that you call his friend, which is me, of course. Do you understand?"

The president shook his hand, and Noah could see the tears that wanted to spill over. "Of course, yes. Thank you, Mister Colson, and may Allah go with you."

Colson walked out of the office, and found Morgenstern sitting next to the young man called Starling. The ambassador was carefully looking down at the floor, making certain that his eyes never touched the computer monitor on Starling's lap. When Colson appeared, he leapt to his feet.

Colson looked to Starling. "Hey, you ready to go? Pause your game, or whatever?"

Starling looked up and grinned. "Actually, I just won the game, so I'm ready whenever you are." He closed the laptop and unfolded himself from the chair.

"Everything go okay?" Morgenstern asked.

"Went great," Colson said. "I think we can make this work."

Morgenstern looked at him for a few seconds, then nodded and turned to walk out of the office. Colson and Starling followed, and they were met immediately by Mahmoud, who escorted them back out of the building, and was careful to reclaim the temporary IDs he had given to Colson and Starling.

Once the men were safely inside the limousine, the ambassador looked at Colson. "I'm actually very surprised that the president was willing to meet with you alone. That's quite unlike him."

Colson shook his head. "Not really," he said. "It might be out of character for President Habib, but it's not a bit unusual for Papa Habib. When we walked in together, we met the leader of the country. When you stepped out of the room, I met with a frightened, worried father. Unfortunately, that worried father is in a position to do serious damage to American relations with Africa, and if I can't allay his fears, he's going to. He and the Prime Minister have already agreed that if they don't have Selah back by the day before the deadline, they're going to give in."

Morgenstern let out a sigh. "If the Russian president gets a strong enough foothold in Mauritania, he'll sweep through the rest of Africa like the proverbial plague of locusts. Can you imagine what would happen if Russia gets control of all of the potential military power present on this continent?"

Colson shrugged. "I don't have to imagine it, that's for diplomats like you. All I've got to do is find the bastards who took this girl, and kill them."

Starling suddenly grinned. "And now we get into the real game," he said. "Just wait till I show you the pieces I managed to score while we were there."

Morgenstern rolled his eyes. "That's another thing," he said. "I can't believe you actually hacked into their computer network while you were visiting with the president of the country. Do you have any idea what would've happened to all of us if they had detected your little computer intrusion?"

"That's why I brought Neil—I mean, Starling. He's the best there is, and nobody detects what he's doing."

"Yeah," said the skinny kid. "I could've hacked them from the hotel, and they'd never have known. The trouble is that they have multiple Wi-Fi networks in that building, and some of them are about as close to hack-proof as you can get. Getting into them from outside would take forever, but every network has some sort of back door built into it, so that the IT people can get in even if some idiot manages to change the password and forget it. Back doors are hard to find, unless you're a true IT expert, like me. Once I found it, I just tried some of the most common IT passwords. These guys almost always use one of them, just in case something happens to them and another one has to take over. I went through half a dozen of them and got in. Then it was just a matter of copying the files from every computer on the network. Oh, and that included the president's computers, both the official one and the personal one that he probably keeps hidden somewhere in the office."

Colson nodded. "You can show me what you got after we get back to the hotel. I don't want to compromise Ambassador Morgenstern any more than we already have."

Morgenstern's eyes bulged. "Compromise me any more? Are you kidding? The stuff you got on that computer needs to be gone through by my intelligence people at the embassy."

Colson shook his head. "That's not within my orders," he said. "You can put in a request to my boss for a copy of it all, but I don't know if that will work."

Morgenstern, his eyes still bugged out, stared at him for a moment. "Colson, no one will even tell me who your boss is! Hell, I don't have a clue who you work for. How do I put in a request for a copy?"

Colson shrugged. "Okay, I see your point. I'll put the request in for you."

TWO

22 Hours Earlier

"Okay, here's what we've got," Donald Jefferson said. One of the senior executives of E & E, it was his job to be sure that each team leader was as prepared as possible for his or her missions, and this often included delivering the briefings himself. "President Habib of Mauritania has a daughter who has been kidnapped. Her name is Selah, and she is seventeen. That's a photo of her on the screen behind me. Apparently, the president was informed that if his country does not enter into an alliance with Russia, one that they've been resisting for a long time, his daughter will be dismembered and killed. Mr. Habib told our ambassador about the kidnapping a couple of days ago, who sent it up the line until our own president heard about it, and he dumped it in our laps. Your mission is to track down who took the girl, kill the sons of bitches and bring her back safely. Sounds fairly easy and straightforward, right? The problem is that we have absolutely no idea who took the girl or where she might be held. You're going to have to find her on your own."

The four people sitting there listening to him all

glanced at one another, but only the blonde-haired man spoke. "We talked about this," he said. "None of us have any actual investigative experience. I'm curious why we are being sent on this mission, rather than a team that's done this sort of thing before."

The woman sitting beside Jefferson leaned forward. "I'm sending you because you're the best we've got. Noah, this mission is so important that it has to be handled by someone who won't hesitate. That's you, as we all know. And while you may not have experience in investigations, you have a mind that works like a computer. I'm quite confident that if anyone can find this girl in time to save her life and save the day, it will be you."

Noah Wolf nodded, and stayed silent. After a moment, Jefferson began again.

"You're flying out tonight for Mauritania. Our embassy there has been briefed through diplomatic parcel on your arrival. I'll be giving each of you temporary identity kits, so as always, be sure you learn your names and don't mess up. The initial phase of the mission is two-fold: Noah, you'll meet with President Habib and question him about the situation. Try to get him to dig deep in his memory of the phone call that told him about his daughter. There might be something there that will help you figure out where to start." He turned to look at Neil Blessing, Team Camelot's computer expert. "Meanwhile, Neil can be working his way into the computers in the Presidential Palace. Somewhere in those computers should be a recording of that call, and you want to find it and listen to it."

"Oh, goody, something to keep me busy," Neil said. "I'm getting awfully bored with all the games I play, it'll be nice to have something fresh to work on."

"What about me?" asked a big man. In another setting, he might well have been mistaken for a professional football player. Moose Conway was Noah's backup muscle, always ready to jump into the fray with any kind of weapons, or just with his fists.

"In this initial phase," Jefferson said, "you'll just have to wait at the hotel, along with Ms. Child. It's highly doubtful the girl's being held right there in Mauritania, so we expect you'll be flying right back out. As soon as we know a destination, we'll make sure that everything you need will be waiting when you arrive there."

Sarah Child, who was Noah's driver and transportation expert, simply nodded and shrugged. "Works for me," she said. "Means I can sleep in."

Jefferson managed to suppress a smile, and then passed out the temporary IDs. The three men each received a small box, which contained a cell phone, a wristwatch and a wallet with driver's license, Social Security card, a number of photos, several folded and creased receipts—some of which were several months old—and lots of other wallet trash, as well as a passport with the same name. Sarah was given a purse, and she grinned as she looked through it. The wallet inside, like the ones the men had received, had ID, passport, photos and lots of flotsam and jetsam, but the other contents of the purse delighted her. She also received a cell phone, but instead of a watch she received a necklace with a heavy pendant. All of the makeup and other things inside were of brands that she liked. She glanced up at Allison, who smiled at her.

"Hey, Sarah, us girls gotta stick together, right?" Allison asked. "I told the Identities Department to be sure they checked your preferences before they put the purse together. No sense giving you stuff you don't want."

"Thanks! Some of the other stuff makes me break out."

"Okay, okay, let's get serious, people," Jefferson said. "The cell phones you received are satellite enabled, so you should never find yourself without signal. The watches and necklace contain GPS-satellite tracking devices, making it possible for us back here, and Neil in the field, to keep track of your whereabouts at all times. Each of the identities has a complete backstory, so if anyone checks them out, they'll hold up. To simplify things, each of your identities grew up in the same towns that you did, went to school where you did, and for those of you where it matters, followed the same work history that you did. That way, if you're challenged and have to provide details, you can."

"Okay, wait a minute," Neil said. "So you're saying that this Eric Starling character did everything I did? If you'll recall, I didn't even get to graduate from my own high school, because I was locked up in the Chicago Youth Authority. Did Starling hack into a bank and get caught, too?"

"No, he didn't, and we were going to explain this to you, anyway. Eric Starling went to work for the State Department right after graduating high school because he has some amazing skills at pattern recognition. He's a mathematical genius, which is what brought him onto government radar."

"I'm a mathematical genius, and the government never came after me for that," Neil said, his voice almost whining. "They waited until I got in trouble, let me suffer for months. Was that fair?"

"Grow up, Neil," Moose growled, but the smack he sent to the back of the kid's head was gentle and friendly. "Nobody wants to hear about your bad luck."

"All right, settle down," Allison said. "Noah, how do you plan to approach the situation?"

"I want to talk to President Habib, first off. Is there anyone else who knows any details about the girl's disappearance?"

"Ndiaye, the Prime Minister," Jefferson said. "We know that Habib has told him what's going on, and discussed it with him. As for anyone else, we have no idea. The security on this is so tight it's unbelievable."

"I can imagine," Noah said. "One of the most consistent things I've found in human nature is the determination of a parent to protect a child. What about the girl's mother?"

"She died four years ago, complications from what should've been a routine surgery. There was a nanny until the girl turned sixteen, but she's had a lot of free reign since then. The Habib family does have security from their version of the Secret Service, but it's not anywhere near as good as ours. Seems that she's been known to slip away from them quite often, and apparently she did on the day that she disappeared. She was supposed to be shopping with friends, but never made it to the mall."

"So, basically, we have no idea where she might have been when she was grabbed?"

"I'm afraid that's the case," Jefferson said. "Frustrating, but true."

"Then that tells me that the case has not received any publicity, or a thousand people would be screaming that they saw what happened. One or two of them would be telling the truth, which might've helped, but now we have no way of finding any witnesses."

Allison leaned forward, putting her elbows on her knees. "I warned you, this is a rough one. I hate to throw you into it, as fresh and new as you are, but you're the best shot we have at a mess like this. If Team Camelot can't do it, then I don't think anyone can."

"One thing did occur to me," said Jefferson. "We could give you an investigative specialist, just for this mission. He'd be under your command, but he may know what to do when you're confused or lost."

Noah stared at him for several seconds. "Who is it? Are we talking about somebody with experience in this type of case?"

"I'm not sure there has ever been a case like this before, or at least not one that was so important. This guy was FBI, just retired last year, but he's an old friend of mine and he's bored. I asked him point blank this morning, early, if he'd be willing to work with an E & E team on a mission of vital national security importance, and he didn't even hesitate before he said yes."

"He was FBI," Noah said, "and he's got a clearance high enough to know about us? How did that happen?"

"A couple of years back, he got dragged into something to do with Homeland Security, a case of potential terrorism here in the USA. It was necessary to tell him things that were classified at our level, and when he identified who the terrorists were, it was up to us to go in and take them out. It was all handled so quietly that the press never even got wind of it, which is the way the president wanted it. Anyway, it left Stanley with enough clearance to know about us, and he and I became good friends. He lives in Kirtland, and acts as a consultant for us at times. This is the first time we've ever considered using him on a team mission."

"I'll take him," Noah said. "He does understand that he has to follow my orders, right?"

Jefferson nodded. "He does." He took out a cell phone and dialed a number. "Stan? You still up for that field-work we talked about this morning? Then pack a bag and come on down to my office. My secretary will show you where I am. Really? Good, that will speed things up. See you soon." He looked at Noah. "He got so excited when I mentioned it this morning, that he's already packed and ready to go. He'll be here in fifteen minutes."

"Won't he need an ID kit?" Noah asked.

Jefferson grinned, reached into his jacket pocket and produced another wallet and passport. "Let's just say I was pretty confident that you'd both agree to it."

"I'd rather just say you're a cocky SOB," Allison said. "I don't know about the rest of you, but I'm ready for a coffee break. Anybody else?"

They all agreed, so Allison called for an aide to bring in coffee and doughnuts. They were all happily partaking of the treats when the new fifth member of their team arrived.

"Noah, Neil, Moose, Sarah, let me introduce you to Stanley Decker, retired from the FBI. Stan, this is Noah Wolf, Neil Blessing, Moose Conway and Sarah Child. Team Camelot."

Stan Decker was a tall, well-built black man who appeared to be in his late 50s. A quick once-over told Noah that he was a very confident man, and probably quite capable.

Decker extended a hand, and Noah took it. "Mister Decker," Noah said, "it's good to meet you. Mister Jefferson's told us a lot about you."

"Yeah, well, don't believe half of what he says. I can't leap tall buildings in a single bound, and I haven't quite managed to outrun a speeding bullet yet, though I have been known to try a couple of times."

Noah put a grin on his face. "That stuff wouldn't impress me all that much, anyway," he said. "What I like is the idea that you'll be able to help me figure out what to do with this nightmare of a mission."

"I'm certainly going to try," Decker said. He took a moment to greet and introduce himself to the others, and was welcomed warmly into the team.

Jefferson went through the briefing again, for Decker's sake, gave him his own ID and password kit, and asked the entire team if they had any questions. Decker was the first one to raise a hand.

"What do we know about the kidnappers themselves? Anything?"

Jefferson shook his head. "Not yet. President Habib is reluctant to allow any information to make it into a diplomatic pouch, on the theory that someone else's spies might be as good as our spies. He doesn't want to take the chance that either the kidnappers or Russia will find out that we've offered to help."

"And how soon can we meet with him, to discuss the situation?"

"We've already arranged for Noah, in the guise of a diplomatic attaché, to meet the president tomorrow morning. It's very doubtful that we could get you in on such short notice, as well, so be sure to brief Noah on the questions you want him to ask. He'll be carrying an undetectable recording device, so you'll be able to hear Habib's answers. I know that isn't the optimum solution, but it's the best we can do right now."

Decker nodded. "I'm sure we'll manage," he said. "What about weapons and gear?"

"Everything you need will be going with you. You're not going on a commercial flight, but on a diplomatic one. When you leave here, Noah will take you to the armory and you can sign out whatever weapons you want. Noah, put it on the team's tab. We haven't had time to set Stan up with one of our department ID cards yet."

Noah smiled and inclined his head. "Not a problem, Sir." He turned to Decker. "Mister Decker, be sure to let me know exactly what you want me to do, or ask. Investigation isn't something I've done before, and this is an incredibly important mission. I appreciate anything you can do to help us accomplish it."

Decker nodded back to him. "It's just Stan," he said. "Noah, I understand that you're the team leader, and that you're in command. Just bear in mind that I'm an old fart, and sometimes it may seem that I'm contemptuous of your youth. Please don't believe that, because the truth is that I'm jealous. Donald has told me about you, so I know who and what you are." He grinned. "Punk kid, you've got the job I always wanted!"

Noah looked him in the eye, then glanced at Jefferson. "He knows, then?" Noah asked his bosses.

Allison nodded. "I authorized Donald to brief him about you, Noah. Yes, he knows it all."

"Noah," Decker began, "what they told me is that you are a man who suffered a terrible tragedy as a child, and as a result, you are without emotion or conscience. Donald and Allison are convinced that you are the most effective operative they've ever had, and frankly, I feel honored to be able to work with you."

"Good," Noah said. "I have to pretend to be human in front of most people, and it feels good to be able to relax and be myself with the team. If I don't have to keep up an act for you, that will make things even easier for us to work together."

"Oh, please, I wouldn't want you to. I'm looking forward to the chance to observe you in action. From what I've heard, it can be quite amazing."

"Not the word I'd use," Neil said. "I'd go for something more like 'terrifying' or 'shocking.' One thing you need to understand to work with Noah is that if he decides you're in the way, he will put a bullet in your head and never even hesitate. We all know that, in the team."

Moose and Sarah nodded their agreement, and Decker smiled. "Any leader worth his salt," he said, "would do the same. When you're out in the field, the mission or the assignment always takes precedence, even over personal friendships and feelings. That's how it has to be."

"Oh, that's just ducky, you're going to fit right in!" Neil said, making a face.

There didn't seem to be any more questions, so Jefferson turned to Allison. "Anything else?"

Allison looked at the entire team for a moment, then pursed her lips and turned her gaze on Noah. "Yes," she said. "I'd like to speak with Noah and Sarah alone for a moment."

Jefferson raised his eyebrows, but didn't make a comment. He gathered Neil, Moose and Decker and took them down the hall to his own office.

In the conference room, Noah met Allison's gaze with his own, while Sarah looked nervous.

"I'd be willing to bet pretty good money that you know why I asked you to stay behind for a moment," Allison said. "There are certain rules in place that you seem to ignore, both of you. Care to guess which ones I'm talking about?"

Noah didn't blink. "You're referring to the fact that on our last mission, Sarah and I broke the rule about avoiding intimacy while in the field."

Sarah looked down at the floor, and her hands began fidgeting with the fabric of her jeans. Allison glanced at her, then looked back at Noah. "Precisely. That rule is in place for a reason, you know. We determined long ago that intimacy between team members during a mission can cause emotional problems that might interfere. Now, I'm aware that you are a different case, Noah, but one of the things that made me determined to recruit you was your record of obeying orders. I'm a little concerned that you seem to think this one doesn't apply to you."

"He does it for me," Sarah put in without looking up. "When we're out there, I need some kind of contact to help me stay focused, and he gives it to me."

Allison looked at her. "I know you've been pretty close here at home, and I have no objection to that. When you're out on a mission, though…"

"Sarah chose me specifically because I won't have any emotional investment in the relationship," Noah said. "It isn't emotional intimacy she's looking for, or she would've chosen Moose or Neil. I've seen this before, and I'm sure you have, too. Some people just need to feel a human touch, especially during a stressful situation. I determined that her ability to function at optimal level falls under my responsibility to keep my team in top shape."

Allison crossed her arms and huffed. "I didn't say that I can't understand it," she said, "I said there's a rule against it." She stared into Noah's eyes for more than a minute, but he never blinked. "So—since I don't seem to have any choice in the matter, I'm going to give you an official verbal reprimand right now. Intimacy between team members in the field is strictly forbidden."

She met Noah's eyes for another five seconds, then looked at Sarah. "Now, unofficially, I'm going to tell you both that I understand, and I'll look the other way. Just don't let it blow up in my face, you both got that?"

Sarah slowly raised her face so that she could see Allison, and there was the ghost of a smile on her lips. "Got it, Boss Lady," she said.

Allison nodded, then led the two of them to Jefferson's office. When they got there, she released the team to begin preparing for their departure a few hours later. Decker followed them out of the building, and they all climbed into Neil's big Hummer for the ride to the armory. Since the armory was not publicly acknowledged around Kirtland, it was in that part of the compound behind the Restricted Access fences. They were stopped at the guard shack, but Jefferson had called ahead to let the guards know that Mister Decker would be going to the armory with Team Camelot, so they were waved through after only a moment's delay.

The armory was set up like some sort of super gun store, with every kind of weapon they could imagine on display. There were a number of firing ranges in the back of the building, where department agents could take weapons to test them, or get the feel of them. There was also an outdoor range that allowed long-range shooters to zero in their weapons, and a combat course that actually shot back at them with paintballs. Moose and Noah had begun running that course after they returned from their first mission, and so far, neither of them had been hit.

"Holy crap," Decker said. "This is incredible! What in the world would you do with half of this stuff?"

Neil chuckled. "Oh, nothing serious, maybe just take over a third world country or start a revolution. Doesn't that sound like fun?"

Decker grinned at him. "Depends on the country," he said. "And don't ask me which one I'd prefer, because I don't want to end up in some federal nuthouse."

Each of them went their separate ways inside the Armory, though Noah and Sarah seemed to wander in the same direction. It hadn't taken Decker long to figure out that the girl was quite infatuated with the team leader, and would probably follow him right through the gates of hell. As they walked away, he caught her asking Noah for advice on choosing a new pistol.

Decker, having been with the FBI for thirty years, was a handgun man. He had always been faithful to the Smith & Wesson thirty-eight caliber, but the incredible assortment that confronted him gave him pause. It took him forty-five minutes and three trips to the indoor range to settle on the forty-caliber Glock. He also chose three extra magazines and two boxes of ammunition, then waited for Noah to come back up front.

He didn't wait long. Noah and Sarah appeared only a couple of minutes later, with Sarah holding a pair of Kimber mini-45s, while Noah had a fifty-caliber Desert Eagle in his hand. Each of them got some extra magazines and ammunition as well, and by the time they were done, Moose and Neil had returned. Both of them declined to get new weapons, choosing instead to stick with the ones they already knew.

They drove back to the office building, where Moose and Decker climbed out and got into their own cars. Moose would go home to pick up his bag and weapons, then meet the rest of them at Noah's place. Since Sarah spent as much time at Noah's as she did at her own apartment, she had enough clothing and toiletries there to pack for the trip, and Neil lived in a mobile home on Noah's property.

Decker decided to just hang out with the three of them, since he had everything he needed with him already. He backed his Chevy Trailblazer out of its parking space and fell in behind the Hummer to follow it home.

Temple Lake Road was full of curves, so much so that Decker was reminded of some of the roads farther up in the mountains. The drive out to Noah's place took almost 30 minutes, before they turned onto County Road six forty. The house was only a short distance up that road, and he followed the Hummer as Neil dropped Noah and Sarah off at the big house that sat on the property. Noah waved for Decker to park in his driveway and follow him and Sarah into the house, while Neil drove across the yard to get to his trailer.

"Come on in, and make yourself at home. There's soft drinks and beer in the refrigerator, maybe some wine and iced tea. Choose your poison. We're going to go get packed for the trip tonight, be out in a few minutes."

Sarah shook her head at Noah, then walked into the kitchen and opened a cabinet door. "The glasses are in here," she said, then turned and followed Noah into his room.

Decker smiled, then opened the refrigerator and took out a bottle of Bud Light. He twisted off the top and tossed it into the trashcan, then reached up and closed the cabinet she had left open. He took a sip of the beer as he walked back into the living room and sat down on the couch. There was no sign of Noah or Sarah, and he figured it would take a little while for them to pack up their things, so he picked up the remote control that lay on the coffee table and turned on the big-screen television on the wall.

Down the hall, Sarah had closed the door behind herself after following Noah into his room. It was no secret among the team that she often spent the night with him, nor was it a problem.

"So," she said, "how long before we have to leave?"

Noah had been pulling a duffel out of his closet, but he turned at her question to look at her. Her shirt and bra were already on the floor, and she was pushing her pants down her legs.

"Hour and a half," he said. "Plenty of time." He dropped the duffel on the floor, reached down and yanked back the covers, then began stripping out of his own clothes.

Forty-five minutes later, Noah and Sarah joined Decker in the living room, where he was watching old reruns of *The Beverly Hillbillies*. He grinned as they entered the room, and Sarah blushed.

"Stan," Noah said, "is there anything you want to go over or ask, before we head out in a little while?"

Decker shrugged. "I can't think of anything. Can you?"

"No," Noah said, shaking his head. "I just thought I should ask."

The three of them sat and watched the antics of the Clampett family for the next few minutes, and then the episode was followed by another one. Sarah and Decker chuckled at a couple of points, while Noah simply watched the show and filed the actions and reactions of the cast away in his memory. It was always possible that he could use them someday.

Moose pulled in just before that episode ended, parked in the graveled area outside of Noah's garage and knocked on the front door. Sarah got up to let him in, and he headed for the kitchen to grab himself a soft drink, then came and sat down in the living room with the rest of them. Neil came wandering in a few minutes later, not even bothering to knock.

"You know, Neil," Sarah said, "it's a good thing we were expecting you. It's probably not very safe to just walk into the home of a professional killer, you know what I mean?"

Neil flopped sideways into one of the big overstuffed chairs, and shrugged his shoulders. "If he shoots me, it just means I don't have to put up with all this crap anymore. I'm willing to take the chance, but I haven't quite decided if it's worth it or not. If it isn't, I'll make a point of coming back from the dead to let you know."

THREE

Their plane landed at Nouakchott International Airport at twelve minutes before eight AM local time, and they were escorted directly into a diplomatic limousine that took them to the Hotel Halima, where each of the five was installed in a separate room on the floor reserved for the US Embassy. Ambassador Morgenstern, they were told, would meet Noah at the embassy in an hour.

Moose and Sarah, since they would not be needed for at least a few hours, announced that they were going to relax and try to catch up on some much-needed sleep, the seats on the diplomatic airplane not being among the most comfortable they had ever used. Noah and Decker met in Noah's room to discuss the upcoming meeting with President Habib, while Neil set up his computers and began working on hacking the presidential palace network.

"The most important questions you need to ask the president," Decker said, "are about the phone call that told him his daughter had been kidnapped. We need to know as much as we can about the caller, such as his accent, any particular mannerisms, anything he might have let slip about himself, and about any background sounds the president might have heard. Sometimes, it's what you hear in the background that can make all the difference. Encourage him to wrack his brain, try to remember any sound that may have come through the phone. Everything that he heard is there, in his memory, and all he's got to do is shake it loose."

"What about the daughter? Is there anything I should be asking about her?"

"Not specifically. Donald gave me a dossier on the girl, everything that our intelligence had on her. We know that she had a tendency to shake her security detail, and seems to have done so the day she disappeared. From what we know, she was planning a day out with friends. It's doubtful he would know anything about where she might have gone prior to being taken."

Noah shook his head. "It wouldn't break my heart if you were able to go with me to this meeting, but apparently it was hard enough just to get me in. I'll do all I can, and go over it with you as soon as I get back. Then we..."

They were interrupted by a knock on the door, and Noah opened it to find Neil standing there. The skinny young man pushed past him as soon as the door was wide enough. "Okay, I've got a little problem," he said. "Getting into the main network was easy, but all it really told me was that there are multiple networks there, and some of them are so secure that even I can't crack them in less than a year."

"Neil, you've only been at it for a few minutes," Noah said. "Wouldn't you expect it to take a little time?"

Neil shook his head vigorously. "You're not getting it," he said. "Three of the networks are using a security algorithm so tight that it would take me weeks to get all the digits of the pass code. Unless I'm mistaken, we don't have that much time. There is another way, though, but it involves getting me inside that building."

"Explain."

"Okay, every network is set up by an IT guy, and every IT guy who sets up a secure network like this builds himself a back door. That's because there's always some idiot on every network who will find a way to mess it up, change the password or whatever. There has to be a permanent way to get in, one that nobody can access but the IT people. If I can get inside that building with my computer, so that my computer is trying to log on to their network, I can get that back door. That way, I can access every computer on the network from right there, and I've got a masking algorithm that will prevent anyone else from seeing that I'm logged on."

Noah looked at him for a long moment, thinking it over. "Okay, then you're going with me. All you have to do is get inside the building, right?"

Neil nodded. "That should do it, but it would be best if I can get as close to the router as possible. Worst case, I just need to be on the same floor with it."

"All right, then, we'll say that you're my assistant. Then all you have to do is hope we can find a place where no one will pay attention to you while you do your thing."

"Got that covered, Boss. I've got a program that looks and sounds like a video game, but I can be siphoning off every bit of data on the entire network while it runs. Just park me in a chair somewhere, I'll do the rest."

Decker grinned at the two of them. "You guys blow my mind," he said. "Neil, somewhere in those computers is likely to be an actual recording of the call the president got from the kidnappers. If you can find that,

that would be fantastic."

Neil smiled broadly. "If it's there, I'll get it. We'll just have to hunt for it on my computer when I get back."

"Let's go, then. I'll have to explain this to the ambassador as soon as we get there."

Neil ran back to his room to grab the laptop he would carry into the presidential palace, and was back in less than a minute. He followed Noah down the elevator and out to the limousine that was still waiting for them. The driver raised his eyebrows at seeing two passengers instead of one, but said nothing. He held the door open for them, then got behind the wheel and put the car in gear.

The drive to the embassy took less than fifteen minutes, and an aide met them at the door. "Gentlemen, if you will follow me," he said, and led them to the ambassador's office.

Dwight Henry Morgenstern was a short, stocky man, but there was a sense of power and presence about him that even Noah could feel. He shook hands with each of them in turn.

"Good to meet you, Mister Ambassador," Noah said. "I'm Alexander Colson and this is my assistant, Eric Starling."

"Mister Colson," the ambassador said, "I was given to understand that you would be arriving alone."

Noah smiled. "As I told you, Eric is my assistant. He goes wherever I go. Is that a problem?"

Morgenstern explained that the meeting Noah would be going into had been hastily arranged, and that security was tight in the presidential palace. It might not be possible for Starling to accompany him, but the two men offered no objection. Moments later, they left the embassy to meet with the President of Mauritania.

An hour later, the meeting concluded, the limousine dropped Morgenstern off at the embassy before driving Noah and Neil back to the hotel. Neither of them mentioned Neil's computer during the ride, nor in the hotel until they were safely inside Noah's room. Noah picked up the phone to let Decker know that they were back, and the retired agent joined them a few moments later.

"How did it go, guys?" Decker asked.

Neil was sitting at the desk in the room, going through the files he had copied. He had plugged in a set of ear buds, and was listening to something while Noah and Decker talked.

"I think it went pretty well," Noah said. "The main things I got from the president were that the caller seemed to have an American accent, and that the only background sound he could remember was a loud roaring noise that seemed to come and go. He said there was also another man speaking in the background, but he didn't think there was any connection between that man and the caller. The man in the background seemed to have a British accent, may have been Welsh. He also said that it seemed the man had a scolding tone in his voice, so he may have been speaking to a child."

Decker closed his eyes and pursed his lips. "An American accent," he repeated. "But the voice in the background seemed to be British? That's interesting. That sounds like the call came from somewhere very public, possibly somewhere that might be visited by tourists. That could account for the different accent of someone in the background."

Noah nodded his head. "I had a similar thought," he said. "One of the most common places where you're likely to find a mixture of accents is at an airport.

Apparently, the call came in a reasonably short time period, after the girl left her home, but before she met up with her friends. I wonder if perhaps she was being hustled out of the country on an airplane. Habib said the caller told him that his daughter had been taken out of Mauritania, so it's possible that the kidnappers handed her off to someone else who took her onto a plane, then called the president once the plane was airborne."

Decker's eyes opened, and he looked at Noah. "That's a very interesting hypothesis," he said, "and probably better than mine. I've been given the name of the CIA station chief here, and he's supposed to give us any cooperation we need. Let me call him and see if he can get me any information about flights that left the country that day, in particular flights that might have left with a young woman who was unconscious. It's reasonable to assume that she would have been drugged before they put her on the plane, so that she could pass for a medical patient or something similar." He took out a cell phone and dialed a number. "Mister Adcock," he said when the phone was answered. "My name is George Russell. I was told to give you a call when I got into town, and ask you to give me some idea of the best restaurant to eat at." He listened for a moment, then looked at his phone and tapped a code onto the dialer. "Okay, I've got it scrambled. You know who I am and why I'm here, right? Good, that will save us a lot of time. I need some information. I'm looking for flights that left the country on the day the president's daughter was abducted, flights that might have taken a young female medical patient out of the country. Actually, any flight that left the country within an hour before the president got the call, regardless of the presence of medical patients. How soon can you get me that?"

He listened again for a moment, and then smiled. "Excellent, yes. Let me know when it's ready, and I'll put our computer guy on it." He ended the call and looked at Noah. "He'll get me the information I asked for, and send it to my phone as a multimedia message attachment." He glanced over at Neil. "He'll be able to open it and read it, right?"

Noah nodded. "I guarantee it," he said. "That kid's about the best there is with a computer, which is why he's with me. They gave me the best support team they had, and I've seen them all at work."

Decker smiled. "I don't doubt you," he said, but he was interrupted before he could say any more.

"*Bingo!*" Neil shouted. He snatched out his ear buds and unplugged them from the computer. "You guys gotta hear this," he said. He tapped a couple of keys, and voices came from the speakers.

"*Marhabaan?*" That was the voice of President Habib. Neil whispered, "That means hello, in Arabic."

Another voice spoke. "*Astamae li beinaya,*" it said. "*Hadha hu hawl abnatik!*"

"Listen carefully," Neil translated, "it's about your daughter."

"Hold it, hold it," Noah said, and Neil paused the playback. "Are you telling me you speak Arabic?"

Neil looked surprised at the question. "Do you know how many hackers are in the Middle East? If you don't speak Arabic, you don't ever talk to some of the best."

Noah's eyebrows went up, but he shrugged. "Okay, go on, then."

Neil resumed playing the recording, which was obviously of the call that told Habib about his daughter's abduction. There were a couple of moments of Arabic, wherein the president complained about the caller's accent, and then they switched to English.

"Yes," said Habib, "I can understand you now. What is this about? Where is my daughter?"

"She's already out of the country," said a man in what Noah would agree to be a Southern drawl. "She'll be perfectly safe, as long as you do what we want you to do."

There was a moment's pause, before Habib spoke again. "And what is that?"

"Your Prime Minister is meeting with the leaders of Syria and Russia at a summit meeting in Geneva on the twenty-third. At that meeting, he will agree to and publicly announce a strategic alliance with both countries, an alliance that would include the construction of military bases within Mauritania, and the expulsion of Western military presence. If he does, then your daughter will be returned to you alive and in one piece. If not, then I'm afraid you'll be getting her back in several different packages. Do you understand?"

Habib hesitated, and in the brief pause they could hear a man in the background. He did indeed sound British, as he said, "...Too late, we can't go back for it now. Come on, then, we'll just have to get you a new one, that'll be right, won't it?"

"How do I know you truly have my daughter?" Habib asked at that point.

The caller chuckled. "Well, how else would I know about that little birthmark she's got on her left thigh, right on the back of it, just underneath her butt? You're her daddy, I'm sure you can remember when she was a baby, that little birthmark of hers? Sorta looks like a little bird, doesn't it?"

Another pause, and the man in the background said, "… No time for this, just no time! You should have made sure to get it before we left, we'll just…"

"How can I contact you? The Prime Minister may wish to…"

"You don't need to contact me," the caller said. "All you want to do is tell the Russian ambassador that they've got a deal, that the alliance is a go. Then, once that goes public, she'll be dropped off safe and sound at your doorstep. Otherwise, her next ride will be to the butcher shop."

"Why are you doing this? You don't sound like a Russian or Syrian?"

"Me? I'm neither one, I'm just an independent contractor. I got hired to do this because I've gotten results in the past. There's nothing like a proven track record to make you popular in this business, know what I mean? Like I said, do what I tell you and everything will be fine. You can count on that, but you can also count on the consequences if you don't." The caller hung up, and a second later the line went dead.

Noah looked at Decker. "What do you make of it?"

Decker frowned. "That accent is definitely Deep South USA, but I don't think it's real. It sounded just a bit too forced, to me."

Noah nodded. "I agree. Some of the drawl was held out just a little too long, the way an actor might do it to make sure people caught it. If you listen to the sibilants, the breathy consonants like *s, z, j* and the *ch* sound, they're very clearly pronounced. Southerners don't do that. The only place you're going to find carefully pronounced sibilants like that is New England."

Decker looked at him, and his eyebrows rose. "Good point, I missed that. So we're probably looking for someone from the Northeast, then."

Neil was tapping on his keyboard. "I'm running a snippet through the NSA's voice print database, now. If this guy is really a player on the international scene, they're likely to have him in their files, somewhere."

Decker nodded. "If that doesn't turn anything up, try the FBI database. Ours is pretty good, too."

"That's where I'll go next, if I need to, and after that I'll hit the Russian database. They've been doing that sort of voice print recognition longer than anybody, and they use it almost exclusively for their intelligence people."

"Okay," Noah said, "what about the guy in the background? Definitely sounded British to me."

Decker was nodding again. "I agree, no doubt about it. And the background noises, if those weren't jet engines, I don't know what they were. I'd lay good odds that our girl was on one of the planes that we could hear taking off."

"Maybe," Noah said, "or maybe that's just what somebody wanted us to think. It seems a little convenient that we got good background noise and an identifiable British accent. Those lead us to the conclusion that the call came from the airport, which causes us to suspect that Selah was taken out of the country by air. What if this is nothing but a smokescreen?"

Decker shrugged. "That's certainly possible," he said. "It does seem a little easy, these clues. Let's face it, the caller would have known he was being recorded. Why wouldn't he have gone into someplace quiet, why risk somebody overhearing him?"

"Because he's just plain cocky?" Neil asked. "I got a hit on the voice print. According to the NSA database, there is a 99.8 percent certainty that the caller is Jeremy Pendergrast. He's originally from the Hamptons, son of a wealthy family who developed a bad streak during his college years. He worked briefly for the CIA in Italy, compiling information from Middle Eastern news sources, then apparently just decided to go out on his own. He's been linked to a number of abductions and extortions, but there's never been enough evidence to take any action against him." He clicked the link on his monitor and scanned the page that appeared. "Seems the NSA keeps a close watch on this boy, monitoring all of his movements. Want to guess where he was the day Selah disappeared?"

"Right here in Nouakchott?" Noah asked.

"*Ding, ding, ding,*" Neil said. "We have a winner! He flew in two days before that and stayed in this very hotel, then flew out two hours after that call was made. He is, or was a half hour ago, in his apartment in London, where he lives alone. Look at the screen, that's a photo of him." The image on the screen showed a stocky man with sandy hair and brown eyes.

Noah and Decker looked at the photo, then at one another. "Sounds like he must be our man," Decker said. "Still seems way too easy, though."

Noah nodded. "Yeah, we're being led on a wild goose chase. The trouble is, we can't afford not to chase the goose. Whether he's a decoy or not, this Pendergrast is somehow involved in all this, and I plan to find out how." He took a phone out of his pocket and dialed a number, and waited for it to connect. Almost a minute later, he got an answer.

"This is Allison," his boss said as she answered.

"It's Camelot," Noah said. "We have a lead, and need to go to London."

"Hang on a moment," Allison said, and the line went silent as she placed him on hold. Noah waited for about three minutes, listening to Neil tapping on his keyboard and cursing under his breath, but he didn't want to ask questions while he was still on the phone.

"Okay, I'm back," Allison said. "I'm sending a charter jet after you, but it won't get there until almost nine o'clock tonight, your time. I would suggest you get as much rest as you can, after the flight you just had."

"That's what we'll do. Have we got a team in London at the moment? I'd like to keep tabs on someone until we get there."

"We don't have a team there, but we do have an asset. Who do you want her to watch? I'll put her on it right away."

"The guy's name is Jeremy Pendergrast," Noah said, "and the address is..." Noah picked up a pencil that was lying on the nightstand beside his bed and threw it at Neil.

"Ow! I'm getting it, I'm getting it—okay, it's Number Fifteen Aberdare Gardens, Apartment 7B."

"Number Fifteen Aberdare Gardens, Apartment 7B. Apparently the NSA is keeping an eye on him, too, but I'd be more comfortable if I had one of our own watching him."

"I'll get her on it. It's almost noon in London, and you won't get there until nearly three AM. I'll have a car waiting for you with a driver, and reservations in your name in the Cavendish Hotel. Good work, Camelot, and good luck."

The phone went dead, and Noah shoved it back into his pocket. "We get to rest up for a while, but we're flying out of here at nine o'clock tonight. Neil, go tell Moose and Sarah. I don't think any of us got any sleep on the plane coming here, and we're all worn out. Let's meet downstairs in the hotel restaurant for dinner at seven, and that should leave us plenty of time to get to the airport after we eat."

Neil nodded, picked up his computer and walked out of the room. Decker stayed behind for a moment, and once the door had closed he looked up at Noah.

"You really think this is a wild goose chase?"

"I think there's a good chance of it," Noah said. "I still feel like this was a little too easy, so I can't help but wonder if Mister Pendergrast wasn't hired just to be a decoy."

Decker shrugged. "Neil says the NSA believes he's done this sort of thing before. Maybe he just got sloppy, this time."

"People like him get sloppy only when it's to their advantage. I need to know what he knows, no matter how little it is."

"True, and at least it's something to start with. I'll let you get some rest, while I go do the same." He got up and walked out the door without another word.

Noah began stripping immediately, and headed for the shower. He stayed there for nearly 20 minutes, just letting the seemingly endless hot water run over him. When he felt that it was actually raising his body temperature slightly, he turned the temperature down and let it cool him, then got out and toweled off. He walked naked out of the bathroom, and wasn't surprised to find Sarah already in his bed, sound asleep. He slid under the covers as quietly as he could, and rolled onto his side. A moment later, he felt her spoon herself against him, and then he relaxed and let himself drift off.

FOUR

Moose, Neil and Decker were already seated in the restaurant when Noah and Sarah arrived, both of them freshly showered. Neil stifled a grin, but wiggled his eyebrows at Sarah, who flipped him the bird.

"Don't start with me, Neil," she said, picking up a menu. "Anybody got any clue what's edible here?"

"They got a rotisserie chicken with vegetables, that's what I'm going for," Moose said. He leaned over and pointed at a line on her menu. "It's this one, *Yassa poulet.* Hopefully, they can't do any harm to chicken."

"I'm with you," she said. "Chicken for me. Oh, look, they got Coke!"

"We've all decided on the chicken," Decker said, grinning at Noah. "Are you gonna be the odd man out?"

"Not me, chicken sounds great." He looked around. "Do we have a waitress?"

"Waiter," Neil said. "Apparently, women don't work in restaurants here. All I've seen are men."

"Okay, then where's the waiter?" Noah asked. Almost as if his question had signaled it, a waiter appeared and approached the table. The orders were taken, and they were surprised at how quickly the food arrived.

"Talk about fast food," Neil said. "They must have a lot of this cooking back there. And did any of you know we were each getting a whole chicken? I figured it would be, you know, shredded or something."

"You're complaining?" Sarah asked. "You forget, Neil, I've seen how you eat."

"Complaining? I'm not complaining. But if any of you can't finish your chicken, just let me know. And I don't know what these vegetables are, but they're delicious."

They ate casually, without rushing, and were finished well before eight o'clock. They each went to their rooms to get their bags, and met again in the lobby a few moments later. Two taxis took them to the airport, and they entered the private flight area to find a man standing there holding a sign that read "Alexander Colson."

Noah stepped up to him. "I'm Colson," he said.

The man was wearing what looked like a pilot's uniform, and he broke into a smile. "Good on yer, mate," he said, in an obviously Australian accent. "We're all set to fly, soon's we get you all on board!"

"Then just lead the way," Noah said. The man tossed his cardboard sign into the nearest trashcan as he led them through the building and out onto the tarmac. A Gulfstream IV sat awaiting them, and they all climbed aboard while another man took their bags and stowed them in the luggage compartment.

The airplane had only a dozen seats, each of which was as big as a comfortable easy chair and reclined so that the passengers could lie back and go to sleep. Everyone settled in as the pilot closed the doors, and then they heard the engines start up. The plane turned around and began to taxi toward the runway, and only a few moments later, they were in the air and on the way to England.

The flight was easy, the seats comfortable. Decker and Neil actually took naps, but Moose, Sarah and Noah were wide awake. Sarah's seat faced backward, just in front of Noah's, while Moose was in the seat across the aisle. It made it easy for the three of them to talk.

"So, is there any particular plan when we get to England?" Moose asked.

"I'll have to improvise a bit, but the basic plan is simple. We're going to grab Mister Pendergrast and shake him the way a dog would shake a snake, until he tells us everything he possibly can. If he makes me happy, he might even live through it." Noah winked at Moose. "No promises on that score, though."

"Grab him?" Sarah asked. "And where are we supposed to take him once we do?"

Noah shrugged. "Anywhere out in the country, I guess. Someplace nobody will pay attention when he screams."

"Sounds wonderful," she said, rolling her eyes. "Think there's any chance the girl is actually in London, somewhere?"

"I don't know, but I do have my doubts. Decker agrees with me, this is going too easy. I feel like we were supposed to find Pendergrast, like we're being set up, somehow. I want all of you on your toes, watching everything you possibly can. Something about this just doesn't feel real."

"It's like blind man's bluff," Moose said. "We're feeling around in the darkness for the players, but one of them is making noises to attract our attention."

Noah nodded. "Yes, that's what I'm trying to say. It's like Pendergrast is the sacrificial pawn in a chess game,

stuck out there in front where he's bound to be captured, but clearing the way for the Rook or Bishop or
Queen to do something more serious. The question is,
who are the other players?"

"Bad thing about a pawn is that he's usually nothing
but a foot soldier, somebody who doesn't know any answers. That way, he can't give away the plan when he's
captured. If this guy doesn't know who's behind it, then
this could be a wasted trip."

"I don't think so," Noah said. "There's a reason why
that pawn was advanced, and whoever he was fronting
for will be watching him. We've got to snatch him, and
I'm going to try to get any information out of him that
I can, but the real reason for the snatch is to make whoever is behind him start to worry and come looking for
him."

Sarah moaned. "That could take days."

Noah looked at her. "You got something better to be
doing?"

"Yeah," she said. "This *is* my very first trip to London,
you know. I could go shopping."

"Oh, don't worry," Noah said. "You'll be going shopping, first thing tomorrow. We need a van; a regular car
isn't going to work for this one. And while you're doing
that, the rest of us are going shopping for a place in the
country."

Sarah, her eyebrows low and menacing, stared at him
for several seconds. "Any chance it will have a pool?"

"I doubt it," he said. "I'm thinking more of a secluded,
out-of-the-way, hard-to-find place with no neighbors
for miles and miles. I doubt those come with swimming
pools and tennis courts."

"No," Moose said. "But something tells me it might

come with cows or sheep. Better watch where you step."

"You guys figure that out," Sarah said. "Something tells me I'm not going to get a lot of sleep in the next few days, so I'm going to go ahead and sleep while I can." She reached down beside her seat and picked up a blanket, then reclined the seat and pulled the cover up over herself. "Good night," she said. "Wake me up when we get there."

Moose and Noah decided to follow her example, and soon all five of them were sleeping peacefully, despite the snoring that was coming from Neil and Decker.

A building storm in their path caused the pilot to have to detour, so the plane didn't land until almost four AM. The five of them stepped onto the tarmac and were met by an elderly gentleman with a limousine.

"You'd be Mister Colson, then," the old fellow said with a smile. "Rum Charlie they call me, and I'm here to take you to your hotel."

"Rum Charlie?" Sarah asked, muttering.

The old fellow laughed, and winked at her. "Rum Charlie, right, Miss, but not because o' me drinking. I ain't touched a drop of liquor in more than forty years. Back in the tail end of the big war, though, when I was but a lad of ten or eleven, I had me a deal with a rum bottler to let me carry a half-dozen bottles out to where all the soldiers were at and sell them every night. My old dad was gone off to fight on the mainland, you see, and was up to me to help mum all I could. The soldiers liked me, and would give me big tips, so that we got through the war all right. The name, though, it just stuck with me, and I reckoned there's no sense to get fretted about it now, oy?"

The old man kept up his running monologue, talking

about anything he could think of as he drove them into the city. The Cavendish Hotel was in St. James, Central London, near Piccadilly Circus, so it wasn't a terribly long drive. Each of them contributed a word or two now and then, just to let Rum Charlie know they were listening, but they all felt a sense of relief when they finally got out of the car.

Rum Charlie opened the trunk and let them all get their luggage, then bid them farewell and drove off into the night. Noah led the way inside the hotel.

The desk clerk, despite the early hour of the morning, looked up at him with a smile. "A good morning to you, sir, and welcome to the Cavendish Hotel. Would you have a reservation?"

Noah smiled. "Yes, indeed," he said. "The name is Alexander Colson, and there should be five rooms reserved."

The clerk entered the name into a computer, and smiled back. "Yes, sir, five rooms on the twelfth floor. I also have a message waiting for you." He passed over a card for Noah to sign, then handed him an envelope and the keys for all five rooms.

Noah waited until he had gotten away from the desk to open the envelope, then read the message inside.

Mister Colson,

As requested, I have been watching the real estate listing you inquired about, and have not observed any activity at this point. As it is getting rather late, I shall be back on this project in the morning. Feel free to call me eight-ish or thereabouts, and I will happily give you an update.

I am at your service,
Catherine Potts

A telephone number was written under her name. Noah refolded the note and stuck it into his pocket. Key cards were passed around, they all rode up together on the elevator, and then each of them disappeared into a room.

They were to meet for breakfast in the hotel's dining room at eight AM, so Noah set an alarm on his phone for seven. Plenty of time to shower, shave, etc., and still make it down to join the others on schedule. He got into bed and was back to sleep only seconds later.

Noah's alarm went off right on time, but he was already up and in the shower by the time it did. He canceled it once he got out, then got dressed for the day. The weather report predicted sunshine and fair skies, so he opted for casual slacks and a polo shirt. He was in the dining room by twenty to eight, surprised to find Sarah and Neil waiting for him.

"I have had all the sleep that I can stand," Neil said, "at least for the next few days. Give me something to do, boss, keep me busy, please?"

"No problem," Noah said. "Get on Craigslist or whatever they use here and find me an extremely secluded place in the country within, oh, say eighty kilometers of London. Something off the beaten path and with no neighbors, something we can get without having to sign a long lease."

Neil rolled his eyes. "That'll take me ten minutes," he said. "Got any other suggestions?"

A waitress interrupted, and Noah ordered coffee and a muffin before turning back to Neil. "How much can you find out about the area around Pendergrast's apartment building? I'd like to have some idea of the layout of his apartment, the design of the building, traffic in the area...Can you give me that kind of stuff?"

Neil squinted for a moment. "I can probably get blueprints of the building," he said. "As long as he hasn't changed any of the physical design of his apartment, that should give you what you want internally. As far as traffic goes, I can look for traffic cameras in the area and scan news reports. Someone is always complaining about traffic everywhere, so there's bound to be some general information."

Noah nodded. "That's a good start." He turned to Sarah. "I'm sending Moose with you to get a van, one without seats in it. Let him rent it under his ID, I don't want anyone remembering a pretty blonde girl getting an empty cargo van."

She made a confused face at him. "Why would anyone remember me?"

"Because it's always possible we may have to burn the vehicle before we're done with it, and things like that tend to make people remember who they dealt with last. If they remember a big guy who looks like a football player, no one will be terribly surprised. We're going to use it in a kidnap operation, so it could end up bloody or with bullet holes in it, and we want to eliminate any clues that might lead back to us. Try to get a white one, or beige. That'll make it easier to disguise it as a utility vehicle or something."

She shrugged and nodded. "You got it, Boss." She nodded toward the dining room entrance. "Here come the slow pokes."

Noah glanced that direction and saw Moose and Decker coming toward them together. He waited until they had taken seats and placed their orders before he addressed them.

"Stan, you're coming with me this morning, after Neil gets us some recon intel on Pendergrast's apartment building. I'm hoping we might be able to spot and tail him for a bit, get an idea of his daily routine. Moose, you're going with Sarah. The two of you are going to get us a van to use when we snatch him. Get one without any markings, preferably white or light colored."

"So you want us to avoid U-Haul, right?" Moose asked. "That shouldn't be too hard."

"Right, and I want you to rent the vehicle with your ID. Roll your sleeves up and muss your hair a bit. If we end up having to destroy the van I want them to remember that they rented it to a tough-looking outlaw type, okay?"

Moose nodded. "No problem. Want me to use an Italian accent?"

"Whatever works," Noah said. "Keep Sarah out of sight, I don't want them to remember her at all."

"Noah," Decker said, "what about weapons? Should any of us be carrying today? The Metropolitan Police go unarmed, for the most part, but since handguns are essentially banned in the UK, they have special officers ready at a moment's notice to deal with anyone who is carrying one."

"Good point, there's really no reason for any of us to be carrying a weapon today. Of course, we're not looking to get into any kind of conflict with the local police, anyway, but let's not give them a reason to worry about us if we happen to get pulled over. Moose, if you get pulled over in the van, say you're planning on doing some shopping for antiques over the next few days. Sarah, if you get pulled over, just smile and look as confused as possible, then ask directions back to the hotel."

Sarah made a face that was supposed to look innocent and lost. "Oh, officer, I'm just so confused with driving on the wrong side of the road and everything. Can you please tell me how to get back to my hotel? Pretty, pretty please?" She fluttered her eyelids for effect, and the men all grinned.

"That ought to work," Decker said. "Tell them your GPS is taking you on a wild goose chase, they'll believe it. The British tend to think us Yanks just don't know how to follow directions, because so many people complain about getting lost, here."

Their breakfast orders arrived, and they began eating. Neil, who never seemed to get enough to eat and was often teased that his skinny frame must be hollow in order to accommodate all the food he shoved down his throat, had ordered the hotel's famous Full English breakfast, which consisted of three eggs sunny side up, four slices of bacon, a large sausage, baked beans, hash browns, grilled tomatoes and eggplant, and something called a black pudding that looked like another very dark chunk of sausage.

"What on earth is that?" Sarah asked, pointing at the black pudding.

Neil cut off a piece and forked it into his mouth. "Mmm," he moaned. "I don't know, but it's good. I have to find out, so I can order it again."

Decker grinned at him. "It's called black pudding," he said. "It's made of pork blood, with fat and oatmeal."

Neil froze in mid chew, and his eyes went wide. He swallowed hard, then looked at the rest of it on his plate. "Pork blood? Does that make me some kind of vampire?"

The retired FBI agent laughed. "No, it doesn't. Black

pudding is one of the most popular dishes in the UK. They do it like that at breakfast, but you can also get it batter-dipped and deep-fried, or you can eat it cold, right out of the wrapper."

Neil stared at him for a long second, then shrugged and stuck another bite in his mouth. "Oh, well, it still tastes good. As long as it isn't going to turn me into a zombie or vampire or something, I can live with it."

The rest of them chuckled at him, as they finished their breakfast. It didn't take long, and then they were each off to carry out their part of the day's mission.

Noah and Decker followed Neil to his room, and Noah took out his phone to call Catherine Potts. He dialed the number from the note, and it was answered on the first ring.

"You've got Catherine," came a pleasant voice.

"Catherine, this is Alexander Colson," Noah said. "How are you doing today?"

"Oh, just wonderful, Mister Colson. I'm on your project right now, would you like to get together to talk about it?"

"I think that would be a wonderful idea," Noah said. "I guess you're somewhere near the property?"

"I am, sir, just a wee distance away. There's a little chip shop at the corner, would you care to meet there? It's easy to find, you can't miss it. It's only a few hundred meters past the property, where Aberdare Gardens meets up with Goldhurst Terrace."

"That'll be perfect," Noah said. "My associate and I should be there within the hour."

"Very good, sir, I shall be waiting. I'm wearing a paisley dress, I should be very easy to spot."

"And you won't have any trouble spotting us, either," Noah said, "since my associate and I look like salt-and-pepper. We'll see you shortly."

He ended the call, and he and Decker sat quietly while Neil hacked into the necessary databases to find the information he wanted. Within half an hour, he had downloaded blueprints of the building and gotten into the apartment complex's security video system. This gave Noah a clear visual representation of the building, including the hallway outside Pendergrast's apartment.

"Is that a live feed?" Noah asked, and Neil nodded. "Then keep an eye on it, and if you see him leave his apartment, call me."

Neil held up a finger, then started tapping keys again. "Okay, like I told you before, he's on an NSA watch list. According to the NSA, he's still in his apartment right now. I'll keep watching, and let you know."

"Good job," Noah said, then hooked his head at Decker. The two of them left the room and went down the elevator to the lobby. There was a car rental agency inside the lobby, and a moment later they were handed the keys to a new Jaguar F-type.

As they walked to the car, Noah looked over at Decker. "Apparently you've been here before?"

Decker nodded. "A few times. I had the pleasure of working with Interpol on a couple of cases that brought me here. I can't say I know the city all that well, but I can probably find the important places without resorting to GPS."

Noah tossed him the keys. "In that case, you drive. I want to reconnoiter the area, get a feel for it, and I can do that better if I'm not the one behind the wheel."

Decker caught them deftly and slid into the driver's

seat, unlocking the passenger door so that Noah could climb in. "Yeah, I'm kind of used to driving on the wrong side of the road here," he said. "It makes you a little crazy, the first time or two."

"I'll just bet it does," Noah said. "There are people who would tell you I'm as crazy as I need to be, already, so we'll just let you do the driving at the moment. Hope Sarah can handle it, but I'm willing to bet she can."

"I'm sure," Decker said, but further conversation was cut short when Noah's phone rang. He looked at the display and saw that it was a call coming in on the special number he had given to President Habib.

"This is Colson," he said.

"Mister Colson," said the president. "I hope you'll forgive a worried father, but I just needed to know that you are working toward bringing my daughter home. Have you made any progress?"

"We've identified and located the person who called you to tell you that your daughter had been taken hostage," Noah said, "and we are zeroing in on him even now. I'm hopeful that he will be able to provide us with more information that will help us find her. I wish I had something more to tell you, but that's where we stand at the moment."

President Habib uttered a sigh. "Thank you," he said simply. "It gives me hope just to know that you are truly doing what you can. I will let you get back to your work, and continue my prayers for your success."

The call ended, and Decker looked over at Noah. "I've worked a lot of kidnapping cases," he said. "The one thing that never changes is that the victim's loved ones always need constant reassurance. Being a world leader isn't going to change that for him."

"I know," Noah said. "Simple human nature."

Pendergrast's apartment building was in South Hampstead, a half hour's drive from the hotel. Decker had punched it into the GPS on his phone, and followed the directions as he maneuvered through the city. Aberdare Gardens, the broad street on which it was located, was lined with apartment buildings that all seemed to be very much alike. Still, they had no trouble finding the right one.

Since they had not heard from Neil, it was a safe bet that Pendergrast was still holed up in his apartment, so they drove past the building toward the intersection. They found the little restaurant known as a chip shop with no problem, and parked the car in front of it. Both of them spotted Catherine as soon as they entered the building, and she looked up and smiled as she waved them over to her table.

"I'm Catherine," she said as they took seats. "Which of you might be Mister Colson?"

Noah smiled. "That would be me," he said. "This is James Mitchell, my associate."

Catherine shook hands with both of them as a young waitress approached their table. Despite the fact that they had eaten breakfast only a short time before, both men ordered snack-sized portions of cod and chips, the beer-battered fish and fried strips of potato that reminded them of French fries, with Coca-Cola. Their orders were delivered only a moment later, leaving them in relative privacy.

"This is a bit of an upscale chippy," Catherine said. "In most, you have to stand in line to place an order, but here they like to think of themselves as a restaurant, rather than just a chip shop. We can speak freely in here. This place is often used for clandestine meetings by Interpol and other agencies."

"I gather from your accent that you're a native here?" Noah asked. When she nodded, he went on. "I was given to understand that you work for the same people we do. Is that correct, or am I missing something?"

"It's correct. I'm the station chief for E & E in London, the agency's liaison and supply officer. If there's anything you need while you're here, you need only to let me know. So far, all I know is that you wanted me to keep an eye on the subject, and that's been very easy to do. In fact, there are so many different agencies watching him that we've been bumping into each other. Someone from NSA spotted me yesterday and wanted to know what my interest was. As far as they know, I'm with British intelligence, so I simply let them think I was looking into some of his local activities."

"British intelligence?" Decker asked. "A story like that won't blow up in your face?"

"Oh, not at all," Catherine said. "I truly am with MI6. It's a special arrangement between E & E and the SIS. Only a very few MI6 top staff have any idea of my real identity and affiliation, but letting me maintain an identity with SIS means they can occasionally put in a request to our boss for the type of services we offer. They're quite happy with the arrangement, and as far as the rest of the British government knows, I simply work in the liaison office that coordinates with Yank agencies."

Decker grinned. "Sounds like a terrific cover. So, what can you tell us about Pendergrast?"

"Jeremy Pendergrast is forty-seven years old, a former CIA employee who now dabbles in information marketing. He's known to provide certain other ser-vices, as well, such as negotiating secret deals between governments and facilitating certain types of clandes-tine operations. Here in the UK, he's fairly well known for having a lot of dirt on a lot of people. Occasion-ally, some of our less desirable citizens go to him when they feel that the government is getting too close to the things that they do. He knows the strings to pull to make excess scrutiny disappear, or even get rid of pend-ing criminal charges. Unfortunately, he has dirt on far too many people for anyone to be willing to take action to shut him down."

"Do they want him shut down?" Noah asked. "I'm planning to take him on a little vacation, to discuss a pretty important situation with him. I need to know what his involvement in it was, but it isn't necessarily important to me that he ever gets to come home."

"I don't think we're done with him just yet. Believe it or not, a sod like him can come in handy from time to time. If possible, I suspect we'd like to have him back when you're done with him, and more or less in one piece." She paused and smiled. "All right, perhaps two pieces."

"I'll do my best."

FIVE

When they finished their snacks, Catherine went with Noah and Decker to give them a tour of the neighborhood. The entire area was predominantly populated by apartment buildings, although a few small businesses dotted the area here and there. It wasn't hard to develop a staging plan for the abduction, as long as Pendergrast didn't throw a monkey wrench into the works by slipping off unobserved.

While they were touring the neighborhood, Neil called. "Hey, Boss man, I think I found what you're looking for in a safe house. Almost due west about fifty miles is a little village called Twyford, isn't that cute, and there's a farm house a half-dozen miles outside of it that is about as isolated as you can possibly get. According to the listing, the nearest neighbors would be in the village itself. It's available on a month-to-month rental, but it's pricey. Comes to about three thousand American dollars for a month, plus a thousand dollars worth of security deposit. Belongs to some rich guy in London, who rents it out to people who like to hunt. It's available right now. Do you want to look at it, or should I just snatch it up?"

"Sounds like it'll work," Noah said. "Go ahead and get it, and send me directions."

"You got it!" A moment later, Noah's phone beeped as it received the directions by text message.

"Neil found us a place to do our magic," Noah said to Decker. "Catherine, can we drop you back off at your car?"

"That would be dear," she said. "I left it at the chippy, so leave me off there."

Decker drove back to the chip shop and let Catherine out, and then headed for the M4 highway. Noah had punched Twyford into his GPS in order to simplify things, and they were on the way moments later.

Neil called again while they were traveling, to let Noah know that he had made the arrangements to rent the place under the name of Alexander Colson, so Noah could stop at the estate agent's office in Twyford to pick up the keys. Noah punched in the agent's address to his GPS, so when they got into town it was easy to find. The agent turned out to be a portly older man named Withers.

"Good to meet you, Mister Colson," Withers said. "Your man tells me you're a writer, eh?"

Neil hadn't bothered to mention this little detail, but Noah smiled and went with it. "I try to be," he said. "I'm working on a novel, it'll be my first. Some of my friends in the business told me that the best way to get any writing done is to set myself up in the English countryside."

Withers nodded his head vigorously. "Oh, aye," he said. "You'll be the fourth or fifth writer to use the estate for some quiet and solitude. I hope it goes well for you."

He gave Noah the keys to the house and a printed map that showed a number of landmarks to watch out for, in order to be certain of making the right turns. The estate was large, encompassing well over a thousand acres, with a river and a small lake on the premises.

The road leading to it was little more than a wagon trail, and Decker had to slow down in spots where runoff had left some deep holes. It took them almost twenty minutes to get to the house, but both men were amazed when they finally saw it.

The house had three stories, as well as a full basement. The agent had explained that it was nearly 200 years old, and had once been a private holiday residence of Lord Liverpool, who had served as prime minister of England under the reign of George IV in the 1820s. It was incredibly well furnished, and many of its pieces were antiques dating back to that period.

In addition to the house, there were several outbuildings on the property. Two large barns gave mute testimony to the estate's farming history, though the only occupants the men found were a number of stray cats that seemed to have taken up residence there. There was what appeared to be a chicken house, surrounded by a pen that would've allowed them a generous area in which to run and scratch, as well as what was obviously intended to be a garage for vehicles and equipment.

"Look at this," Noah said, as he and Decker were exploring one of the barns. He pointed upward to where a block and tackle hung from the highest point of the roof. "I'm guessing that's about fifty feet up, what do you think?"

Decker nodded. "I'd say you're about right. It blows my mind that the British seem to like these huge barns, but I guess having three hay lofts comes in handy for their winters."

"I guess. Right now, I'm thinking that if we hang Pendergrast off that hook up there by his hands, and just let him think about things overnight, he might be ready to do some serious talking come morning."

Decker stared upward at the hook. "You'd need to run him right up tight to the ceiling, so he doesn't have any slack. Probably still be a good idea for us to keep a watch on him, though."

"I was planning on it, but whoever is watching will stay out of sight. I want him to think he's alone, that we just hung him up and left him there to rot. Most people don't realize it, but there's very little more frightening than to think you're going to die slowly from thirst or starvation, and all alone. I want him to reach that point before we actually start to question him."

They got back into the car and started on the trip back to London. Noah called Neil to tell him the house was perfect and to be ready to move later that day.

"Oh, come on boss, I was just getting settled in here," Neil whined. "The window beside my desk has a fantastic view of the pool, do you know how many bikinis are out there right now?"

"When we get this job done, you can actually put on your trunks and go join them, but for now we got work to do. Pack it up."

"Me, put on trunks and go to the pool? Boss, have you seen the chicken legs I got stuck with? I'm trying to impress a girl, not scare her away forever! Don't worry, I'll be packed by the time you get here."

Noah ended that call, then dialed Sarah's number.

"Hola, Señor?" Sarah said as she answered.

"Sarah? It's Noah. How are things going on your end?"

"Hey, our job was easy. We got a white Maxus van, it's parked outside now. We're back at the hotel, in case you're wondering."

"Okay, that's good. Go ahead and start packing everything up, we're checking out this afternoon. The house that Neil found for us is ideal, so we'll be staying there for the rest of our time in England. What kind of car are you driving?"

"Range Rover, an SUV. Why?"

"That's good, the road to the house is pretty rough. Have everyone load their gear into your car, I want the van empty. We'll be there in an hour or so, and get our stuff packed up."

"Okay," Sarah said. "Hey, how many bedrooms are in that house?"

"I counted eight, so there's plenty. Just be ready to go when we get there."

It was well past noon by the time Noah and Decker got back to the hotel, so they joined the others for lunch after they packed everything up and loaded it into the Rover. Noah explained his plan, that Sarah and Neil would go on to the house, making a stop for groceries along the way, while he, Moose and Decker would pay a call to Mister Pendergrast. Noah had decided on a direct approach, simply snatching the man right out of his apartment. He called Catherine Potts to fill her in on the plan.

"Right, then," she said. "The tricky thing will be getting him packed up and hauled away without setting off too many alarms. Between NSA, Interpol and heaven knows who else, he gets watched pretty closely."

"What I'm counting on is that we can convince him to just walk out with us and get into our vehicle. It should look like three guys just going for a ride."

"All right. I'll just stay on station for a couple of hours after you leave, then. Everyone else seems to be watching me at the moment, curious why I'm watching him. If I stay put, they'll think I know what's going on and that I expect Pendergrast to be back soon. That should give you a head start, at least."

"What if I get you in any kind of trouble?" Noah asked.

"Oh, not at all," Catherine answered. "Those blokes are all visitors, here, and I'm MI6, as far as they know. Don't worry about me, luv, I'll be in the sunshine."

Noah thanked her and ended the call, turning back to Moose and Decker.

"Okay, when we make the snatch, Stan will be driving," Noah said, "since he's already familiar with the way out to the house. Moose, you and I will go inside the building. We'll knock on his door, and hopefully he'll open it up, but if he doesn't we'll kick it in."

"I sat there and watched his building security video all morning," Neil said, "and he never left his apartment. He had one visitor, a woman who went inside for about an hour, then left."

Moose gave a snort. "He seems to be a cocky one," he said. "Neil says he doesn't seem to have any kind of security, no bodyguards, nothing. You think he'll put up a fight?"

"There will be two guns pointed at him, so I doubt it. He might be a badass, but nobody can fight a bullet. We'll knock, and as soon as the door starts to open, we'll force our way in. That should knock him down, disorient him so that we can get control of the situation instantly. You'll stand back out of reach and keep him covered, while I put my gun to his head and explain that we're taking him with us."

They finished eating, and left the hotel. Decker had turned in the rented Jaguar when they had gotten back, so he, Noah and Moose got into the van while Sarah and Neil drove off in the Range Rover.

Noah dialed Catherine's number. "Hello," she answered cheerfully.

"Catherine, it's Colson again. Any change in the situation there?"

"Not even a bit," she said. "He had a visitor a couple of hours ago, a professional lady if you take my meaning, but it's been quiet since then."

"All right, we're on the way. We're in a white van. Call me immediately if anything changes before we get there, okay?"

"Will do," she said, then hung up the phone.

It took them nearly 30 minutes to drive back to Pendergrast's building, and there had been no calls. A parking space was open just in front of the building, and Decker pulled into it. Moose and Noah stepped out and walked nonchalantly up the walkway.

The two men entered the building by the main entrance and quickly found themselves standing in front of apartment 7B on the second floor. Noah reached out and knocked, while he and Moose both tried to keep their faces impassive.

There was silence on the other side of the door for a second, and then they heard footsteps approaching. There was a hesitation, probably while Pendergrast looked through the peephole to see who was at the door.

A second later, the door opened. As soon as it was obviously swinging inward, Moose plowed his weight into it, slamming it open and causing Pendergrast to fall back. He crashed into a hall table that had been covered in knickknacks, shattering it as he fell to the floor.

"What the…" That was as far as he got before he realized that the muzzle of a large automatic pistol was shoved against his cheek. That realization caused him to clamp his jaws tightly shut, while he stared into Noah's eyes.

"Smart man," Noah said. "Here's the situation. My friend and I would like you to take a ride with us. We have absolutely no qualms about killing you if you refuse or try to draw attention to yourself, so really, the only thing you can do is get up and walk calmly and peacefully out the door with us. If you so much as make a face at someone to try to say that you're in trouble, I will shoot you dead, and then I'd probably have to kill the other person, too. You wouldn't want that to happen, now would you?"

"Depends," Pendergrast said. "Apparently you're planning to kill me anyway, so what would I have to lose?"

"I have no intention of killing you, if I can avoid it. In fact, all I really want is to have a little talk with you, but under certain controlled conditions. Once that talk is over, I'll be happy to drop you off here once again. You only get killed if you make a mistake. Understand?"

Pendergrast flicked his eyes to Moose, who hadn't said a word and was standing just inside the now-closed door with his own pistol aimed at Pendergrast's head. He kept them on the big man for a moment, then looked back at Noah.

"Fine, you want to talk. Why can't we talk here?"

"Because I don't want to be interrupted, and I don't know who might be dropping by to visit you. We do this my way or no way, and if we do it no way, that's where you end up in trouble. Now, I'm going to back away and help you get up, and then we're going to walk out the front door like old friends, the three of us. Just remember that your old friends, here, each have a pistol in their pockets that are pointed at you. Got it?"

Pendergrast nodded once, and then accepted the hand Noah offered him to help him up. He didn't attempt to fight, and only looked around at the broken table and ceramics for a moment before dusting himself off. "Well, guys, you ready to go? I sure am."

Moose and Noah tucked their guns into the pockets of the light jackets they wore, and Moose opened the door again. Pendergrast smiled and stepped out, then waited for the two of them to take a position on either side of him. Side-by-side, the three of them walked down the hall to the stairway, and a moment later they walked out the front door.

Decker had stayed in the van as planned, and the side door was standing open. Pendergrast and Moose climbed in the side, while Noah took the passenger seat up front. Moose closed the side door, and Decker put the van in gear and drove away from the curb.

Moose produced some large zip strips, and quickly bound Pendergrast's hands behind his back, and then bound his feet together. Pendergrast cooperated, saying nothing during the procedure. Sitting on the floor of the van, he was unable to see out the windows, so he had no idea where they might be going.

They rode in complete silence for about twenty minutes, but finally Pendergrast's nerve broke. "Okay, can you at least tell me where we're headed? Is it going to be much longer before we get there?"

Noah looked around at him, but said nothing. A moment later, he turned back to look out the windshield. Pendergrast let out a sigh, and leaned against the side of the van. "I thought you wanted to talk," he said.

"I do," Noah said, "but I'll tell you when."

"Look, man, I'll tell you whatever you want to know. We don't have to do the rubber hose and spotlight treatment, just tell me what you want to know. I don't have a lot of secrets."

Noah turned to look at him again. "Okay, let's test that theory. Where is Selah Habib?"

Pendergrast scrunched his eyebrows together. "Who? I have no idea who you're talking about."

Noah smiled. "That was your one and only chance to avoid what's coming." He turned around and looked out the windshield again.

"No, wait," Pendergrast said. "Seriously, I don't know who we're talking about. Who the heck is Sheila whatever?"

Moose, who was also sitting on the floor of the van, kicked Pendergrast gently in the leg to get his attention. When he had it, he simply shook his head and put a finger to his lips. Pendergrast let out another sigh, then leaned back and shut up. The rest of the ride was in silence.

When they got to the house, Decker drove the van right into the barn and parked it under the hoist they had looked at earlier. Noah climbed out and opened the back door of the van, and Moose slid Pendergrast out until he was sitting on the edge of the van floor. A moment later, he took out a knife and cut Pendergrast's hands free.

The man rubbed his wrists and looked down at his bound ankles, but Moose shook his head. He produced another pair of zip strips and put one around each of Pendergrast's wrists, linking them together again, but this time in front of his body.

Noah had gone over to the wall and untied the rope that led to the block and tackle. The mechanism was well maintained, because the weight of the hook was enough to bring it down smoothly as Noah paid out the rope. When it hung just about Noah's height from the floor, Pendergrast suddenly had a look of understanding on his face.

Moose and Decker took the man by an arm each and put his zip-stripped wrists onto the hook, and then Noah began pulling on the rope. The block and tackle had been designed to lift several bales of hay at a time, so Pendergrast's weight was almost nothing to it. His feet left the floor only a second after Noah began pulling.

"Hey, wait a minute," he yelled. "The rope looks pretty old, come on, you don't want to do this! How high we going? Come on, man, you said you wanted to talk, let's talk."

"We tried that," Noah said, "but you decided to lie. I'm done with your lies. The next time I ask you a question, I want the truth." He kept pulling on the rope, lifting Pendergrast even higher.

"So ask," Pendergrast yelled. "I'll be honest, I swear!"

Noah didn't say another word, but just pulled on the rope until Pendergrast was hanging from the center beam of the roof. More than forty feet of nothing but air separated him from the concrete floor at the bottom, and the look of terror on his face told Noah he had chosen an appropriate technique.

Noah went to the wall and began climbing the ladder, going all the way to the third loft. The floor of that loft was just about even with where Pendergrast was hanging, and Noah walked right up to the gap.

"You ready to give me the truth?" Noah asked.

"Oh, yes, and you bet! Ask me anything, I'm ready to talk!"

"It's the same question I asked you before. Where is Selah Habib?"

"Oh, geez, I told you, I don't know who that is! Ask me something I can answer!"

Noah stood there and looked at him for a moment, then shook his head. "I don't think you will ever give me the truth," he said. "Here's the deal. I'm going to ask you one more time to answer that question, and if you don't, if you continue to tell me you don't know who I'm talking about, then my friends and I are going to get into our truck and drive away. I've rented this place for a month, so no one will be coming out here for at least that long. Do you want to know how long it would take you to die of thirst, hanging there? About four days, that's what I'm guessing. You might manage to make it five, but I don't think there's any hope of going beyond that. In the meantime, you will piss and shit yourself over and over while you hang there, and if you were to manage to shake yourself loose, you'd fall to the concrete floor. That would almost certainly break several bones, and make it impossible for you to go anywhere to get help." He paused and just looked into Pendergrast's eyes for a moment. "Where is Selah Habib?"

This time, Pendergrast hesitated. "Look, man, I swear

I don't know who that is."

Noah turned away without a word, walked back to the ladder and started down.

"Oh, come on, I'm trying, here!" Pendergrast yelled. "If you ask me something I can answer, I will, I swear." He continued shouting as Noah climbed all the way down, and motioned for Moose and Decker to get into the van. They drove out, and within seconds the van was completely out of range of Pendergrast's hearing.

They drove up to the house and parked, then went inside. Neil and Sarah had not yet arrived, but they found some teabags in the cabinet, along with a canister of sugar, and they each made themselves a cup of tea with the microwave.

"You really gonna let him hang there all night?" Moose asked.

"Yep. I figure that will soften him up, and he'll be ready to tell me whatever I want to know by morning."

"Thirst will be working on him by then," Decker said, "so that will help. He seems to be somewhat terrified of heights, too, so that won't hurt anything."

"He'll be trying to swing his way over to the loft floor," Noah said. "As soon as it gets dark, Moose, I want you to go out there and climb up to that loft as quietly as you possibly can, then just sit in the shadows and watch him. I don't think there's any chance he'd actually escape, but let's not take any risks."

Moose tapped on his phone for a moment. "Sundown isn't until eight fifteen tonight, so that'll be a few hours. At least it will give me time to eat some dinner first."

As if on cue, they heard the Range Rover drive up just outside the door, and all three got up to go and help bring their things in. Moose and Noah grabbed bags of groceries first, and carried them in to the table, then went back to get their own bags. Each of them chose a bedroom, except for Sarah, who carried her things into the room Noah had selected.

Since it was still only midafternoon, they all helped to put the groceries away and then sat down in the big living room and turned on the television. It was a large flat-screen model that was mounted on the wall, and the remote was lying on the coffee table. They watched a few minutes of a news program that was almost over, then flipped channels until they found a comedy movie that was just coming on.

When the movie ended, Sarah declared herself hungry and went to the kitchen to see what was available to make for dinner. Most of the food they had bought was simple fare, since they didn't really know how long they would be there. She opted for chicken salad sandwiches, and opened a big bag of rippled potato chips to go with them. She made each of them a sandwich and put it on a plate, along with a pile of chips, then yelled for them to come and get it. Everyone took a plate, although Neil stopped to make himself a second sandwich, and then they went back to the living room to watch more television.

"Sarah," Noah said, "how come you never make this at home?"

She shrugged her shoulders. "Because you usually do the cooking," she said. "This is the first chance I've had."

"Really? Remind me to change that."

SIX

Moose, for all his size and muscle, could move silently when he chose to do so. This was partly due to his Navy SEAL training, but he had also developed the skill on his own as a kid, always finding ways to sneak up on his friends during their various combat games. Getting up the ladder silently had not been difficult for him, and he had made himself comfortable on a couple of hay bales as he settled in to watch Pendergrast hanging.

Periodically, the man would start yelling for help, and would keep it up until his voice gave out. He reached the point that his voice sounded scratchy even when he first began talking, and Moose knew that the guy was on his way to cracking. Very few people could handle hanging this way and still manage to resist questioning. After only a few hours, Pendergrast—like most people— would be ready to do anything at all to get down from his position and survive it.

Noah could probably have questioned the guy right then and gotten the answers he wanted, but he insisted on leaving him hanging all night. Moose didn't know why, but he was learning to trust Noah's instincts. Letting him hang overnight might cause Pendergrast to spill even more beans, and Noah had demonstrated in the past that he could adapt quickly when the situation called for it.

The night wore on, and finally, Pendergrast stopped yelling and just hung there. His head was drooping onto his chest, and it dawned on Moose that the man had actually managed to fall asleep. *Don't think I could do that,* Moose thought to himself. *How can a guy sleep when he's hanging by his wrists like that?*

The answer, apparently, was that he couldn't sleep long in that position. The nap lasted about twenty minutes, before Pendergrast began groaning and woke up. He tried weakly to yell for help, but it was obvious that his spirit was not in it.

After another hour, he seemed to drift off again. Moose didn't know exactly what time it was, and he didn't want to light up his phone to find out, just in case Pendergrast were to look in his direction at that moment.

When the sun began to rise, peeking over the horizon, Moose went down the ladder again just as quietly as he had come up it. Pendergrast was still hanging where they had left him, and seemed to be nearly catatonic.

Moose slipped into the house, being quiet so that he wouldn't wake the others, but it was too late. They were already up, having coffee and breakfast at the table. Moose poured himself a cup and grabbed the plate with two big pancakes that Sarah had set aside for him on the warmer. He sat down at the table and smothered it with butter and syrup, then began eating.

"Since you're calm enough to eat, I gather that our guest is still hanging around," Noah said. "Am I right?"

Moose nodded, his mouth full. He chewed and swallowed quickly, then said, "Yep. Would you believe the guy actually managed to get some sleep? Dozing off, sleeping for about twenty minutes or so and then waking up."

"I'm not surprised," Noah said. "I would imagine it's pretty exhausting, just hanging there. Did he yell much?"

Again, Moose's head bobbed up and down. "In between naps, like clockwork. Kept yelling for help, even though I'm pretty sure he could tell nobody was coming."

"It's the survival instinct," Decker said. "Even when we know it's hopeless, we always try to hold onto some kind of hope. Somebody trapped in a ravine will continue to call for help until they die of dehydration, somebody facing a firing squad will imagine a sudden, last-minute reprieve, right up to the moment when the guns go off. It's just human nature."

"I don't know," Moose said. "I don't think I could go to sleep like that."

"You would if you hung there long enough," Noah said. "Exhaustion sets in, and there's nothing you can do about it. You get depressed, because you start to feel like there's no way out, and that's when the exhaustion will get you. I was counting on it." He shoved the last bite of pancakes into his mouth, and washed it down with coffee before getting to his feet. "I think it's time to pay him a visit. I want the rest of you to come out to the barn and stand underneath him, just looking up. Don't say anything, just stare at him."

Everyone but Moose was pretty well finished, and he shoved the rest of his own breakfast into his mouth as quickly as he could. When he was done, they all rose to follow Noah out to the barn.

The barn where Pendergrast was hanging was about a thousand yards from the house, so it took them a little while to walk out there. When they arrived, Moose, Sarah, Neil and Decker all went to stand just underneath the man while Noah climbed the ladder.

Pendergrast was awake, and began yelling at them to let him down. None of them responded, but just continued to stare up at him, keeping his attention while Noah moved as quietly as he could across the loft floor. He came up behind Pendergrast, out of the man's line of vision.

"You see those people down there?" Noah asked, startling Pendergrast. "They asked me to give you one more chance to be straight with me. This is the only chance you're going to get, and I want you to understand that. When I ask you a question, I want a straight answer. Do you understand me?" He moved around the hole in the floor so that Pendergrast could see him.

Pendergrast's lips were covered in spittle, and there was a dark stain on the front of his pants. The man had pissed himself. "Yes, yes, whatever you want," he shouted. "I'll tell you anything you want to know, I swear it!"

"That's good," Noah said, "because whether you live through this or not depends on how honest you are with me right now. So tell me, Jeremy, old pal, where is Selah Habib?"

"Look, they just hired me to deliver a message, okay? I never had anything to do with the girl, I just had to make a phone call, that's all."

Noah shook his head, and started to turn away.

"That's not the answer," he said as he took the first few steps back toward the ladder.

"Wait! Wait, please! I never saw the girl, myself, that's the truth, I swear, but you need to know that she was never really kidnapped! She made a deal with the Russians, to help her run away with her boyfriend. He's a Russian, from the embassy there in Nouakchott. She'd been keeping it a secret, because her father would never approve, but I guess it got pretty serious. They're living somewhere in Russia, but I have no idea where, I swear I don't."

Noah had stopped when he began talking, and turned back to face him. "Who hired you?"

"He was SVR, Russian foreign intelligence service. I've known the guy for years, his name is Vladimir Sokoloff, he works as an attaché in the Russian Embassy in London. He called me up a couple of weeks ago and told me he wanted me to negotiate a deal for him. It was all set up, already; the girl and her boyfriend were loaded onto a diplomatic flight back to Moscow, and all I had to do was deliver the message. It was just a pressure move —no one's really going to hurt the girl."

Noah stood still and stared at him for a long moment, then stepped back up to the edge of the hole. "Can you arrange a meeting with Sokoloff?"

"Yes, yes, all I got to do is call him. We've done business together for a few years, now; if I ask him to meet with me, he will. I don't have to tell him what it's about, I can say I've got a lead on some new information they might want." He licked his lips with a very dry tongue. "Just one thing, though—you can't let him go when you're done with him. You've got to kill him, promise me that. If you let him go, he'll know I set him up, and I'll be a dead man."

Once again, Noah just stared at him for a moment. "What if it turns out that he's more important to me than you are? Maybe it would be worth it to me to let him have you."

"Oh, come on, man," Pendergrast said frantically. "Do you have any idea how much information I can provide you? You keep me safe, and I can get you just about anything you want!"

Noah crossed his arms and looked into Pendergrast's eyes. "Can you get me the location of the girl?"

Pendergrast opened his mouth, but then closed it again. He licked his lips once more, then said, "I can, but you'd have to trust me. You'd have to leave Vladimir alone and let me handle him."

Noah smiled, the kind of smile a shark might wear just before it bites you. "What makes you think I would ever trust you, Jeremy?"

Pendergrast burst out laughing. "Right now, whoever you are, you got my life in your hands. Do you think I'd be stupid enough to cross you? You took me in broad daylight, right out of my apartment! You're obviously an American, but you're not CIA or NSA, so I got a hunch you're somebody a lot darker than that. I know that both of those keep tabs on me, so the chance I could ever hide from you would be pretty slim, right? Yeah, you can trust me. You can trust me because I know damn well that if I get sideways with you, you're going to make me a dead man, yourself, and I suspect it wouldn't be anything I'd want to experience on the way. Good enough?"

Noah stood there for a moment longer, then nodded. "I think you're being sincere," he said. "Hang tight for another minute, and I'll let you down. Just remember what you just said, though, and understand that if you cross me, your death will be as slow and painful as I can possibly make it. Got that?"

"I've got it, believe me, I've got it."

Noah traced his steps back to the ladder, and made his way down to the ground floor. He untied the rope from the hook that locked it in place, then slowly let the rope play through his fingers until Pendergrast's feet touched the floor. The man collapsed, unable to stand, and Moose moved in to pick him up.

Noah walked over and unhooked him from the block and tackle, and then Moose tossed Pendergrast over his shoulder and carried him up to the house. It was a long walk again, punctuated now and then by grunts and groans from Pendergrast.

Moose dropped him into a chair at the table, and then cut the zip strips to release him. Sarah went to the sink and got him a glass of water, cautioning him to sip slowly at first. Pendergrast nodded, but even by taking small sips, he emptied the glass within a minute.

"I think I'm getting some circulation back," he said. "Would it be possible to get to the bathroom?" He looked down at himself. "And could I maybe borrow a pair of pants from someone?"

Noah nodded, and Moose grabbed the man by one arm and helped him stand. He was still weak, and his legs were unsteady, so Moose had to help him all the way to the bathroom. Stan Decker went to his room and got a pair of his own Dockers and brought them to him, and stayed in the bathroom with him as he stripped and showered, leaning against the walls of the stall to stay on his feet. When he was finished, he managed to walk back to the table with only minor support from Decker.

"So, what's your plan?" Noah asked him. "How are you going to give me that location?"

"I'll need a phone," Pendergrast said. "I'll call Vladimir and tell him that the Israelis are on me, and I need to prove to them that the girl is unhurt. I can convince him that I have to go to her and get a photo of the two of us together in order to keep the Mossad off our backs. Israeli intelligence scares the hell out of him, I don't know why, but they do, and even though Israel and Mauritania don't maintain diplomatic relations, Israel would be dead set against this alliance with Russia and Syria. If they got wind of it, I guarantee you they really would be on top of me and anyone else they thought might know something. Vladimir would know that, too, so he'll believe me."

Noah cocked his head to one side and squinted at Pendergrast. "But why would they only want proof the girl is alive and unhurt? Wouldn't they be working to stop the alliance?"

"Not publicly, not right now. Once it's announced, then you'll see Israel all over it, but not till then. For now, they would just want to know whether the leverage is intact. If it is, meaning that the girl is safe and still in Russia's custody, then Israel would have to sit back and wait to see what happens. On the other hand, if they found out that something bad had happened to her, they could leak that information to President Habib and scuttle the whole deal. That's exactly what the Russians would be afraid of, and that's why I can use it this way. I'll get on a plane to Russia, to go get that supposedly necessary photograph, and all you have to do is follow me."

Noah shook his head. "That sounds like such a stupid plan that it's bound to work." He nodded to Neil, who produced a cell phone and handed it to Pendergrast.

"I hope you know the guy's phone number," Neil said.

"Trust me, it's embedded in my memory." He dialed a number quickly, then held the phone up to his ear. "Vladimir? It's Jeremy. Listen, buddy, we got us a problem. You want to guess who just paid me a visit? Yeah, Abner Ben Yousef! Well, what do you think he wants? I guess their people got wind of what's going on in Mauritania, and somehow they found out I was involved." He listened for a moment, then scowled. "I didn't leak anything," he said emphatically. "As far as I knew, only you and I knew that I was involved in this at all, but knowing how many leaks your organization has, I'm not surprised they found out about it. Well, it had to come from your place, nobody else knew! Okay, okay, calm down! All he wants is to know that the Habib girl is still alive and well, and they want me to get them proof of that. I'm supposed to go to her and come up with a photo of me and her together, or they're going to blow this whole thing wide open on us." He paused and listened again for a couple of minutes. "Yeah, yeah, I'm free right now. I don't have anything going on, so it's good timing. Just tell me where she is and I'll go get the photo, get these bastards off our backs."

He suddenly motioned for something to write with, and Sarah quickly produced a pen and notepad. Pendergrast clamped the phone between his ear and his shoulder, while he scribbled notes on the paper. "Okay, yeah, I've got it. I'll get on the next flight out to Moscow. You're sure that's where I'll find her, right? Okay, good enough."

He hit the end button on the phone and handed it back to Neil, who confirmed with a glance that the call was ended. Pendergrast looked at Noah.

"They're in a small town called Kubinka, about thirty-five miles southwest of Moscow. I've got to fly out as soon as possible, and he'll have someone meet me at the airport in Moscow to take me to them. You can follow me, but you got to figure out how you're going to cover me. If you're going to go in and take the girl, I don't want anyone thinking I led you to them. Can you manage that?"

Noah grinned. "That won't be a problem," he said. "We'll make sure no one suspects you. For right now, though, we need to get you back to your place so you can get cleaned up and ready to go. Ready for another ride?"

Pendergrast shrugged. "Sure, I guess so."

Noah looked at Sarah. "Can you rig up a blindfold for him? I don't want him to know how to get back here."

She grinned. "Sure, no problem."

SEVEN

ollowing Pendergrast's lead, Noah, Moose and Sarah had booked tickets on the same flight to Moscow, scheduled to depart early the next morning. They had driven the man back to his apartment and stayed with him while he reserved his own ticket, planting some of the nearly invisible, high-tech bugs that Neil had provided to them. The computer geek would be able to listen to everything that went on in the apartment, and had already rigged a tap on Pendergrast's cell phone.

"Why aren't we all going?" Neil asked that evening, as they had dinner.

"Well, you're not going because I don't want you away from your computer for any length of time," Noah said. "You're my intelligence division, remember? If anything is going on, you'll spot it before anyone else, and I need you to be where you can get word to me quickly. Decker is going to stay here with you, just in case Mister Pendergrast decides to pull a double cross and has any idea of this location."

"So what's your plan in Russia?" Decker asked him. "You won't be able to carry weapons on a commercial flight, you know that, right?"

"That's why I called the boss lady a while ago," Noah said. "Turns out our outfit has people in every major city, even though some of them don't know what we really do. Our station chief in Moscow will be waiting with a vehicle when we get off the plane, and everything we need will be inside. Depending on what we run into, it may be a simple snatch job or could boil down to a small-scale invasion. Whatever we have to do, he'll make sure we got the equipment for it."

Neil tossed a napkin onto the table angrily. "Doggone it," he said, "I get left out of all the fun! Why don't I ever get to play cops and robbers with you guys?"

"Because you have the worst firing range scores of anybody the organization has ever seen," Moose answered him. "You'd be more likely to shoot one of us than the enemy!"

The tall, skinny kid rolled his eyes. "Now that's not fair, not all of us can be Wyatt Earp. Some of us have to have real brains, y'know?"

"Hey, just relax, Neil," Noah said. "Maybe one of these days on a mission, the rest of us will get killed off and you'll have to go complete it yourself."

Decker started laughing, but Neil, Moose and Sarah just stared at Noah. "Holy crap," Neil said, "boss man, did you just make a joke?"

Noah looked at each of them in turn. "Well, I tried," he said. "Wasn't it funny?"

Sarah shivered. "Out of anyone else, it might have been, but out of you? Noah, that was downright terrifying."

Decker stopped laughing and looked at them all. "Well, I thought it was funny."

Moose shook his head. "That's only because you're not used to working with the human computer," he said. "If you'd been around him as long as we have, it would've scared you, too."

They finished eating, and retired to the living room to watch some television, but all of them went to their bedrooms before nine. Decker would get up with Noah, Moose and Sarah in the morning, to drive them to Heathrow, and they had to be through security and at the gate before eight AM.

Sarah followed Noah into the room they were sharing, and stepped out of her clothes as he did the same. "I wish we knew more about what's going to happen when we get to Russia," she said. "I hate to think this could be our last night together."

"Then don't think it," Noah said. "Believe me, I have every intention of coming out of this alive, and bringing Moose and that girl with me. I plan to spend a lot more nights making music on that beautiful body of yours."

She smirked at him as she slid under the covers. "I thought you didn't know beauty when you saw it?"

"Not really, but I know it when I touch it. Shut up and come here."

Noah's alarm went off at five AM, and he had to extricate himself from Sarah's arms and legs. Doing so woke her up, and she mumbled something about getting the first shower as she stumbled out of the bed. Noah watched her walk into the bathroom, then followed her and climbed into the shower with her.

"Hey," Sarah said, "I thought you were gonna let me go first?"

"This'll be faster. We don't have a lot of time this morning, so every minute we can save is a good thing."

Twenty minutes later, they walked into the kitchen to find Moose and Decker sitting at the table nursing cups of coffee, and there was a fresh pot on the counter. They each grabbed a cup and sat down with the two men.

"Drink fast," Decker said. "We need to be on the way in about ten minutes. Grab your bags, and as soon as you're ready we can hit the road."

"I'm ready," Noah said as he guzzled his coffee down. He got up and rinsed his cup, leaving it in the sink while Sarah finished hers in a couple of gulps.

"I'm good, let's go," she said. "We might as well get on with it." The four of them walked out the door and got into the Range Rover.

The drive to Heathrow took slightly less than an hour, and was made mostly in silence. Decker was concentrating on his driving, while the other three were trying to mentally prepare themselves for the mission they were going into.

Decker dropped them off at the terminal entrance and they checked in at one of the self-service kiosks, then started through security. Because each of them only had a small carry-on bag, the process went more quickly than it normally does in the US, but since their flight was leaving from the B satellite, they had a long trek ahead of them just to get to their gate.

It was while they were making that journey that Sarah suddenly grabbed hold of Noah's arm and pulled him down so she could whisper in his ear. "Look at your eight o'clock," she said. "It's Pendergrast. He's seen us, but he's pretending not to." She made a little giggle, so that onlookers would think she was whispering something romantic.

Noah didn't even look back at the man. "He's doing exactly what he's supposed to do," he whispered back. "And we're supposed to do the same, not notice him. Remember, there's no connection between us."

"I know that," Sarah whispered. "Just thought you'd like to know he showed up."

Noah caught a slight disappointment in her manner, and suddenly realized that she had been trying to please him. He quickly kissed her cheek and whispered, "And you were right. Thanks, babe."

Sarah smiled up at him, and continued to hold onto his arm as they walked the rest of the way to their gate. Moose, staying in character, walked slightly separate from them. He got to the gate about a minute before they did, and took a seat by himself. Noah and Sarah found a pair of seats together, and continued to keep up the act of a happy little couple.

Pendergrast arrived a moment later, and also took a seat. He had a magazine tucked under his arm that he opened and seemed to be reading while he waited for the flight to be called.

Boarding commenced about fifteen minutes later, and Sarah and Noah were among the first to board. Their seats were toward the back of the plane, and they found them with no trouble. Moose took his own seat, four rows ahead of them, and then they watched for Pendergrast. He was one of the last to board, with a seat near the very front of the aircraft.

The flight to Moscow's Sheremetyevo International Airport took only four hours, most of which was spent sleeping by the team members. They were all awake for the landing, of course, and were up and ready to disembark as soon as the plane stopped taxiing at its terminal.

Getting off the plane was quicker and easier than getting on it, since it wasn't done by section. Everyone simply got to their feet and into the aisle as quickly as they could, and there was a fair amount of pushing and shoving. Sarah stayed close to Noah, who stopped to let Moose step into the aisle in front of him. They walked right past Pendergrast, who caught Noah's eye for a split second and gave him a barely discernible nod.

Once they were off the plane and in the terminal, the three of them slowed to wait for Pendergrast to come back into view. It took only a couple of moments, and then all four merged into the line that formed up at the customs desk. Customs in Russia was fairly relaxed, and since none of them had any items to declare, they queued up in what was called the "green corridor." Bored customs inspectors accepted their declaration forms, which indicated that they were not carrying any restricted or taxable items, and simply waved them through, not bothering to open their bags and check. Moments later, they joined the crowd that was headed for the street outside.

Moose stopped pretending to be separate, and walked along with Noah and Sarah as they approached the entrance. They watched Pendergrast as he was greeted by a portly gentleman, and then Noah spotted the young man holding the sign he was looking for. He veered off toward the fellow with Moose and Sarah in tow.

"I'm Colson," he said to the man.

The fellow broke into a big smile. "Good to meet you," he said in perfect American English. "I'm Larry Carson. Can I help with your luggage? Come on, the car's right outside." He reached out and took Sarah's bag from her, then turned and led the way through the milling crowd to an exit. "I got you a Land Rover, I hope that's okay. It's a brand-new one we had on hand, because everybody else is driving Russian-made vehicles. We got the Land Rover a couple of months ago, but the ambassador felt that if we use it too much, it might send the wrong message."

"I'm sure it'll be fine, Larry," Noah said. "So, you're with the embassy here?"

"Yes, I'm a data analyst. That's my official job, and it keeps me out of the spotlight so that I'm here when you need me." He placed Sarah's bag into the back of the Land Rover, and stood back as Noah and Moose added their own. "Incidentally, I've got a couple of helpers watching your subject, so that we'll know what car he gets into, and I got everything on the Christmas list that was sent to me, as well. It's all in the storage space under the back seat."

Noah nodded. The "Christmas list" referred to the list of weapons Noah had requested. Since he anticipated a hostile environment, they would be a necessity. "What about extraction? Is it set up yet?"

"It is," Larry said. "I've arranged a Gulfstream five, chartered as a diplomatic flight. It's sitting out on the tarmac right now, waiting for delivery of some important files. In reality, of course, it's waiting for you and whoever you're bringing with you. When you get back to Moscow, you just call me—here's my card, by the way—and I'll meet you here to make sure you get onto the plane okay." He suddenly reached up and touched his left ear, where Noah could see an ear bud in place. "I just got word, your pigeon just got into a Mercedes limousine. It should be passing us in about a minute, so here are the keys, and she's all yours."

Sarah snatched the keys out of his hand, causing his face to register surprise as she jumped behind the wheel. Noah slid into the passenger seat in front, while Moose got into the back seat. Larry stepped back up onto the sidewalk as the Mercedes limo slid past, and Sarah let the clutch out. They were the second vehicle behind the Mercedes as it made its way toward the M2, the loop highway around Moscow.

"I'm gonna let one or two more cars get between us," Sarah said, as they merged onto the A130 toward Kubinka. "We don't want the driver to pay too much attention to us."

Noah nodded. "Sounds like a good idea," he said. "Just don't lose them. We know where Kubinka is, but we don't have an exact address."

"I won't," Sarah said with a smile. She slowed a bit to let a couple of vehicles come around her, then resumed her speed. The limousine was still in plain sight, and the intervening vehicles were keeping up with it.

In the back seat, Moose slid to his knees on the floorboard and lifted the seat up to look underneath. He gave a low whistle. "Man, we got some toys here. Three Glock 45s, four Uzis, and enough ammunition for a small war. There's a sniper rifle, too, looks like a .30-06, but I only see two magazines. They all have sound suppressors on them."

"That's everything I asked for, and it ought to be good enough," Noah said. "We want to hit them hard and fast, don't want to give them a chance to see what's coming before it's on them. I want to get them while Pendergrast is still inside, and we've got to leave him injured, but not seriously. That means we need a couple of the others to survive, as well, so that it doesn't look fishy that he's still alive."

"You think we're gonna find that many of them there?" Moose asked.

"Even if the girl really did run away on her own, she's being used as a pawn in a major international political game. Russia is going to have some kind of security on her, you can bet on it. I'm guessing there will be at least two bodyguards inside, plus two or more watching the grounds, and then there's the boyfriend. She met him at the Russian embassy, so it's quite possible that he's a Russian agent. Wooing this girl might have been his entire assignment, but that doesn't mean he hasn't been trained in combat. We'll need to watch him, and if possible, leave him alive."

"So we fire to incapacitate, rather than kill, right?"

"On the inside, anyway. Anyone on the outside who tries to get in our way is fair game. We need to eliminate them as quickly as possible, because they will alert the guards inside whatever house or structure we're dealing with."

Moose chuckled. "There's a very good silencer on the sniper rifle," he said. "If we can spot external guards, I can take them out at a distance."

"Good, then that's another option. Let's wait till we see the lay of the land, then I'll decide how to handle it."

"Then, what I'm going to do is cruise past wherever they stop," Sarah said. "I don't want them to pay a whole lot of attention to us. Once we see where they're at, I can circle the area to give you a better chance to look things over."

Noah nodded his head. "That'll be perfect," he said. "We want to get out of the car some distance away from whatever house or building they go to, so that we can approach from an unexpected direction. This is the kind of situation where stealth is key."

They rode in silence for a few minutes, and then Sarah glanced over at Noah. She turned her eyes back to the road. "Does it get to you, when you know you're going into a situation like this? Does the adrenaline start pumping?"

Noah turned his head to look at her. "No," he said. "I know what you mean, because I've heard other people talk about it, but I've never experienced it." He held out his left wrist to her. "Check my pulse if you want to. Strong and steady, and I've had doctors who have gone crazy trying to figure it out. I guess it's part of my disorder, but I don't get excited or apprehensive before I go into a conflict situation."

Sarah swallowed hard. "My heart is racing," she said. "I'm sure my blood pressure is probably up, too, even though I'm not the one who's going to be shooting people or getting shot at. I get—I don't know, I get all swelled up inside, whenever I know you're going to..."

Noah watched her for a few seconds. "Going to what?"

She made a nervous smile and shrugged. "When I know you're going to kill someone. It gets me all—pumped up, excited..."

"It turns her on, man," Moose said from the backseat. "Sarah, don't let it get to you. That's perfectly normal. I guarantee you, as soon as this mission is over, Elaine and I are going to lock ourselves into my place and not come out for a week."

Noah glanced at him, but then looked back at Sarah, who was blushing. "He's right about it being normal, at least for anyone but me. I don't have that reaction, for some reason. I just go in and do my job." He reached his hand up then and caressed her cheek with the backs of his fingers, then leaned over and whispered in her ear. "The only thing that ever gets me that excited is you."

Sarah's eyes went wide, and her head spun to look at him for just a second before it snapped back to the road. Noah saw the smile that she was barely able to suppress, but said nothing.

He hadn't lied to her; she definitely did get him excited, especially in the night. Noah had had girlfriends in the past, though he'd never had a relationship that lasted more than a few weeks. He had learned long ago, back when he and his best friend Molly were teenagers and casual lovers, that his libido was just as active as any other male's, but the truth was that he would find himself aroused and excited whenever he was in the company of a willing young woman.

As she'd told Allison, Sarah had decided that, since E & E operatives could not have normal relationships, a "no-strings" relationship with Noah would be the next best thing, and his body certainly enjoyed the physical pleasures she brought along, but he occasionally wondered if she expected more from him that he was able to give. The way his mind worked, he would willingly do things to make her happy, but if the situation required him to walk away or abandon her, Noah would do so without a moment's remorse. It wasn't that he didn't care about her, it was just that he was incapable of having such feelings, for her or anyone else.

"We're getting close," Sarah said. "Kubinka should be coming up within the next five miles or so."

"All right, then keep that limo in sight, but try not to be too obvious about it."

Sarah smirked. "Chill out," she said, "this is my specialty, remember?"

EIGHT

Kubinka owed a lot of its history to the Soviet Union's military. It had once been the home of the USSR's tank proving grounds, now housing the Russian tank museum, and had a fairly large military airbase. Most of the current town was made up of former barracks, many of which had been converted to homes or apartment buildings, combined with a number of small villages that had cropped up around the area. In fact, it had not even been known as a town until 2004.

Since then, however, there had been an influx of citizens, as jobs opened up due to manufacturing facilities coming into the area. As a result, there were some very nice homes in town, several of which were just off of the main road in town, known as Naro-Fominskoye. This was a broad street that ran north to south, and led into a more affluent area.

The interesting thing about the town was that it seemed to be built within a forest. Many of the houses and buildings were surrounded by trees, with dense foliage that made it almost impossible to see one house from another.

The limousine turned left onto a side street, but then

immediately turned into a driveway of the house on the corner. Sarah cruised past as if uninterested, but then turned left herself on the second street after that one. She took the first left she came to then, and circled back around until they could see the limo still parked at the same house.

"This is amazing," Noah said. "The trees are thick enough to cover our approach, but they've almost certainly got security in there, as well. Sarah, go up another block and let us out. Moose, give me a Glock and an Uzi, and you bring the rifle and a pistol. I'm hoping we can spot them before they spot us, and we'll see just how good you are with that sniper scope."

Moose handed him the weapons he asked for, then picked up his own. Sarah came to a stop at the next corner, which was hidden by trees from every direction, and the two men slipped out. Noah looked at the girl before he closed the door, and said, "Park somewhere that lets you keep an eye on the house, and I'm pretty sure you'll know when to come pick us up."

"Stay safe," she said as he shut the door, and then she drove away.

Noah and Moose stepped into the wooded area beside the road, moving slowly and quietly toward the house where the limo had stopped. According to Pendergrast, that would be the location of President Habib's daughter. In other circumstances, Noah would have preferred to make this assault at night, rather than in the middle of the afternoon, but there wasn't time to wait. It was possible, probably even likely, that the Russians would decide to move the girl after this visit from Pendergrast, so Noah had decided to take her immediately.

Each block on the road was approximately a thousand feet long, and while there were a few houses scattered around the one they were crossing, they were far enough away that Noah wasn't concerned about being observed. The two of them moved stealthily through the woods, and finally came to the street that divided one block from another. The house they wanted was across that street, but when they went to cross it they would be completely exposed for a few seconds.

"Boss," Moose said, "I'm thinking the best way to do this is for you to run across first and hit the ground. If anyone fires on you, I should be able to spot where they're shooting from and take the shooter out."

"That'll work," Noah said. "Set yourself in position, and signal me when to go."

Moose put himself beside a tree and braced the sniper rifle's barrel against it. He leaned left, then right, checking his field of vision, then said, "Go!"

Noah rushed out from behind the trees that were concealing him, and hurried across the road. As soon as he got into the cover of the woods on the other side, he dropped to the ground and watched for any motion in the woods around him.

There was nothing, which surprised him. He had been sure that the Russians would have security in the woods around the house, but it was possible that they were keeping it closer to the building. He held up a hand and hooked a finger at Moose, who came running across the road a second later and dropped down beside him.

"No motion, no activity," Noah said. "If they got anybody in the woods, they're keeping them close to the house. Let's move, slow and quiet."

The two men began leapfrogging, with Noah going first and moving forward five yards, then letting Moose pass him by an equal distance. After each dash, they would stop and wait, watching and listening for any activity that might indicate security had seen them.

They reached the point where the house was barely visible through the trees, with Moose in the lead. He stopped and listened, and then suddenly held up a hand to tell Noah to wait. Noah watched as Moose carefully and quietly adjusted his position, and then pointed with two fingers in two different directions.

Looking carefully, Noah saw what Moose was trying to show him. Two men, dressed in camo fatigues, were crouching beside a couple of trees, about fifty feet apart. Each of them held what looked like an HK MP5, and Noah had no doubt they knew how to use their weapons.

Moose held up two fingers, and then made a gun with his hand and dropped the thumb twice, signaling that he was going to take out both of them. Noah stayed put as Moose carefully lined up his shots. The rifle coughed once and the nearest of the two men fell over backward, obviously hit in the forehead. The second man suddenly rose, but he didn't have the sense to duck behind a tree. Moose's rifle coughed again, and that fellow simply dropped where he stood, a large part of his head suddenly missing.

Moose and Noah held their positions for a moment, waiting to see if anyone had realized what had happened. When there was no activity after a few seconds, Noah moved up beside Moose.

"Good shots," he whispered. "I think we might want to go around the south side of the house, because there might be one or two more of them there. We're far enough from the house with these two to make me think it's worth checking out."

"Yeah, I get it. You first?"

Noah nodded, then moved off to the left, angling slightly to the west, to position himself to see any activity south of the house. He paused, but when he could sense no one ahead of him, he signaled Moose to make his next move.

Moose ran a crooked path to his next position, and after a moment he signaled Noah to go ahead. Noah rose to his feet and ran quietly past Moose, then dropped to the ground and froze. Twenty yards ahead of him, a third man stood leaning against a tree, his back to Noah.

Noah could see the man's left shoulder and hip, but he didn't have a clear shot. He glanced over his shoulder at Moose, but the big man's view of the target was no better. Noah rose silently to his feet again, letting the Uzi hang from the shoulder as he extended the pistol ahead of himself, and walked carefully and quietly toward the security guard.

He had gotten within ten feet of the man when a slight crunch under his feet caused the fellow to turn and look in his direction. Noah squeezed his trigger once, and the man's eyes and nose seemed to blow out the back of his head. He dropped like a stone where he stood, and probably hadn't even had time to realize that he was about to die.

Still standing, Noah looked around and knew that there was no one else in the woods but himself and Moose. He signaled Moose to join him, and began moving toward the house.

The limo was still in the driveway, and the driver was standing beside it. There was unfortunately no way that they could get to the door without being seen by the driver, so Noah pointed at the man and nodded to Moose. A few seconds later, the driver fell prone beside the car, his brain splattered across its windshield.

They burst forward, running straight to the back door of the house, where Noah paused to try the knob. To his surprise, it turned easily, and he yanked the door open and rushed inside with Moose right behind him. The kitchen and living room seemed to be one big common area, and Noah saw several people gathered there. Selah Habib, Jeremy Pendergrast and another man were gathered together in the center of the room, while a woman pointed a camera at them, but two other men were holding MP5s, which they began to raise toward the intruders. Noah fired twice, and both of their heads disintegrated. The girl began to scream, and the woman with the camera simply froze, staring at Noah and Moose with her eyes wide and her mouth open.

"What the hell is this?" Pendergrast demanded, being sure not to show any recognition of the invaders. "Do you have any idea who…"

Noah turned his pistol toward Pendergrast and fired once. The bullet cut a groove along the left side of the man's head and he fell without another word, his eyes rolling back into his head as he lost consciousness. The woman holding the camera finally screamed as Noah grabbed her hair and shoved her into a chair, and the remaining young man simply stood beside Selah, looking calmly and coldly into Noah's eyes as she, whimpering, tried to hide behind him.

"We've come for the girl," Noah said to him. "You don't have to die, but it's your call."

"Vasily?" Selah said. "Don't let them take me, I want to stay with you!"

Vasily continued to stare into Noah's eyes, but he spoke over his shoulder to Selah. "I have no choice, my dear," he said with a distinct Russian accent. "If I try to resist or keep you, he will simply kill me, and take you anyway." He turned his face back toward Noah. "You work for her father?"

Noah smiled coldly. "You wouldn't even want to know who I work for," he said. "Just take it as a given that most people don't survive a meeting with me. You can be the exception, and all you have to do is sit down and be quiet."

Vasily smiled back. "I won't resist you," he said. "I will tell you this, however—this will not be the last time we meet."

"For your sake, Vasily, you better hope it is. Next time, you might not have the option of living through it."

The young man winked at him. "I suppose we shall have to see how things turn out, then, won't we? Perhaps I shall surprise you."

"Not a good idea," Noah said. "I'm not fond of surprises. Now sit, and be very quiet."

Vasily moved to the side and sat on the sofa, while Selah began to cry. He looked at her. "Compose yourself," he said. "I have no doubt these men are simply taking you back to your father, and that you'll be safe. We shall have to make—other arrangements, so that we can be together again. Go with them quietly, and just wait for me. I will be in touch soon."

Moose stepped forward and grabbed Selah by the arm, dragging her toward the back door. Noah kept Vasily covered, walking backward as he did so, and waited until Moose had taken the girl outside before he stopped and looked at the Russian boy again.

"Sometimes, I change my mind at the last minute." He squeezed the trigger, and a third eye appeared in the center of Vasily's forehead. The woman who had been taking the pictures began to scream once more, and Noah put a bullet into the back of the chair, just missing her, as he turned and sprinted out the back.

The Land Rover slid to a stop at the end of the driveway, and Moose shoved the girl into the back seat, then got in beside her. Noah ran and jumped into the front passenger seat, and Sarah shoved the big car into gear and dumped the clutch. Gravel flew as the car leaped forward, and she maneuvered her way through various streets of the town, making her way back to the highway.

"Did anyone get a look at the car?" Sarah asked.

Noah shook his head. "The only one who could have would have been too scared to try. I think we're in the clear, for at least the next twenty minutes or so. Let's get on the highway and head back to Moscow, and I doubt anyone will bother us."

"Vasily will come for me," Selah said. "He will come for me, and he is a man who knows how to handle criminals like you!"

"Oh, shut up, bitch," Sarah said. "Just shut up!"

"Selah, did you know that the Russians are claiming they kidnapped you?" Noah asked. "Did you know that they claimed they were holding you against your will, and threatened to kill you and chop you up if your father did not do what they want him to do?"

Selah stared at him. "That is a lie," she said. "Vasily and I are going to be married, and there is nothing my father can do to stop it. He is telling you lies to make you come and find me, but Vasily will come for me again."

Noah shrugged. "That might be a little difficult," he said, and then he leaned his head back against the head-rest and closed his eyes. "Wake me up when we get close to Moscow, okay?"

"Sure," Sarah said, glancing at him out of the corner of her eye. She watched him for a second, then turned her eyes back to the road.

The drive was uneventful, but Sarah decided to take a slightly different route back to the airport, anyway. The path took her through part of Moscow, and she was amazed at just how much greenery she saw. It seemed that almost every block of the city had its own small piece of forest, despite the urban sprawl that threatened to displace it all. Even areas of the city that were obviously commercial or industrial seemed to be almost overgrown with trees. Many of the signs were in both Russian and English, and she saw some pointing toward the Kremlin, Saint Basil's Cathedral and Red Square.

Noah was awake, and pointed at the signs indicating those landmarks. "Wish we had time," he said. "Architecture always fascinates me."

Sarah smiled. "Maybe you can bring me back on vacation, someday."

"Like any of us are gonna live long enough to have a vacation," Moose mumbled. "I'm half surprised we're still alive, right now."

Selah, who had been leaning against the window on her side, said, "You won't be for long, not when Vasily finds you."

Noah turned in his seat to look at her. "So, you're not the little innocent you're hoping to make us believe you are."

The girl looked at him, trying to look confused.

"What? I only know that Vasily can get very, very angry. He will not be happy by the time he finds you."

"No, that's not what you said a minute ago. You implied that you knew Vasily would kill us if he caught us, so that tells me that you know exactly what kind of man he was. Since you knew that, then I have to figure you knew exactly how you were being used to pressure your father into this political mess, right?"

"I know nothing about that, as I told you. I don't know if Vasily would truly kill you or not, but I know that he will be angry enough to do so."

"I seriously doubt it," Noah said. "It's pretty hard to be angry when your brains are blown out."

Sarah gasped and looked at Noah, and Selah stared at him in shock.

"You are lying," Selah said. "You would not dare to kill him, you would not dare to risk..."

"You listen to me, little girl; my orders were to find you, bring you back and kill everyone responsible for you being taken. At this point, Vasily is the only one I can find that could be held responsible, so putting a bullet through his head just sort of made me feel good. He's dead, bank on it. What I want to know is what it is you think I wouldn't dare risk."

"You are a liar!" Selah screamed at him. "Vasily is alive, he's alive, I know it! If you had killed him, you would never get out of here alive! No one would ever willingly anger Nicolaich Andropov!"

Noah cocked his head at her. "And who is Nicolaich Andropov? What makes you think I'd be afraid of him?"

Some part of Selah seemed to be reaching the point of believing that Vasily was dead, because she leaned back against her seat and let her eyes close, her head resting against the window as tears streamed down her cheeks. "He is a director of SVR," she said slowly, "a man who decides who lives and who dies, and he is Vasily's father. If you have killed Vasily, then you have ordered your own deaths. It will not matter who you are, or who you work for. He will never stop until he has seen you dead. Nicolaich will never stop."

Selah ran down, and Noah turned to face forward again. They were nearing the airport, so he took out his phone and called Larry Carson.

"Larry, it's Alexander Colson. We got our package, you got the plane all warmed up?"

"Great guns, am I glad to hear from you! We've got SVR crawling all over this airport, and from what I understand, every other airport is just as busy! Word is, they're looking for a group of five men, possibly Israeli, who killed several people down in Kubinka and made off with some sort of political asset. Since I know you were headed for Kubinka, I just can't help wondering if this mess might be connected to you."

"I'd say it's pretty much a certainty," Noah said. "What's this going to do to us getting on the plane?"

"Well, you're not Israelis, but you're not Russians, either. The SVR has roadblocks set up at every entrance and exit to this airport; they're checking everybody coming in or out. If they recognize your package, or get suspicious because you don't speak the local lingo, there is a pretty good chance they're never going to let you get near that plane."

"Is there any kind of back way in, that will get us close to the plane?"

"I don't know of any," Larry said. "How far out are you?"

Noah glanced over at Sarah and repeated the question. "About three minutes, we're on the E105," she said.

"About three minutes on the E105. Any suggestions?"

"Yeah, turn around and go back towards Moscow, just past the loop. Go to the parking lot of the Nescafe Imax theater, and I'll have someone meet you there. He'll take all the weapons from you, and give you something to help keep that package quiet. Stuff it into the compartment under the back seat, and then my buddy there will give you some things to prove you've just been cruising around Moscow for the last couple of hours. We've already modified some flight records to make it appear that you were just here on a layover, on the way to Hong Kong, and he will also give you tickets that would get you on the next flight."

"Wait a minute, what happened to the Gulfstream?" Noah asked.

"I've still got it waiting, but we have to get you inside the airport safely. The SVR has checkpoints set up on all the roads leading in and out, but once you get inside the grounds, here, then we can divert you over to the diplomatic gate. Just come all the way up to the terminal, as if you're dropping someone off, and I'll be waiting for you."

Noah ended the call, then told Sarah to turn the Land Rover around. He punched the Nescafe IMAX theater into his phone's GPS and handed it to her. "That's where we have to go," he said. "Larry's got somebody waiting there for us."

The pretty blonde shook her head, but took the next opportunity to turn the car around and began following the phone's spoken directions. Eight minutes later, she pulled up into the parking lot and stopped. Another car whipped in beside them only a few seconds later, and a young man jumped out of it as Noah stepped out of the Rover.

"Mister Colson? I'm Harold Frank, I work with Larry Carson at the embassy. I've got some things for you, and I understand you have some things for me."

Moose shoved Selah off the seat and lifted it up, then began passing the guns out to Noah, who loaded them into the trunk of Harold's car. The girl didn't protest, and almost seemed to be catatonic, until Moose tried to push her down into the storage compartment. Then she objected, but Harold leaned in through the open door. In his hand, he held a hypodermic syringe, the needle of which he jabbed into the girl's thigh. She squealed, and tried to kick at him, but only a few seconds later she suddenly relaxed and seemed to drift off into a deep sleep. Moose arranged her in the storage compartment as comfortably as he could, then put the seat down over her and sat on it again.

"Larry said he thought that might come in handy, so I brought it along," Harold said. "I've also got some other things for you." He handed Noah some paperwork, which included three tickets on a connecting flight to Hong Kong, a rental agreement on the Land Rover, a large stack of tourist brochures from popular tourist attractions in the city, a digital camera that was chock full of photos of many Russian buildings, bags from a Russian carryout restaurant and three large cups from Starbucks that still had residual latte in the bottoms. "Make sure whoever stops you sees all the trash, and be sure to be enthusiastic about all the things you saw while you were here. Apparently the witnesses to what happened are confused about how many people were involved, but they both seem to agree that they were Israelis. That's who the roadblocks are looking for, so they probably won't even look you over very hard." He nodded toward the back seat. "She's going to be out cold for about thirty minutes, which should be plenty of time to get you past the checkpoints. Still, you don't want to waste moments, so you better get going. Best of luck!"

Harold got back into his car and drove away quickly, while Noah slid back into the passenger seat of the Land Rover. "You heard the man, let's get moving. We need to be catching up with Larry before she wakes up."

NINE

They fell into line for the checkpoint, which was luckily not very long. Only a few moments later, it was their turn as two gruff Russian agents shoved their faces in through the front windows. One of them spoke in Russian, but Noah shook his head.

"Sorry, we don't speak Russian, just English. What's going on?"

The agent rolled his eyes. "We are looking for some criminals who may be trying to get out of the country," he said. "Please show me your passports and identifications."

All three of them handed over their passports and ID, and Noah made a point of showing the agent their connecting flight tickets. "Is this going to take very long, sir?" Noah asked. "We're supposed to go back through security pretty soon, our next flight leaves in about an hour."

The two Russian agents glanced through the passports and at the tickets, and then looked around the interior of the vehicle. There were food bags on the front seat between Noah and Sarah, and another in the floorboard of the backseat. Sarah had a stack of brochures on the seat beside her leg, and there were coffee cups in the cup holders.

The agents passed the paperwork back to Noah, and stepped back as they waved the Land Rover through. Both of them looked somewhat disgusted at the "American tourists," but they said nothing. Sarah drove forward, and a moment later they spotted Larry standing in front of the terminal.

Larry slid into the back seat beside Moose as they stopped for him, and gave Sarah directions toward the diplomatic gate. "I was starting to worry," he said. "I take it everything went all right at the checkpoint?"

Moose shrugged and grinned. "I got the impression that the guys looking us over don't care for tourists, but other than that it went fine."

Larry smiled. "That's pretty normal, for those guys." He patted the seat. "And your package is safe in here?"

"Yep," Moose said. "Your buddy's sleepy juice helped a lot."

"Good, good. Okay, turn in through that gate up there on the left, then follow the yellow line on the tarmac. That's the plane, right over there." He pointed at a Gulfstream that was waiting beside a large hangar. "Pull in between the plane and the hangar building, and we should be able to get the girl out and onto the plane without anyone seeing."

Sarah parked where she was told to, and Moose waited until Larry slid out, then lifted up the seat. He reached in and grabbed Selah by her shoulders, pulled her up and out and tossed her over his own shoulder, then walked straight up the stairs into the plane. Sarah and Noah grabbed the carry-on bags from the back of the Land Rover, and followed a moment later.

Larry waved as Noah stepped inside the plane, then

slid into the driver's seat of the Land Rover and drove away. A man in a copilot's uniform closed the door and then walked into the cockpit area, as a young woman dressed as a flight attendant did her best to ignore the fact that one of her passengers had obviously been drugged.

Moose had parked himself in the seat beside Selah's, while Sarah and Noah took another pair, facing backward toward them. The flight attendant checked to see that they were all buckled into their seat belts, then stepped into the cockpit for a moment. A few seconds later, she came back out and took her own seat, as the engines started up.

It took only a few minutes to get everything warmed up and ready, and then the plane began to taxi toward the runway. As it turned into the wind, Noah heard Sarah breathe a sigh of relief, and then the ground was rushing past as the plane gained speed. The nose lifted up, and a moment later the sound of the wheels on the asphalt came to a sudden end as they left the runway.

"A little nervous, were you?" Noah asked her.

She stuck her tongue out at him. "Not all of us can be perfectly calm all the time," she said. "Some people know what it feels like to worry. Just because you don't, that doesn't mean you can judge me for it."

"I'm not judging," he said. "There's a part of me that wishes I knew what it felt like, just so I could feel normal, I guess."

"Be careful what you wish for, boss," Moose said. "I've been a nervous wreck from the very moment we landed here, and it hasn't let up yet. Diplomatic flight or not, if they knew we had her on this plane, there's not much doubt in my mind that they'd blow us out of the sky."

"Oh, don't you just have the most wonderful thoughts," Sarah said. "I was actually starting to calm down, starting to feel better, but no, you can't let me relax! You got to make sure I keep right on worrying, don't you?"

"Hey, I just calls 'em like I sees 'em," Moose said. "Trust me, I'm just as worried as you are."

"Just relax, the best you can," Noah said. "It's not like you can do anything about it."

Selah gave a groan, and began to wake up. The plane leveled off and a moment later, the copilot reappeared. He stopped beside Noah.

"You're Mister Colson, right?" Noah nodded. "Okay, I was told to let you know that we're on the way to Nouakchott in Mauritania. Our flight plan actually calls for us to be headed for London, but we're being diverted, and I'm supposed to tell you that your other associates back in England will be returning to the states later today."

Noah nodded. "Thank you, I appreciate it." The copilot returned to the cockpit, and Noah reached into his pocket for his cell phone. It showed four bars of service, so he quickly dialed the number that would connect him to his boss, Allison.

"Camelot," she said as she answered. "I understand some congratulations are in order."

"Well, we managed to find her," he said, "and we have her with us on the way back to Mauritania. I terminated the one person I'm sure was involved in taking her out of her own country, but it appears that there are some bigger people involved. Do you know anything about Nicolaich Andropov?"

He could hear Allison tapping on computer keys.

"Hmmm, checking the file on this guy. Deputy director of SVR, handles a lot of wet work. Sounds like their version of me. What about him?"

"If the girl is telling the truth, then the man I killed is his son. He was also, again according to the girl, planning to marry her. To be honest, I didn't get the impression that he was too invested in that idea. He seemed a lot more interested in the political uses he could make of her."

"Typical," Allison said. "We're bringing Neil and Mister Decker back home today, and you and the others can come home after you've dropped Selah off to her father. Ambassador Morgenstern will be letting him know shortly that you're on the way with the girl, so there should be a diplomatic reception waiting for you when you land. There will also be a new crew waiting for the plane you're on, to turn around and fly you back to Denver. I understand that plane is pretty comfortable, so you can get some sleep."

"That will be appreciated," Noah said. "If there's one thing I'm learning about this life, it's that you don't get as much sleep as you want."

"Yeah, but we pay you pretty well. You can't have everything, right? Hopefully, I'll see you in a couple of days. I can't wait for the debriefing on this one, and from what I hear, there may be some commendations in it for you and your team."

"See you then, boss lady," Noah said. He ended the call, and looked over at Selah. "Well, hello there, young lady," he said. "We'll be landing in a few hours, and I understand your daddy will be waiting for you when we get there. I don't know how much trouble you might be in, but I suspect it's going to be more than just the usual grounding."

She shook her head. "My father could beat me and imprison me, and I would still be better off than you. I only met Nicolaich a few days ago, but I have heard so much about him, about how he never fails, and you have painted targets on your heads. On the other hand, if Vasily is really dead, then Nicolaich will probably be coming for me, as well. If he gives me the chance, before he kills me, I shall tell him everything I know about you. I shall describe each of you to him, so that he might find you and take his vengeance."

Noah sat and stared at her for a moment, and then smiled. "Be sure to tell him this, too," he said. "Tell him that I said I'll be waiting."

The flight attendant offered to make them lunch, and all but Selah accepted. It was simple fare, consisting of roast beef sandwiches, potato chips and soft drinks, but it was welcome. Once they had eaten, Noah and Sarah drifted off to sleep, while Moose sat up to watch Selah.

The flight lasted almost seven hours, and was uneventful. Noah woke up after about three hours, and let Moose get some sleep for the rest of the trip.

Shortly before they landed, Selah turned to look at Noah. "Do you know what you have done? I have spent the last two years trying to get away from my father, trying to be free of his manipulations and threats, and you have taken that away from me. I had found someone who loved me for me, someone who was good to me and would not use me, the way my father tried to do. Now, if Nicolaich does not kill me, I will be forced to marry some potentate of another country that my father wishes to engage in trade or security agreements. I shall be nothing more than a slave of my father, despite the fact that in public, he despises the way women are treated in our country." She shook her head in misery. "And you, you will go back to wherever you have come from, and forget what you have done to me. You will not remember, not until the day when Nicolaich comes for you. On that day, I pray that you will have time, have just one moment, to remember me, before he does to you the same thing you did to Vasily."

Noah looked the girl in the eye, but he said nothing. It was quite possible that she was telling the truth, and would be used as a political slave in her father's administration, but that meant nothing to Noah. In her country, this was acceptable, and there was nothing that he could do about it even if he wanted to.

As for her insistence that Vasily's father would be coming for him, Noah gave it little credibility. Nicolaich probably knew nothing of the existence of E & E, but even if he did, this operation did not fit the way the organization usually operated. If it happened that they identified him and Moose as the shooters, they would only find the names that were used on their passports for this mission, with no possible way to trace them back to their true identities. There was very little chance that Nicolaich Andropov would ever be any threat to Team Camelot.

The captain announced over the intercom that they were about to land, and Noah woke Moose and Sarah. The plane touched down fifteen minutes later and taxied to an area that had been cordoned off and was surrounded by Mauritanian military and police vehicles.

As soon as the plane stopped moving, the copilot appeared to open the door, and three men rushed inside. One of them was President Habib, who threw both arms around his daughter and wept as he clung to her.

Morgenstern was present, as was the Prime Minister, and both men congratulated him on the success of his mission. As they spoke, the flight crew exited the airplane, and another crew entered. Noah watched the girl's face as her father held her, and saw nothing but contempt.

"Mister Colson," the president said, "there are not words to express my gratitude for what you have done. You have returned my daughter to me, and I am forever in your debt. And if there is ever anything I can do for you, you need only let me know."

They shook hands, and a moment later the president escorted his daughter off the plane. There was something in the way he kept his hand on her arm that told Noah that she had been at least somewhat honest with him about the situation she would be facing, but it was still not his concern. The new flight crew informed the three of them that they would be flying nonstop to Denver, as soon as the plane was refueled, and the door was closed only a moment later.

Refueling took almost 20 minutes, but as soon as it was done they returned to the air. The flight would take almost 11 hours, and Moose announced that he planned to spend most of it sleeping. Noah and Sarah opted to watch a movie on a screen that folded down from the ceiling, but when it was over they both decided to get more sleep. All three of them awoke after several hours, and the flight attendant was happy to offer them breakfast.

The plane landed in Denver a couple of hours later, and Noah was delighted to see his friend Marco waiting for them. "It's about time you got back," Marco said. "I've got a nice, comfortable SUV waiting to take you home. You got any luggage to grab or anything?"

"No, just our carry-ons. All the rest was with our other team members in London, so I guess they brought it back with them."

Marco grinned. "Okay, then, let's get you folks home. The Dragon Lady says to let you get some R and R for the rest of the day, but then she wants to see all of you first thing in the morning for debrief."

He led the way out to the big Ford Expedition he was driving, and they all climbed in. Noah let Moose take the front passenger seat, while he slid into the backseat with Sarah. Moose took out his phone and called Elaine, his girlfriend—who also happened to be the daughter of Donald Jefferson, their supply officer—to let her know that he was back and dying to see her. From the sounds that were coming from the phone, she seemed quite excited at the prospect.

Sarah suddenly slid across the seat to lean into Noah, and he put an arm around her. They rode like that all the way to his house, where Moose got into his own car and headed for home. Noah and Sarah went to the door, where they found a note from Stan Decker. It simply said that he would see them at the debriefing, and thanked them for letting him be a part of the team, even for such a short time.

It was still relatively early in the day, and neither of them were terribly tired. After twenty minutes of staring at the television screen and finding nothing worth watching, Noah suddenly grabbed Sarah's hand and pulled her to her feet.

"What? Where we going?" Sarah asked, but Noah only put his finger to his lips. He pulled her out the back door, and she suddenly realized he was taking her to the boathouse. They had only been out on the boat a couple of times, and she let out a squeal of delight when he opened the door and led her inside and onto the boat. He used a remote to raise the big overhead door that led onto the lake, then fired up the big Mercury engine and eased the boat out of its slip. When they were out of the boathouse, he turned it around, then shoved the throttle and the big boat shot forward like it had a rocket in its tail. They cruised out to the middle of the lake, and then kicked back on the deck to just enjoy the sun and the wind and the waves.

They stayed out on the water until they began to get hungry in the late afternoon, then headed in and put the boat away. Neither of them felt like cooking, so they got into Noah's Corvette and headed out to the Sagebrush Saloon, their mutual favorite eatery. Neil was washing his Hummer as they drove away, and they waved at him as they went by. Neither was terribly surprised when the big yellow Hummer suddenly pulled out on the road behind them and followed them out to the Saloon.

"Good to see you guys," Neil said, as he climbed out of the Hummer beside them in the parking lot. "Hope you don't mind if I join you for dinner?"

"Of course we don't mind," Sarah said. "Come on, let's get a table. The booths are too hard, and the chairs have padded seats."

They sat down and put their orders in, then chatted a bit about the mission. Noah and Sarah filled Neil in on how things had gone in Russia, while Neil simply complained about Decker driving him crazy while they were stuck in London.

"Did you know that man never, ever shuts up? He talks, and he talks and then he talks some more."

"Really?" Noah asked. "He didn't seem like that with me."

"Of course not," Neil said, "but you guys won't let me carry a gun, remember? Trust me, I would've shot him. At least three times I would've shot him."

"Oh, come on," Sarah said, "he isn't that bad. I sat with him when you and Noah went to the presidential palace, and—well, yeah, he talks a lot, but I think it's just because he's lonely."

"Do I look like I care?" Neil asked her. "Trust me, I don't care. He just about drove me crazy, while I was trying to keep focused on what was going on with you guys and that Pendergrast idiot. And that reminds me, how come you never called me to see what he was up to?"

"Because we were watching him the whole time," Noah said. "I didn't need you to tell me what he was doing when I was looking right at him."

Neil looked at him for several seconds, his mouth opening and closing twice. "Okay, I guess that makes some kind of sense. But you could at least make me feel like I'm contributing once in a while, you know, call and ask me a question, even if you do know the answer. Makes me feel like part of the team, you know what I mean?"

Noah squinted at him. "No, I don't. You are part of the team, why do I need to make you feel like you're part of the team?"

Neil shook his head. "That's what I get for trying to get sympathy from a robot," he said. He turned to Sarah. "You understand what I'm saying, right?"

She smiled, and reached over to pat his hand. "Yes, I understand, and I'll try my best to explain it to Noah later."

Neil looked over at Noah, shaking his head again. "Good luck with that," he said.

They sat at the Saloon for a couple of hours, enjoying their meal and enjoying each other's company. Noah and Sarah opted for dessert, but Neil declined, uncharacteristically. When they did leave, Sarah convinced Neil to come over to the house and hang out with them for a while.

Noah parked the Corvette just outside his garage door, and Neil pulled the Hummer in behind him. They met up at the door, and Noah reached out to unlock it, but then suddenly froze. He had carefully locked the door behind him as they left, but now it was open by half an inch.

Not one of them was armed, so Noah whispered to the others to stay outside for a moment. He stepped inside the house and reached out for the light switch. When the lights came on, he looked around and saw that nothing had been disturbed near the front door, so he began moving through the rest of the house.

After a few moments, he went back and told Sarah and Neil that it was all right to come in. "I can't find anything missing, and nothing seems to be disturbed. I'm sure I locked the door behind us, but I can't see any sign that the lock was picked, either."

"You locked it," Sarah said. "I saw you, it was locked. Who would be stupid enough to try to play games like this? I mean, especially with you?"

"It was probably Moose," Neil said. "Remember, he's got muscle, not brains."

Sarah shook her head. "Moose wouldn't do that, he's got more respect for Noah than to do that." She looked at Noah. "Noah? Do you think there's any chance they've actually tracked us down?"

Noah scowled. "The Russians? Nicolaich? No way. Even if we concede that it's possible, it would take weeks to crack through all the subterfuge that went into that mission. There isn't even anyone who could have sold us out, because no one we dealt with had any idea who we really are. No, I think this is somebody around here, and maybe it was just a prank. Still, I'm going to let Allison know about it, and I'm going to install a security system."

"Well, we can do all that tomorrow," Sarah said. "For this evening, let's just go find a decent movie and pretend we're just normal people, okay?"

TEN

Allison was in her conference room when they arrived the next morning, with Donald Jefferson and Stan Decker. They all got up to shake hands with the team, and there were some mutual congratulations before they got down to debriefing. The debrief went smoothly, and took only a short time.

"Once again, you've got everybody in the organization talking about how brilliant I was to recruit you," Allison said. "Of course, we all knew that already, but it's nice to get some confirmation once in a while."

"I spent a good part of this mission," Noah said, "feeling like maybe things were going too easy, too smoothly. I mean, we found Pendergrast so fast that it just seemed almost like it was set up. Couldn't Habib's security people have found him just as easily?"

"Not necessarily," said Jefferson. "I'm not sure they have access to the voice recognition databases that you ended up using. Of course, if we had put even regular CIA on this, they would have tracked him down, so in one sense, the answer to your question would be yes. Our people would have cooperated with theirs, and shared that information."

"But for some reason, they didn't want CIA involved,

right?" Noah asked.

"That's correct," Allison said. "And I completely understood where they were coming from, because the normal intelligence agencies are all full of interconnections that could conceivably leak something important like this. They couldn't take a chance that someone from SVR would find out that they were digging into it. Maybe they wouldn't really have killed the girl, but no one knew that for sure. Hell, we still don't."

She turned to Jefferson. "Donald? What do you think?"

Jefferson chewed on his bottom lip for a moment, then leaned his head to the left. "It's quite possible that Noah is correct," he said. "It does seem that somebody left some big clues, and made sure we had a way to get to the girl's location. If that's true, then I have to say that the whole thing may have been nothing but a fishing expedition. If the Russians got wind of what we're doing, here in our outfit, it's quite possible that this was set up specifically to draw us, or some of our people, out into the open."

Allison looked at him. "Do you suspect that Habib might have been in on it?"

"I have my doubts about that, mostly because he acted genuinely like a frantic father. That doesn't mean that someone else in the Mauritanian government might not have been involved."

"The Prime Minister," Noah said. "According to President Habib, he only discussed it with the Prime Minister and our ambassador. If the PM was part of it, he could have been the one to suggest not letting the CIA get involved. If they didn't want any of the standard agencies involved, then it was a pretty safe bet that the president would turn to us, right?"

Allison was nodding. "I think you hit it," she said. "We were called in on this one, even though we don't normally get involved in anything investigative. The others do all the snooping work, and we just go in to clean up the messes."

"And that leaves the question of how they might have found out about us," Jefferson said. "Who in the intelligence world would know enough about us to be able to tip them off?"

Allison shrugged her shoulders. "There are a few people at Langley, and a few at DHS, maybe even a few at NSA. We're talking about people with the highest possible clearances, though, people who would be highly unlikely to ever give out anything like this."

"Somebody did," Noah said. "Or have we pulled off enough missions that it would become obvious we exist?"

"Not likely," Allison said. "Most of our missions look like genuine accidents, or natural causes. It's a very rare case when we actually want anyone to know that the target was assassinated. Normally, we just want them to go quietly into that good night." She shook her head. "I'm afraid Noah is correct; somebody has sold us out."

"There's something else," Noah said. "Last night, Sarah and Neil and I all went out to the Sagebrush Saloon for dinner, and when we got back, my door had been unlocked. It was open just a tiny bit, even though I locked it securely when we left, but I couldn't find any sign that anything had been disturbed."

Allison's eyes went wide. "Good Lord, Noah, why didn't you call it in last night?" She turned to Jefferson. "Get somebody out to sweep that house, today! Noah, did you discuss anything about the mission after you got back home and inside the house?"

"Only briefly," Noah said. "Sarah asked if I thought there was any chance that Nicolaich might have tracked us down, and I mentioned his name when I said I didn't think so. I had considered the possibility, at that point, that we may have been sold out even before this mission began."

"I think we have to consider that possibility now," Allison said. "I'm going to demand a security shakedown of everyone outside of our organization who knows anything about us. We'll find out who it could've been."

"Just a question," Noah said, "but can we be certain it came from outside our organization? Is it possible someone inside might have tipped the Russians off?"

"I sincerely doubt it," Allison said, "but we won't discount the possibility until we're sure. I think that everyone is going to be taking a polygraph test. We'll get that set up, and let everyone know."

Neil and Moose had been whispering in the background together, and they suddenly sat forward. "You know," Neil said, "it's possible that the setup wasn't before the mission. If the Prime Minister was in on this, then the president probably told him about meeting with Noah, so he would've had a chance to let the Russians know about it. It could be that finding Pendergrast so easily was just a fluke, one they didn't expect, but it gave them a way to tail us. If they followed Noah all the way to Russia, and let him get away with taking the girl back, then they could also follow him all the way back home. That could explain the break-in at his house."

Allison looked at Neil for a moment, then turned to Jefferson again. "Donald, I'm afraid it's going to be up to you to try to get to the bottom of this. We need to know what's happening, and we need to know as soon as possible. I'm leaving it in your hands, because I'm going to be leaving today for DC. I plan to sit down and ask the president exactly who knows that we exist."

ELEVEN

Since they were already in Kirtland, Noah and the team decided to get in a workout. They drove out to Allie Town, the area on the outskirts of Kirtland where most of the E & E facilities were located, heading to the PT field. Jackson, the PT instructor, smiled when he saw them all piling out of Neil's big yellow Hummer.

"Come for a run?" Jackson asked as he shook Noah's hand.

"Yeah," Noah said. "We thought we'd come down and see what your newest batch is like. Got anyone that can give us a run for our money?"

"Nah, all I got is a bunch of pansies this time. You want to run with them, or go out on your own?"

Noah, Moose and Sarah all decided to run the parkour course on their own, but Neil, who for all his long legs couldn't seem to run very far, headed into the gym. It was state-of-the-art, with many of the finest exercise machines. Neil enjoyed lifting weights, so the gym was more his speed.

The other three set out at a jog, not pushing themselves too hard. Their run took them downtown, as always, and Moose and Sarah enjoyed the looks of startlement on the faces of the people they passed. Most of those people were accustomed to the intrusions, believing that the runners were athletes preparing for competition, but they still found it annoying.

Parkour, of course, is the science of getting from one place to another by using every obstacle in your path to help you move more quickly than usual; they ran through stores, office buildings and even leaped from roof to roof. As a workout, it was intense and satisfying, but it also kept them ready and able should they ever have to pursue a target or flee from attackers.

The run lasted a couple of hours, ending back at the PT field. Neil was already finished with his own workout and was sitting on a bench outside, nursing a soft drink. Moose and Sarah collapsed onto the bench beside him as Noah went to the vending machine to get drinks for the three of them.

"It just ain't fair," Moose said. "It's all I can do to breathe, and he ain't even winded."

"That's because he does this almost every day, when we're around home," Sarah said. "I gave up trying to keep up with him. I come running with him a couple of times a week, but most of the time I stay in bed while he does this."

"Hey, I can run steadily like this for two solid hours, and all I do is run this course once a week. I figure that's good enough; if somebody can catch me within that two hours, fine, then, we'll just fight it out. I don't need to be able to run for a week straight."

Sarah accepted the bottle of Coke from Noah and clinked hers against the one he gave to Moose. "I hear ya," she said. "Besides, I don't plan on having to do any running on foot. If I have to race somebody for my life, I want wheels under me and a big engine."

"At least you can run," Neil interjected. "I make it about fifty yards and my feet forget which order they're supposed to operate in. All of a sudden, my left foot will try to take two or three steps in a row, while the right foot is sort of waving in the breeze. You know what happens then?"

"Yeah," Moose said. "You end up on your face, and we all laugh."

Neil glared at him. "You do realize, don't you, that I'm a genius? That means I can devise ways to kill you in your sleep, and you won't even see it coming. Keep picking on me, I dare you."

"He isn't picking on you, Neil," Sarah said. "He's just trying to tease you so that you'll keep working at it until you get better."

"Nope. I'm picking on him."

Noah stood a few feet away, just watching the repartee. A part of him wanted to be able to join in the banter, but he didn't want to have to plan out his comments. Since they knew about his emotionless nature, they would realize that he was faking it. Noah yearned to know what it felt like to truly be part of their friendly camaraderie.

His phone rang, and he pulled it out to see that the caller was Donald Jefferson. "Donald?"

"Just got the report from the sweep team," Jefferson said. "Your house seems to be clean, no bugs or any other kind of electronic equipment. I had them look for unknown fingerprints or any other sign that someone had been in there, and they found nothing. Are you certain you locked the door behind you?"

"Yes, I'm sure I did," Noah said. "It's possible it didn't

latch all the way, I suppose."

"Well, I guess we'll just have to go with that for the moment. Let me know if you find anything else, or if anything like this happens again."

"I will." Noah ended the call as Moose, Sarah and Neil started walking his way.

They climbed back into the Hummer and headed home, dropping Moose off at the office building so that he could pick up his car. He and Elaine were planning a short, romantic getaway. With the debriefing finished, they would have at least a few days to enjoy before another mission might call them back to action.

Back at Noah's place, Neil decided it was time for him to do some housekeeping in his trailer. Sarah said it was about time, since Neil was the consummate bachelor; his kitchen had more empty pizza boxes in it than pots and pans, and there were probably dirty clothes scattered from the front door all the way back to his bedroom. She made a comment about his housecleaning skills and got his middle finger as a response.

She and Noah went straight to the shower, ready to wash off the sweat of their exercise, but that led to exercise of another sort. An hour later, the two of them made it to the kitchen to prepare lunch. Sarah opened the refrigerator, but nothing in the leftovers looked either appealing or edible, so she closed it and opened the freezer.

"Corn dogs okay?" Sarah asked, and Noah nodded. She set the oven to preheat, then took the box out of the freezer and put five of them onto a cookie sheet. "You want french fries with them, or we could just do chips?"

"Chips is fine," Noah said. He reached up into a cabinet and pulled out a big bag of rippled potato chips and set them on the table, then stood and watched Sarah for a moment as she poured two large glasses of iced tea.

Sarah turned around and caught him watching her. "What?"

Noah shook his head. "I don't know," he said. "Sometimes—sometimes I just like to watch you as you're moving around. I can't explain it, it's not like I'm watching you in a sexual way, it's just—appealing, maybe."

Sarah stood and stared at him for a moment. "Is this something new? Have you watched girls like that before?"

Noah hesitated for a second, then shook his head. "No. No, I don't think I have."

She shrugged. "Well, maybe it's a step in the right direction." She walked over to him and reached up to put her arms around his neck, clasping her hands behind it. "I like watching you, sometimes, too. You move so purposefully, like you can't stand the thought of wasting a motion. It's very appealing."

Noah cocked his head slightly, looking down at her face. "You're the first girl I've ever been with who really knew what I am, at least since I was a teenager. Molly used to tell me that I was doomed to be lonely, because I'd never find a girl who could deal with it, but I don't know what it feels like to be lonely. Being alone never bothered me, and when I had a girlfriend it was just sort of a different situation. She was right, though, and it never lasted very long. No matter how I tried to pretend to be normal, I'd make mistakes that would upset them, and when I couldn't explain it, they'd leave."

Sarah grinned. "That was different from us, though," she said. "I do know how you are, and it's not like we're married or anything. I started this because Queen

Allison made it clear that we weren't allowed to have any normal relationships outside the agency, so being with you seemed like a compromise. No strings, no emotional attachment—all I wanted then was the comfort of having somebody touch me, and hold me." She brought her hands down and put them around his back, drawing him closer to her and laying her head against his chest. "Am I going to ruin things if I tell you that it's different, now? That I'm here because I want to be, because I want to be with you?"

Noah raised his eyebrows. "Ruin things? What do you mean?"

Sarah stood there and held him for a moment, then leaned back slightly to look up at him again. "I'm not like you," she said, "I do have emotions. Is it going to cause problems between us if I'm—if I'm getting attached to you? Emotionally attached, I mean?"

"It doesn't cause a problem for me," he said, "but you have to know that it doesn't change anything on my end. I still don't have any way to return those feelings. It's not that I don't want to, it's just that I don't seem to have them inside me."

"I know," Sarah said softly. She rose up on her toes and brushed his lips with hers. "I didn't want to feel anything, it just sort of hit me one day that I did. You may be a robot to everybody else, but to me you're just the most incredible man I've ever known. I won't rub it in your face, I won't tell you I love you or anything like that, don't worry. I just needed to let you know, so that if you wanted out..."

Noah looked into her face, his expression as blank as ever. "I don't want out, but sooner or later you're going to."

Sarah grinned. "Maybe," she said. "But until then, I plan to enjoy being with you as much as I can. That okay?"

"That's okay," Noah said.

The oven beeped to say that it had reached the right temperature, and Sarah let go of him to turn and put the corn dogs into it. She set the timer for eighteen minutes, as it said on the box, and the two of them took their glasses and walked into the living room to find something on the television. Noah found an old episode of *Star Trek*, and they watched until the timer went off.

Noah paused the television as Sarah went to get their lunch. She was back a moment later with all of the corn dogs on a single plate, carrying the bag of chips under her arm. "I figured we could just eat in here," she said.

"Sounds good to me," Noah said. He picked up a corn dog, dipped it into the puddles of mustard and ketchup she had put on the plate, and took a bite while she opened the bag. He picked up the remote and started the program again.

The show ended and they started a movie, a recent action flick with a lot of older action stars. Sarah watched intently, enjoying all of the violence and action, while Noah paid close attention to the way the members of the mercenary team interacted with each other.

When the movie ended, they flipped through the list of movies and programs, looking for something else to watch, but didn't find anything that caught their interest. Instead, they decided to go for a walk in the surrounding forest. Both of them enjoyed being out in nature, watching the wildlife and discussing the things they saw. Noah noticed when Sarah's fingers entwined in his own, but didn't say anything.

It was almost six by the time they got back to the house, and they were looking at options for dinner when Noah's phone rang.

"Hello," he said, and he heard Allison's voice.

"Camelot," she said, "I need you in my office in one hour. Is Sarah with you?"

"Yes, she's right here."

"Bring her along," Allison said, and then the line went dead.

Noah turned to Sarah. "Allison wants us at her office in an hour. You need anything before we go?"

Sarah's eyes were wide, but she shook her head. "No, I'm good. Maybe we can grab something to eat on the way."

Noah nodded, and they went out the door and got into his Corvette. The drive into Kirtland only took about twenty minutes, so they stopped at one of the taco shops and went inside. The place had an all-you-can-eat taco bar, with a selection of meats and toppings so that they could make their own tacos. They made their plates quickly and sat down to eat.

Thirty minutes later, they were parked in the garage under Allison's office building, and rode the elevator up to her floor. Jenny, her secretary, was already gone for the day, but there were lights on inside. Noah tapped on the door and heard Allison call out, "Come in."

They stepped inside, and Noah was surprised to see no one else there. Allison was fumbling with some papers on her desk, and pointed at the chairs in front of it. "Sit," she said. They sat, and waited for Allison to finish what she was doing. It took her another minute or so, and then she looked up at them.

"Sorry for the sudden roust," she said. "I just made a whirlwind flight to DC and back, and I learned a couple of things you need to know. It seems that the Mauritanian Prime Minister may well have been working with the Russians. NSA and CIA both picked up chatter that indicates he was likely involved with the plot to use the girl against President Habib. They've got at least eight clandestine meetings between him and the Russian ambassador, Pavel Gregorich, over a three-month period leading up to her disappearance. In at least one of them, the topic of discussion was the alliance the Russians have been pressuring for, and Ndiaye was heard saying that the only thing standing in the way was the president's opposition."

Noah shrugged. "Well, we beat him," he said. "You don't think they'll try to use the girl again, do you?"

Allison shook her head. "Very doubtful," she said. "And this doesn't really pertain to us, anyway, except that it seems you may well have been correct when you said the whole thing seemed too easy. Our intelligence analysts are examining the possibility that this entire situation was contrived with the sole purpose of drawing E & E out where the Russians could find something leading back to us."

Noah sat there and looked at her for a moment, letting all that she was saying run through the logical filters in his mind. "Why would Russia give a fig about us? Have we taken out some of their people lately?"

Allison's face wore what could only be considered a sarcastic smile. "We're in the assassination business," she said. "Of course we've taken out some of their people. We almost always try to make it appear to be accidental or natural, but just the timing of some of these deaths alone would be too coincidental for a cynical intelligence agency to believe. I'm sure the same is true for other countries, that they know we have cleanup crews, but don't know the details."

"So Russia wants details, then?" Sarah asked. She glanced at Noah, then back at Allison. "What does that mean for us? Would we be exposed, would that get us shut down or anything?"

"I don't think we're in any danger of being shut down; American diplomacy can't get by without us, and we're a deeper secret than the stuff that goes on in the back of Area 51. There are already conspiracy theorists who have stumbled across hints of our existence, but we have a whole division that does nothing but play smoke-screen. Every time we get mentioned or described in an article or blog post, they plant plenty of disinforma-tion and start campaigns to discredit the writers." She leaned back in her chair and steepled her fingers under her chin. "As for Russia wanting details, however, that's a bit more serious. They're not going to worry about trying to expose us, they'll be looking for some way to counter us, keep us from getting to those of their people who become targets for us. That means they want to identify any of our operatives they can, which is why our analysts believe that we were drawn into this mess."

"They used the girl as bait to draw us out, then," Noah said. "That's why it was so easy to find Pendergrast. They were undoubtedly watching him, and knew when we took him. As soon as he called his Russian contact, they knew we were coming. All they had to do was fol-low Pendergrast the same way we did, and see who fol-lowed him."

"It might have been even simpler than that. Once Pendergrast was on his way to Moscow, they probably started watching everyone in our embassy over there. When you met with our station chief at Sheremetyevo Airport, they were probably watching you then."

Noah's expression did not change. "I should have seen that," he said. "I should have realized it was a setup."

Sarah reached over and took his hand, a comforting gesture that was wasted on him, but he didn't resist. "Noah, you did," she said. "You told us all that it was going too smoothly, too easy, but you also said we had to follow through with the mission, anyway. Remember?"

Allison leaned forward again, bracing her arms on top of her desk. "Which was absolutely correct. CIA and NSA are both convinced that the unholy alliance between Russia, Syria and Mauritania would have been a disaster for the whole Western world, and if you had not recovered the girl, it probably would have become a reality. Frankly, I would have sent you in to retrieve her even if I had known it was a trap."

Noah was continually running all of this information through his mind, and he reached a conclusion. "This is Nicolaich," he said. "You said he's their version of you, so he's trying to identify our agents in order to be able to target us. That's why he was using his own son in the operation; I don't think he expected you to kill Vasily. Even a man like this wouldn't put his own son out there as a sacrificial pawn."

"That could be true, but he isn't above using it to his advantage."

"Of course not," Noah said. "Since I killed his son, he's going to call in every favor he can, get everyone possible to help him find us. He's got the perfect scenario. He can claim a father's rage as his motivation for coming after us, and an awful lot of intel operatives are going to either be afraid to get in his way, or want to score points with him by helping. He's not going to pass up a chance like this, even if he's still in mourning. I wouldn't."

Allison and Noah looked into each other's eyes for a few seconds, and then Noah broke the silence.

"Going in and rescuing that girl just painted a target on all of our heads. Nicolaich Andropov isn't just out to identify us, he's out to track us down and destroy us."

TWELVE

"I think you're right," Allison said. "The only question is what we do about it."

Noah shrugged his shoulders. "Why is that a question? The only logical course of action is to take Nicolaich out of the equation. That may not stop his organization from coming after us, but it will send a message that we're not that easy to take out."

"Camelot, Nicolaich Andropov is a ghost. According to many sources, there's never even been a photograph taken of him that we are aware of. The SVR considers him one of the most dangerous men in the world, which is why he is nicknamed the Boar, after the wild hogs that rip people to shreds in the Russian forests and swamplands. He's not going to be easy to locate, and he's probably as deadly as anyone we've got. A mission to go after him would take an awful lot of our resources."

"No, it won't," Noah said. "I'm the one who killed Vasily, his son; if I put myself on his radar, I won't have to track him down. He'll come to me, and when he does, I'll kill him."

Sarah squeezed his hand. "Noah, you're talking about using yourself as bait! That could be suicidal!"

Once again, Noah shrugged. "Leaving him out there would probably be even worse. I'm the one he wants most, so I'd be the irresistible target. If I were him, I wouldn't come at me for the kill, I'd be looking to capture me, try to break me and get information about the rest of the agency. He'll be expecting a trap, but that doesn't mean I can't spring it."

Allison stared coldly into his eyes. "And what if he does manage to capture you? He would break you eventually, and you'd give up everything you know about us. We've managed to keep this whole operation a secret. We can't risk Neverland being hit by an SVR death squad. A single assassin can devastate an organization. Imagine what several of them, working together, could do."

"Body bomb," Noah said. "Give me an explosive belt. Have it made so that it can be triggered remotely, and keep a bug on me. If I'm captured, detonate it. I can't give up secrets if I'm dead, and maybe we'll get lucky and take out Nicolaich along with me."

The woman behind the desk kept her face a mask of stone. "I'd be losing a pretty valuable asset," she said. "We've got an awful lot invested in you, you know that, and we have half a dozen missions in the planning stage right now that count on Team Camelot carrying them out. If we do this, we risk losing you, potentially compromising those missions."

"You've got other teams. I'm sure that with a little modification to the planning, they can handle the missions I'd be missing out on. The issue is whether or not anyone else could get to Nicolaich, and I don't see that happening anytime soon. I'm the best shot we've got."

Allison was silent for almost a minute, and it was obvious that the wheels in her head were spinning. "I want you to meet with Donald tomorrow morning, and begin planning the mission. He'll take you to Wally Lawson, he runs our R&D section. Wally can show you some of the new toys his boys and girls come up with, and make the belt you're talking about." She got to her feet and leaned forward, her hands on the desk. "That belt will be a last resort, though, Camelot. I'm going to go ahead and authorize this mission, but I want you to give me your word right now that you'll do everything in your power to come back. There are an awful lot of people who will be pretty pissed if you go out and get yourself killed on this."

"Yeah, and I'm one of them," Sarah said.

"I'll do all I can, I promise you," Noah said. "The priority has to be killing Nicolaich, though. He's the threat to the agency, and that threat has to be eliminated."

Allison nodded once. "All right, then," she said. "Nine o'clock in the morning, right here. Have your team with you."

Allison sat down and opened the file, signifying that the interview was over. Noah rose and pulled Sarah to her feet, and the two of them walked out of the office. They were quiet as they rode down the elevator, but once they were in the Corvette, Sarah looked over at him.

"Do you really think this is the smart move?"

"I think it's the only move. We got drawn into a situation that could compromise the entire agency, a setup that allowed Nicolaich and his organization to get way too much information on us, on our team. Right now, that's all he's got, but if we don't shut him down quickly he'll find other things tied to us. It's like a trail of breadcrumbs, and as he finds each crumb that gets accidentally dropped, it will lead him to the next one, and the next."

Sarah leaned back against the headrest as Noah drove back toward his home. "And what do the rest of us do, if you get yourself killed?"

"You'll be assigned to another team," Noah said. "All three of you have already proven yourselves, Allison isn't going to give you up just because I'm gone."

They rode the rest of the way to the house in silence, and Sarah followed him inside. Noah went straight to the living room couch and took out his phone. He called Moose first, and then Neil, to tell them to meet at the offices in the morning in preparation for a new mission. Both of them complained, but there was no question of whether they would show up.

Noah turned on the television and began scanning through the movies that were available. After a moment, Sarah got up and went into the kitchen. She returned a few minutes later with a pair of root beer floats, and snuggled up to Noah as she handed him one.

"You pick the lousiest times to volunteer yourself for a suicide mission, do you know that?"

"I have absolutely no intention of making it a suicide mission," Noah said. "Not for me, anyway. I'm planning to make it suicidal for Nicolaich to come after me. I'm only hoping that he's as angry at me about the death of his son as little miss Selah seemed to believe he would be. One of the things I've learned over the years by observing human nature is that anger will almost always cause you to make mistakes. The angrier he is, the more emotional he is, the more likely he is to make a mistake that will give me the chance to take him out before he can do anything to me."

Sarah looked at him for a long moment, then leaned her head on his shoulder. "I just finally got up the nerve to tell you how I feel, and if I lost you now..."

Noah thought for a second, then kissed the top of her head. "I'm going to do my best to make sure you don't," he said. "That's all I can promise you."

Sarah looked at the clock on the wall, and said, "It's early, but how would you feel about going on to bed? I—I need your attention. Your undivided attention, all on me. Is that okay?"

Without a word, Noah picked up the remote and turned off the television. The two of them rose from the couch and walked into the bedroom.

When they left the house the next morning, they found Neil standing outside the garage, sitting on the fender of the Corvette. His Hummer was nowhere in sight, and Sarah grinned at him. "You look like death warmed over," she said.

"I was up most of the night," the skinny kid said. "I can't believe they're sending us on another mission this quick, that's just not fair."

Sarah laughed. "We work for the government," she said, "and you're stupid enough to think they'll do things in a fair way? Besides, you can blame our fearless leader for this mission. It was his idea."

Neil looked over at Noah. "Are you freaking kidding me? What on earth could be so important that you would drag us back out into the field when we've only just gotten home?"

Noah pointed at him to follow them, and led Sarah toward her own Camaro. "Sarah's driving this morning," he said. "You can ride with us. As for the mission, it turns out our last one really was a setup, a scam run by the Russians to draw E & E out into the open. Andropov was apparently trying to get a lead on us, and there is very little doubt that he has photos of me, Moose and Sarah, as well as the names we were using. If he shakes the right trees, he's going to find out more about us until he cracks one of the identities. That could lead right back here to Neverland, and we can't let that happen. Nicolaich just became National Enemy Number One, and moved to the top of our target list."

"So send one of the other teams," Neil said as he climbed into the back seat. "Let us take a break. Isn't there something in our contracts that says they can't send us out too often?"

Sarah laughed again as she started the car and pulled out of the driveway. "You have a contract? I don't. I wish I did, because I'd be going through it trying to find a loophole to get me out of this screwy outfit."

"It's got to be me," Noah said. "While we were in Russia, I killed several of Nicolaich's people, including a man who is supposedly his own son. I'm sure he knows that it was me, even if he doesn't know who I really am. We've got to use that against him, by making him come after me. When he does, then I spring the trap and take him out."

Neil made a snort. "Well, goodie, goodie for you," he said. "And what if he turns out to be better at this game than you are? We end up without a team leader, at which point we might become expendable. Do you know what expendable means in this organization? It means dead, that's what it means!"

"No, it doesn't. When you guys were assigned to me, Allison made it plain that you are each the best in your respective fields. There's no way she's going to get rid of you, just because I get killed. You're safe enough, all they would do is assign you to another team."

"I don't want to be on another team, dammit," Neil said. "One of my many talents is calculating the probability of any particular outcome, based on available data concerning the participants. I applied that talent to figuring out my odds of living to the ripe old age of thirty, and they got a whole lot better once I added you into the equation. They put me with anybody else, and I'm not likely to live past twenty-two! And just for the record, Moose and Sarah probably wouldn't make it a year without you in charge. So dig down deep inside yourself and find just enough compassion to understand that we need you to stay alive and healthy, you arrogant son of a bitch!"

"Neil, chill out!" Sarah said. "At least Andropov doesn't have your picture. The way it turns out, he probably got a whole album full of Noah, Moose and me. We may not even make it out to where we have to go for this mission, and I'm still not sure he hasn't already tracked us back to here. Somebody sure as hell broke into the house the other night, I don't care what Jefferson's people say!"

Neil slapped the back of her headrest, and Noah turned suddenly to look at him. "Don't yell at me!" Neil said. "It isn't my fault I'm freaking out over this! I wasn't expecting to have to go back out into the field this soon, and now you tell me Noah is putting his life on the line?"

Suddenly, there were tears on Neil's cheeks, and Sarah saw them in the rearview mirror. She reached over and put a finger to Noah's lips, cutting off whatever he was about to say to the frightened boy in the backseat.

"Neil, look," Sarah said softly. "I didn't mean to yell at you. This is pretty stressful, I understand that, and I think I know what's really bothering you. You've been pretty much on your own since you were a kid, right? And the team feels like a family, now, doesn't it? That's why you're so scared of losing Noah; he's like your big brother, am I right?"

Neil turned his face to look out the back window, and for a moment the only sound that could be heard was from stifled sobs. "I'm scared of losing all of you," he said. "What if they split us up, if something happens to Noah? What if we each get sent to a different team? We were all brand new when we got assigned to Camelot, but what would it be like to go into a team that was already together? We'd be the new guys, and we'd probably never fit in."

"But we'd still have each other," Sarah said. "You don't think I would turn my back on you, just because we were on different teams, do you?"

Neil sniffled a couple more times, then turned around to face forward again. "No," he said at last. "I just don't know what I'd do without all of you. Even Moose—he picks on me, but I know he'd have my back if I needed him."

Noah turned and faced him. "Neil, believe me when I tell you I'm going to do my very best to make sure I'm the one who walks away from this. I'm going to need you, though, because between your computer and your brain, you're one of my most important assets. We're going to draw this bastard out and eliminate him, before he can do any damage to us. You are going to be a big help in that, and I know that you've always got my back, too."

Neil managed to smile, and the sniffles faded away. When he suggested they all go out to the Sagebrush Saloon for dinner again that evening, Noah made a point of being enthusiastic in his agreement.

THIRTEEN

Moose pulled into the parking garage just behind the Corvette, and parked right beside them. They all greeted one another, and then stepped into the elevator for the ride up to Allison's office. They were surprised to find her standing there waiting when the elevator opened, but she only hooked her head at them and walked off toward the conference room.

Donald Jefferson was waiting there, and there were large cups of coffee on the table ready for each of them. Allison grinned as she took her seat at the table. "I figured we might as well make this as comfortable and cordial as we can," she said. "I can't wait to hear what your mission plan is going to be, Camelot." She picked up a cup and took a sip of the hot liquid.

"Yes, I'm pretty curious about that myself," Jefferson said. "I want you to know this is the very first time I've ever seen the Dragon Lady, here, allow a team leader to declare his own mission. We're breaking a lot of rules and records, here, Camelot."

The team had all taken their seats, and gratefully accepted the coffee. Noah took a sip of his own before he answered.

"It just makes sense," he said. "If Andropov has gone to such trouble to try to draw us out, then we shouldn't disappoint him completely. Now, I'm not interested in giving him what he wants, which is probably my head on a platter and all of yours for side dishes, so it only makes sense for us to turn the tables and use his own plans against him. I killed his son, so I'm going to be number one on his list. If I'm out where he can find me, then he's going to have to expose himself in order to get me. When he does, he dies."

Jefferson glanced at Allison, then turned back to Noah. "The first thing we need to do is clarify whether or not that was truly his son that you killed. I've been digging since early this morning, and I've only found two references to Vasily Andropov. That is definitely the name of Nicolaich's youngest son, but I've only scrounged up one photo of the boy, taken when he was about nineteen." He pointed at the monitor on the wall, squeezed the button on a small device, and a picture appeared there. It showed a young man with dark hair and eyes, mugging for the camera with a couple of his friends. "Is that the face you saw in Kubinka?"

Noah and Moose both concentrated on the image, and then nodded. "Definitely," Moose said, and Noah followed with, "That's him. He didn't look much different, at least until I gave him a third eye."

Jefferson sighed deeply. "Then the situation is every bit as dire as you describe. Vasily's mother died in childbirth, and the little intelligence we can gather on Nicolaich says that he doted on the boy. He has two older sons, and a daughter, but he isn't very close to any of them. Vasily was his pride and joy, the only one of his children who shared his disregard for human life. We haven't been able to come up with any chatter regarding the boy's death, so it's a safe bet Nicolaich is keeping it quiet at the moment."

Noah nodded. "Then, what would happen if I went back to Russia and began letting it be known that I had already taken the kid out, and come back looking for his daddy?"

Jefferson's eyebrows went up almost a half-inch, and Allison's eyes got a bit wider, as well. "Camelot, that would set off a storm...Oh, my God, you'd have all of the SVR crawling all over you."

"I don't think so," Noah said. "Nicolaich is going to want me all to himself. He may not intend to pull the trigger with his own hand, but I'm certain he'll want to be there when it happens. He's the man who gets to decide who lives and dies, remember? Godlike powers tend to make one believe in his own invincibility. He won't hesitate to become personally involved in trying to trap me or kill me."

"Or capture you," Allison said. "That's what you said last night, and I still think it's probably going to be high on his list of priorities. He's not going to want you dead, not at first; he's going to want to bleed you dry before you die."

Noah nodded again. "That's true, but I don't intend to allow that to happen. If it becomes obvious that I'm about to be caught, then I'll use that belt. If I can't, then one of you will have to do it for me."

Moose held a hand up in the air. "Excuse me? What's this about a belt?"

Sarah looked over at him. "Noah came up with an idea for an explosive belt, one that he can trigger himself, or that can be triggered remotely if he isn't able to do it.

The idea is to make sure he can't be captured, so that he can't give up any secrets about E & E or Neverland."

Moose's eyes also went wide at this point. "Can I hold the remote? I can blow them up, if it comes to that."

Sarah backhanded him on the shoulder. "Moose! You asshole!"

"No," Allison said. "I'm sending team Cinderella as your backup. Cinderella will hold the remote, and only use it on my direct order."

"That's fine," Noah said, "but don't let them get in my way. In fact, I would prefer there be no connection between us at all. The last thing we want to do is give Nicolaich or his people any further intel on one of our teams. I don't want anyone else exposed on this mission." He glanced over at Neil, and then turned back to face Allison. "Neil is another one that Nicolaich knows nothing about, and I want to keep it that way. Let's send him and Cinderella together, and put them in the same hotel. They can keep an eye on him for me, while he's keeping his eyes on me electronically."

"Now, wait a minute..." Neil began, but Allison cut him off.

"He's right, Neil," she said. "If anything goes south on this, Noah, Moose and Sarah could all be killed or captured. We can't take a chance that he would get you, too."

Sarah shivered. "If you're worried that Moose and I might be caught, then are we going to be wearing those belts, too?"

Allison gave her a sad smile. "I'm afraid so, dear girl. It's a necessity, in this case. If this were another mission, where the target didn't know who we were, I wouldn't even consider it, but we simply can't take a chance on someone like Nicolaich being able to question either of you. Cinderella will hold your remotes, as well, but they will not be used unless it is absolutely necessary, and then only on my own personal order. I think you know me well enough already to realize that I would never willingly give any of you up."

Moose pointed at Noah. "What did I tell you? I said we weren't going to live long in this job, didn't I? I should have made it a bet, then you'd be paying up, right now."

"Okay, okay, people," Jefferson said. "Let's get back on topic. Camelot, have you devised a basic plan for this mission?"

Noah nodded his head. "I have, and I just gave it to you a minute ago. What I'm planning to do is go back to Russia and start looking for other SVR agents who might have been involved in the plan to use President Habib's daughter against him. That will make it look like I'm simply doing a follow-up on the mission we already completed, and I shouldn't have too much trouble. I already know of one person who was involved —Vladimir Sokoloff at the Russian Embassy in London. Assuming he's still there, I'll snatch him up and twist him for information. I'm fairly sure I can get him to give me at least a few names, which I'll use to work my way back to Russia. Once I'm there, I can make enough noise to get Nicolaich's attention, let myself be caught on some security video and such. I'll make it look like I'm cocky, like I think I'm too smart for him to track me down. Then, when he comes after me, he'll have to expose himself. That's when I'll take him out."

Jefferson pulled a computer that was sitting on the table closer to himself, and began tapping on the keys. A moment later he grinned. "Vladimir Sokoloff is listed as the commercial attaché at Russia's embassy there. NSA keeps close tabs on him, and he's still there."

"Good," Noah said. "That's where I'll start, then. We actually still have the safe house we rented available, so I can use it as our staging area. We'll see how Sokoloff responds to the same treatment I gave Pendergrast."

"Speaking of Pendergrast," Allison said, "I wonder how much he actually knew about what was going on? Do you think he was aware of what the Russians were really up to with this scam?"

Noah shrugged. "I suppose that's possible, so it might be a good idea if I grab him again, too. In fact, putting him and Sokoloff in the same place might generate a little extra intel. Of course, it will mean that Pendergrast will have a target on his head, unless I terminate Sokoloff. Any opinion on whether I should do that?"

Allison looked at Jefferson, who was still reading the file on Sokoloff. "He's done a lot of typical commercial stuff, but he's been tied to a number of purely political operations, as well, including the assassinations of some low-level British and European functionaries."

Allison pursed her lips for a moment, then turned back to Noah. "From what you said in your debrief, I'm going to sanction his elimination. The British seem to feel that Pendergrast has value to them, so let's do them a favor and keep him alive."

"Okay, good. Incidentally, he might be a source of information leading back to Nicolaich. From what he says, he's done a lot of work with the SVR. I'll twist his arm again, too, and see what I can get."

"Camelot, I'm not going to even imply that I'm happy with this plan," Allison said, "but I'll admit that I'd be at a loss to come up with anything better. I'm going to run it past our mission-planning people, just for the sake of keeping them in the loop, but for now you can consider this mission a go." she turned to Jefferson. "Donald, get the IDs and accessories they used on the last mission, and then take them to see Wally. I already got him started on the belts, but he might have some other gadgets that could be useful on this mission. They've got carte blanche, let them have anything he's got that Camelot feels he can use."

"Yes, Ma'am," Jefferson said. He closed the laptop and slid it into a soft case, then got to his feet. "Let's go."

Noah and the team got up and followed him out the door and down the elevator. When they got to the parking garage, he turned to Noah.

"We'll take the van," he said, leading the way to a large Mercedes panel truck. He opened the door in the side and climbed in, and the team followed. There were a number of plush, comfortable seats inside, the kind you might find in a fancy conversion van. Jefferson stepped to the front and slid in behind the wheel, and Noah took the seat beside him on the passenger side.

They rode out of the garage and through Kirtland, past the area they called Alley Town and into the restricted area where the Armory could be found. Noah and Jefferson were quiet, but the three in the back were holding a muffled conversation, something about working out their own plans to keep Noah alive and healthy.

Jefferson pulled into a parking lot beside a large concrete building. Anywhere else, it would have been taken for a factory or repair shop, but Noah knew that he was about to enter a wonderland of weapons and inventions. From rumors he'd picked up around Neverland, Wally was the American counterpart to "Q" from the

James Bond movies.

Jefferson led them through a door into the building, and the team was instantly surprised at how clean the interior was. They could see a number of workstations that seemed to be enclosed in Plexiglas, where men and women were tinkering with various devices. A short, thin man with a receding hairline was waiting a short distance inside, and smiled when he saw them.

"Donald! It's so good to see you," the little man said.

Jefferson smiled and shook his hand. "Hey, Wally," he said. "I want to introduce you to Team Camelot. This is Noah Wolf, Sarah Child, Neil Blessing and Moose Conway. Camelot, this is Wally. If you need something that hasn't been invented yet, he's the guy to come to."

"Really?" Neil asked. "Can I get a time machine? I want to go back a couple of years and beat the snot out of myself for ever thinking about hacking into a bank."

"That wouldn't help," Moose said. "You're such a wuss that neither one of you would actually land a punch."

Wally smiled at the two of them. "Well, I haven't quite cracked the time continuum yet, but I can assure you it's something I'm interested in. If I ever make it, I'll let you know. Meanwhile, I've got some goodies for you to look over. Allison tells me that you have a pretty serious mission ahead of you, and told me to make sure I give you anything you want."

Noah shook hands with Wally. "I appreciate that," he said. "You got the belts ready?"

Wally grinned and nodded his head. "I do, I actually had some already made up in various sizes. We've never used them on one of our own, but you'd be absolutely amazed at how cooperative someone will be when you put one on them and let them see a demonstration of just what they can do. They even have an electronic lock that requires a digital code in order to take them off. I understand the remotes are going with another team, but we're going to give you each an app on your phone that will allow you to take them off when you need to, or set them off should the need arise." He giggled and leaned close to them. "Personally, I hope you don't have to use them. I've heard good things about you and your team, and I'm just dying to build you some equipment."

"Yeah, we hope we don't have to use them, either," Sarah said.

"I appreciate that, Wally," Noah said. "Now, why don't you show us things you think might be helpful."

Those were apparently the magic words, because Wally giggled again, then turned and started off through the maze of workstations. He assumed the others would follow, and he was right. He came to a stop at one cubicle where two young women were working on what appeared to be iPhones.

"These are the phones we're giving you," he said. "I wanted Marcia and Gina to show you what they can do. Come on in." He opened a door into the cubicle and stepped inside, and once again they all followed. "Marcia, Gina, show us what you got."

The two women turned to face their visitors, each of them holding an iPhone. The one on the left bore a nametag that read, "Marcia," and the other was obviously Gina. "Hi, gang," Marcia said. "We've got something here that we think might be pretty useful out in the field. You know about backscatter radiation, right? A way to look right through walls and such?"

The team nodded, and Marcia grinned. "Watch this," she said, then tapped an icon on the phone's screen. She held the phone up in front of Gina with the screen facing forward, and the team saw what appeared to be a clear x-ray of her head. Her entire skull was clearly visible, and the image moved as she did. Marcia moved the device downward, and they saw her cervical vertebrae, then her sternum.

"That's cool, right?" Marcia asked. "But watch this, it's even better." She took the phone away from her work partner and picked up a metal box. "Now, you want to know what's in the box, but it's locked, right? Just use this phone and who needs a key?" She passed the phone over the box, and they could see that it contained a gun and what looked like stacks of paper. She held it in position for a moment so they could all see, then pulled it away and opened the box. A Beretta handgun lay inside, along with three bundles of hundred-dollar bills.

"All you got to do is hold it up like you're taking a picture, and it uses a specially adapted emitter and camera that we designed right here to send out my new, almost undetectable bursts of electromagnetic radiation, then forms an image based on how that radiation is reflected back. You can use it to look through walls, examine the contents of a safe, scan people to see if they've got weapons on them, all that stuff. Pretty awesome, right?"

Noah reached out and took the phone from Marcia, then looked at his own hand through it. Each bone was clearly visible, and he could even see the ripples of muscles and tendons. He passed it to Sarah, who did the same thing and then passed it off to Moose.

Moose looked at his hand for a second, then suddenly held the phone up toward Noah's head. He stared at it for just a couple of seconds, then said, "I knew it! There's a computer in there!"

Everyone laughed but Noah, and even he managed a small grin. Neil was given a chance to look at the phone, and then Wally was ready to show them something else.

Once again, they moved through the maze of cubicles, and they were shown several items. One was a perfectly ordinary-looking forty-caliber Glock pistol, but they were shown that it was connected wirelessly to a ring worn on the hand of one of the technicians. He picked up the gun and calmly fired a shot into a ballistic catcher, then handed it to an assistant who seemed nervous. That fellow pointed the gun at the catcher, but when he squeezed the trigger there was no shot fired. Instead, he dropped the pistol and fell to the ground. His partner reached down and helped him get back to his feet, though it took a few seconds, then explained that the pistol had a stun system built into the grip. If the hand holding it wasn't wearing the ring that matched that gun, squeezing the trigger would do nothing but deliver a shock that would instantly incapacitate the person. Noah and Moose immediately requested their own, and Wally said they would be ready before the team left the building.

They saw other marvels of technology, as well. Besides the pistols, Noah selected a few other items that he found to be interesting. These included a pair of earpieces, similar to the Bluetooth devices that allowed you to remain hands-free with a cell phone. This pair, however, had their own built-in communications structure, working through cell towers and keeping them in constant communication with each other. They were slightly larger than the average Bluetooth headset, but that was because of the special battery they carried that could keep them working for up to seventy-two hours at a stretch.

There were also a number of disguised weapons, common devices that concealed guns or knives. One was a completely normal soda can, and the technician demonstrated how it worked by taking one out of a cooler and opening it. He put it to his lips and took a drink, then held it in front of a ballistic catcher and tilted it as if trying to give a drink to the bullet-catching box. As soon as the liquid inside began pouring out, there was a loud *bang*, and the can leaped out of the technician's hand. "It's a gun," the technician said. "When you open it and take the first drink, it's armed. When it's tilted for a second drink, a forty-five caliber slug is fired straight up through the center. There's a three inch barrel, so it has plenty of punch to blow someone's head off. You can simply hand it to your target and let them open it and literally drink themselves to death, or you can open it yourself, take the first drink so that they suspect nothing, and then pass it to them."

Another disguised weapon caught Noah's eye. It looked like an ordinary black plastic comb, but twisting it so that the ends were at ninety degrees to each other caused a quarter-inch-wide stiletto blade to shoot out of one end. The blade extended for about three inches, and when Noah tested it against a board, he found it to be incredibly strong and was unable to bend it. He twisted it again and the blade slid back inside.

He looked at Wally. "You got one of these I can take with me?"

Wally smiled. "Take that one. Trust me, we've got dozens more."

"Holy crap," Neil said. "Where was all this crap when I was getting the shit beat out of me in high school?" He looked around the building for a moment, then shook his head. "You know what blows my mind? There's as much brainpower in this building as there probably is in Silicon Valley, but here, it's all dedicated to new ways to kill people."

Moose grabbed Neil's shoulders and gave him a little shake. "Neil, Neil," he said. "I know it's hard for you to look at reality, but that's what we do, here. We kill people. Isn't it nice to have a complete laboratory working out new ways for us to accomplish it?"

FOURTEEN

"These guns are awesome," Moose said as they left the firing range that afternoon. Noah had insisted that they take the new Glocks and try them out, since every gun has a slightly different feel to it. These were typical Glock weapons, with the minor addition of electronic grips.

"They handle nicely," Noah said. "I got two-inch groups at twenty yards, firing fifteen rounds from standing. That's better than the Glock I was carrying before."

"Yeah, mine is more accurate than my old gun, too. And it's kind of nice to know that no one can take it away and shoot me with it."

They walked the half-mile to where Sarah and Neil were waiting at a small restaurant. This one was inside the restricted area, so that E & E operatives could grab a bite to eat while they were taking care of business. They stepped inside, and both of them felt relief as the air conditioning hit them. Sarah saw them and waved, and a moment later Noah slid in beside her while Moose shoved Neil over.

"Good timing," Sarah said. "I just ordered us lunch. I hope you both like spaghetti, because it's on special today."

"Spaghetti is fine," Noah said, and Moose nodded his agreement.

"So how are the guns?" Sarah asked. "Does the high-tech stuff mess up their aim or anything?"

"No," Noah said, "if anything, I think they're more accurate than the standard models."

"Really?" Neil asked. "Maybe I should get me one, maybe I could hit the target with it."

Moose laughed. "Neil, these guns have enough recoil to throw your skinny ass backward ten feet. What are you complaining about? We gave you a twenty-five-caliber automatic. That's your gun."

Neil narrowed his eyes at Moose. "Hey, you know what? I looked up everything I could find on the twenty-five-caliber automatic pistol, and you know what it says in some of the best books about guns? It says this is a wonderful weapon if you're hunting mice! Somehow, I don't think mice are going to shoot back, so if I ever really need a gun, I'm going to be pretty well screwed! And if you were half as good a friend as you pretend to be, you'd take me out and teach me how to shoot something serious."

Moose threw an arm around Neil and pulled him over close, then rubbed the top of his head with his knuckles. Neil pushed him away and got loose, and Moose said, "Neil, I'm just picking on you! You want to learn how to shoot? You and me, we'll start going to the range together, how about that? No gags, no joke, I'll teach you how to handle a nine millimeter. That work?"

Neil continued to look sulky, but he nodded his acceptance of the invitation. A few moments later, the spaghetti arrived and everyone gave up talking while they ate. Shortly before they finished, Noah's phone rang, and he walked away for a moment to take the call privately. It was Allison, telling him that the mission was approved and giving him the initial travel details. When he returned to the table, Noah tapped on it for attention.

"Look, guys, we're going to be heading out for London tomorrow morning. This is an incredibly important mission, and I genuinely appreciate each one of you going with me. This isn't one of our usual missions, but I think it could be important for the organization, and for each of us individually."

Sarah nodded. "I agree. If Nicolaich has gotten wind of who we really are, we run the risk of having him and his kind coming into Kirtland. There are a lot of good people here who don't even know what we do, and some of them would probably end up getting in the way and getting themselves killed. We can't have that, not on our own consciences. Nicolaich has to go."

She picked up her glass of iced tea and held it over the center of the table. A couple of seconds later, all three of the men clinked theirs against hers, and unanimously declared, "Nicolaich must go!"

"Anyway, we're all going to need some rest. Neil, you wanted to go out to the Saloon for dinner tonight, and I just want to let everybody know that it's on me. We've got a nine-hour flight leaving Denver at nine AM tomorrow, so if you want to drink tonight, that's okay. You'll have plenty of time to sleep it off on the airplane."

"Commercial flight?" Moose asked.

"No," Noah said. "The Dragon Lady got us a leased Gulfstream V. It's ours for the duration of the mission, with flight crews provided by the company it came from as we need them. As far as they know, we're just travel-ing on business."

The four of them finished their drinks and headed out to Sarah's Camaro, parked beside Moose's Chevy Malibu. Neil was about to climb into the back seat of the Camaro, but Moose called out to him.

"Neil," he said. "Why don't you ride with me? We're all going to the same place, anyway, right? Boss? We going to your place?"

Noah nodded his head. "Yeah, we can relax there a bit until it's time to go have dinner. If you want, we can take the boat out for a while."

Neil let out a whoop. "Boat! Boat! Boat! I've been dying to get out on your boat, how come you never offered before?"

"Because it's a lot cozier when it's just me and him," Sarah said. "Ever heard that expression, three's a crowd?"

Neil shook his head. "I have got to find me a girl-friend, that's all there is to it."

They made a small, two-car convoy out to Temple Lake Road, and arrived at Noah's place slightly more than half an hour later. Noah and Sarah had discussed the idea of taking the boat out, so she grabbed Neil and had him help her load a cooler with soft drinks while Noah and Moose went down to the boathouse to get the boat ready. Twenty minutes later, the big Mercury engine idled the boat out of its slip, and then roared as Noah poured on the power.

The lake was beautiful, and the air was warm. They cruised for about an hour, waving at other boaters out on the lake, and then Noah guided the boat into a small cove-like inlet that was surrounded by trees that hung over the water, creating a shady, pleasant atmosphere.

"This is gorgeous," Moose said. "Wish I'd brought swimming trunks, I'd dive right in."

"Who needs trunks?" Neil asked, stripping his shirt over his head and kicking off his shoes. A second later, he shoved his pants down and stepped out of them completely naked, then ran and dived off the back of the boat. He came up sputtering a few seconds later, and yelled, "Ain't you ever heard of skinny-dipping?"

Sarah burst out laughing, then looked over at Noah and shrugged. "I'm not putting on that good a show," she said, but then she shimmied down her jeans and kicked them off, and followed by taking off the T-shirt she was wearing. In nothing but bra and panties, she took two running steps and followed Neil into the water.

Moose looked at Noah. "What do you think, Boss? I'm not gonna strip in front of your girlfriend unless you say it's cool."

Noah shrugged, then took off his own clothes and dived in. Moose was left alone on the boat, but he hesitated only a few seconds before following suit.

They swam together in the warm, clear water for a couple of hours, but then Noah said it was time to head in. Reluctantly, they all climbed onto the swim platform on the back of the boat, then clambered over the transom and began putting on their clothes. Moose did his gentlemanly best not to stare at Sarah, whose wet underclothes had become essentially transparent, but Neil ogled her openly.

"Geez, Neil," Sarah said, "you'd think you've never seen a girl before! Do you mind?"

"Not a bit," Neil said as she struggled to pull her jeans

up her wet legs. "Please continue."

Sarah mumbled something, but no one caught it. Noah watched Neil for a moment, then picked up his own clothes and put them on. When everyone was dressed and had a bottle of something cold, he started up the boat and they cruised sedately back to his boathouse.

He tied the boat to its stanchions and they all climbed out and headed up to the house. Moose carried the cooler, stopping outside the boathouse to dump out the water from the ice that had melted. When they got inside, he set the cooler on the floor in the foyer, then took the remaining bottles of soda into the kitchen and put them back into the refrigerator.

Their clothes had dried on the way back in, or at least for the most part, but Sarah insisted on taking a shower and changing before they went to dinner. While she went into the bedroom, Noah, Moose and Neil went to the living room and watched another episode of *Star Trek*.

Sarah came out just as the episode ended, wearing shorts and a tank top. She had washed and dried her hair, and put on fresh new makeup, and Neil whistled appreciatively. Sarah grinned and thanked him, then went into the kitchen.

Noah looked over at Moose, sitting beside him. "She's really quite a beautiful woman, isn't she?"

"She is that," Moose said. "Are you starting to recognize that for yourself?"

Noah turned his head and looked toward the kitchen door, where Sarah had disappeared only a moment before. "Logically, I know that she's beautiful because I know what people consider to be beautiful in a girl.

She's well proportioned, her skin is smooth, her eyes are bright and blue and her hair is blonde and long. All those things can be said of many of the girls that people seem to think are beautiful." He turned back to Moose. "I've never felt any kind of excitement or rush just from looking at a woman, no matter how beautiful other people might think she is. Lately, though, I started to feel—I don't know, maybe a sensation that could be called pleasant, whenever I look at her. I wonder if I'm starting to actually notice how pretty she is."

Moose stared at him. "Boss man, are you starting to turn human on us? Aren't you taking this Pinocchio thing just a little bit too far? We sort of count on you being the human computer, don't go all mushy on us now, please!"

"Shut up, Moose," Neil said. "Can you imagine what it would be like to not ever feel any kind of emotion? If he's starting to come out of that, all I can say is more power to ya, Boss."

Sarah came back a moment later, and Noah announced that it was late enough to head out for dinner. This time, Moose offered to drive, so they all piled into the Malibu. Because of his long legs, Noah let Neil sit in the front passenger seat, which required Sarah's tiny frame to sit behind him. Noah squeezed in behind Moose, and they were off.

Elaine Jefferson, Moose's girlfriend, was working that night at the Sagebrush Saloon, and he caught her attention as they came through the door. She made certain to put them at one of her tables, and took their drink orders. When she had time between customers, she would come over and hang out with the four of them, standing beside Moose's chair with an arm draped around his shoulders.

Sarah had pulled her own chair a little closer to Noah, and noticed that Neil's eyes were bouncing between the two couples. She waited until Elaine had walked away again, and then reached over and tapped Neil on the arm.

"Hey, little bro," she said. "You okay?"

"Me? I'm fabulous. Life couldn't get any better, unless maybe there was a beautiful female in my future. Strike that; make it any kind of female at all, as long as she is reasonably close to being human."

"He's lonely," Noah said. "I've seen that before, lots of times."

"Yes, I know," Sarah said. "You didn't have to point it out." She turned back to Neil. "Don't worry, Buddy, there's a girl out there for you. You'll find her, sooner or later."

"If I get an option on that, I'll take sooner, thank you. Later just sounds so—late, y'know? Like, it might never get here?"

Their dinners arrived, and they slipped into normal conversation as they ate. When they were finished, Noah ordered a beer, and the others followed suit. Neil, who was not anywhere close to twenty-one, knew that Elaine wouldn't ask any questions, and happily took a swig of his own bottle as soon as they arrived.

The Saloon was a Bar and Grill type of place, and after seven, it often had a band performing live music. This particular night was one of those, and Moose waited until Elaine had a break, then grabbed her hand and dragged her to the dance floor. Sarah looked at Noah, and he grinned. A second later he was up and leading her onto the floor, as well.

Neil sat at the table alone, watching his friends dance. He finished off his first bottle of beer, and reached over to take Moose's, since he was monopolizing their waitress. He tipped the bottle out and took a drink, then heard a snicker from the table beside them. He glanced over and saw a girl who looked to be not much older than him sitting there, and smiled when he noticed that she was smiling his direction first.

"You took your buddy's beer," she said. "Aren't you worried he'll get mad?"

Neil shrugged. "That's Moose," he said, "he's pretty much always mad about something. I'm Neil."

As soon as he blurted out his name, he wanted to bite off his tongue. There had been times in the past when he had tried to talk to girls, but he never seemed to know exactly what to say. He should have waited to see if she was interested enough to ask for his name, but he had blurted it out, showing that he was desperate. He found himself looking at the bottle in his hand, rather than at the girl.

"I'm Lacey," she said after a few seconds. Neil looked up again, and that's when he realized that she was sitting at a table alone, but where two other places had obviously been occupied a few minutes before. She saw his glance, and grinned. "My mom and dad," she said. "They're out there on the dance floor, too." She pointed, and Neil followed her finger to see the couple she was indicating. A second later, he did a bit of a double take.

"Is that Mister Jackson?" He blurted out the question before he thought about what he was doing, and was about to apologize when he saw that she was nodding.

"Uh-huh," she said. "He's my dad." She leaned as far toward him as she could without getting out of her chair, and whispered, "He works where you do."

Neil's eyebrows shot up. He made a face that he thought would indicate that he sort of understood, but wasn't sure. Lacy grinned wider, then startled him when she stood up and walked over to his table. He sat there looking up at her, suddenly realizing that she was probably at least six feet tall. She waited for a moment; then, deciding that he was not going to offer her a seat, she simply snagged a chair from an empty table and pulled it over to sit beside him.

"Don't worry," she said, "I'm cleared. I work in the Neverland data center. I know who you are, Neil." She indicated the other chairs at the table with her eyes. "I know who all of you are. You're Team Camelot. I just finished compiling your after-action reports on your last mission."

"Oh," Neil said, then mentally kicked himself for sounding so lame. "That sounds like an—interesting job," he finished.

Lacey laughed. "Oh, my goodness," she said, "you're a shy one, aren't you? Don't worry about it, I know I tend to be a little overbearing, sometimes. If I get annoying, just tell me to get lost, okay? Believe me, I won't be offended."

Neil tried to smile, but he wasn't sure if he made it or not until she smiled back. "Oh, I'm not really shy," he said. "I'm just not used to girls who want to talk to me." Again, he wished he could bite off his own tongue, but he followed up with, "I mean, it seems like when you're this tall and skinny, most girls are a little put off. I mean —I'm really messing this up, aren't I?"

Lacey laughed again, and the thought crossed Neil's mind that she had the laugh of an angel. "Neil, relax," she said. "Trust me, I know the feeling. There aren't a lot of guys who want a girl as tall as I am, either. Oh, you know, if I was built like Geena Davis, then maybe that would work, but I don't have her boobs. My dad calls me Six O'clock, because he says I look like the hour and minute hands on a clock at exactly six."

Neil's eyes got a little wider than they already were. "But you're very pretty," he said, and then cringed once more, afraid he was being too forward.

Apparently Lacey didn't think so, because she put a hand on his arm and said with a smile, "Oh, that's so sweet. Thank you."

The music suddenly ended, and Noah, Sarah and Moose all returned to the table. Neil fumbled the introductions, so Lacey took over and introduced herself. A moment later, her father stopped by the table and shook hands with the men.

He looked down at his daughter. "Well, you finally found him," he said, and then he looked up at Neil, who had stood as he approached. "She saw your picture and read your file when you were first recruited, and kept asking me if I had ever met you. When I finally did, and told her so, she drove me nuts with questions for two solid days. I guess it isn't often she spots a guy that really interests her. I hope she doesn't drive you crazy, but if she does, please don't shoot her. Just send her back to me, I'll try to straighten her out."

Neil made a sickly grin, and waved as Jackson walked away. Sarah and Lacey were talking, and it took a moment for Neil to realize that he was the topic of their conversation. He did his best to ignore what they were saying, but it pleased him to know that Lacey had wanted to meet him even before they ran into each other at the Saloon that night.

The five of them sat and talked for a while, but then Sarah asked Noah to take her back onto the dance floor. Elaine was busy, so Moose waved at them to go on, then looked at Neil. "Well, come on, boy, aren't you going to ask the young lady to dance?"

Neil's face went into full-blown panic. "Dance? I have enough trouble walking across an even floor, and you want me to try to dance? Are you insane?"

Lacey laughed out loud again, then got to her feet and grabbed his hand. "You can dance, don't give me that. Anyone can dance. Come on, I'll prove it to you."

Unable to argue, Neil let her pull him to his feet and onto the dance floor. She grabbed his hands and positioned them onto her waist, then took hold of his shoulders and began moving. "Just do what I do," Moose heard her say, and a moment later Neil looked like he was actually enjoying himself.

Out on the dance floor, Neil and Lacey were actually talking more than dancing. She told him that she had read his entire file, but that what had really gotten her interested was watching the hours of video interviews he had been put through as part of his recruitment and initial training.

"You have the quickest comebacks of anyone I've ever known," she said. "I almost fell out of my chair, I was laughing so hard when I watched the one of you and Doctor Parker. Doc can be one of the most cantankerous old buzzards in the world, but you had him so flustered that he figured he had to pass you just to find out what you might do in the future. When he asked about your time in the juvenile jail, and you told him it was a great place to hone your criminal skills, I literally laughed so hard I almost hit the floor."

Neil, who was slowly gaining his confidence back, shrugged and smiled. "Hey, what can I say? I'm a guy who never lets an opportunity for higher learning get away. I learned a few pretty neat tricks in there, like how to beat someone with a bar of soap in a sock. It doesn't leave a mark, but boy, can they feel it the next day!"

They continued to chat as they danced, and Neil found himself relaxing. He was terrified of getting his hopes up, but he wondered if he might have finally found a girl who would actually like him.

FIFTEEN

Because they had a flight the next morning, Noah insisted they leave by ten o'clock that night. The Jacksons stayed until then, as well, since Lacey and Neil seemed to be getting along so well. Mrs. Jackson confided in Sarah at one point that Lacey's problem was that she wanted a guy who was taller than she was, and since the girl actually stood six foot one, they weren't all that easy to come by. They were delighted that she had finally found one.

Ten o'clock arrived, however, and Neil had to say goodnight. Lacey walked him out to the car and stood with him for a final few moments.

"Well," she said, "I hope I get to see you again sometime. Maybe, if you want, you could give me a call?"

Neil's eyes lit up and he snatched out his phone. "I'd like that," he said, and then swallowed hard as Lacey took his phone and put her number into his contact list.

"I know you're going out on a mission tomorrow," she said, "but call me anytime, whenever you can. At least, call me as soon as you get back, okay?"

Still grinning, Neil promised that he would. Lacey handed his phone back and let her fingers linger on his for a moment before she turned and walked back into the bar.

Moose, of course, couldn't let the opportunity to tease the kid go by. "Well, I'll be doggone if Neil isn't growing up," he said. "Did you see that, Boss? I think he even has a girlfriend! Maybe now he'll stop whining about you and me having somebody to snuggle with, you think?"

"Leave him alone, Moose," Sarah said. "Neil, just ignore him. Lacey seems like a very sweet girl, and hopefully you two will hit it off. We can triple date sometime, that would be cool."

Noah didn't say anything, but Sarah noticed a bemused expression on his face. She leaned close to him and whispered, "What?" Noah glanced at her but didn't say anything. He let one eyelid droop in a wink, which she took to mean that he would tell her later.

They arrived back at Noah's place, and since they had to leave for Denver by seven AM, Moose just crashed on Noah's couch. Neil went across to his trailer, promising to be wide awake and ready to go on time.

When they got into the bedroom, Sarah stripped down quickly. "Who knows when we'll get another chance? I'm not going to skip this one, so get your butt in bed, Mister."

Noah grinned at her, something she had noticed him doing more often lately, and quickly got out of his own clothes. After a quick trip to the bathroom, he slid in under the covers with her.

"Oh! Stop that, your hands are cold!"

They were both up at four, and got a quick shower before getting dressed. When they came out of the bedroom, they could hear the shower in the main bathroom running as Moose got ready to go, so they went into the kitchen and put on a pot of coffee. Moments later, a tap on the door signaled Neil's arrival. He joined them in the kitchen for coffee, but Sarah didn't think he needed any. Neil was more lively and cheerful than she had ever seen him before. It didn't take a rocket scientist to figure out that Lacey had a lot to do with that.

Moose joined them only a few minutes later, and guzzled a cup of coffee as they all got ready to go. Neil had brought over his big Hummer, and they put their bags into the back and then climbed inside. Neil started the SUV and put it into gear, and they were off to the airport.

When they arrived, Neil drove right up to the charter flight gate so that their luggage could be loaded onto the plane, and then a courtesy driver with a golf cart followed Neil out to long-term parking and brought them back. Five minutes later, they were all inside the big Gulfstream and getting comfortable as the pilot started up its engines.

Within another fifteen minutes, they were in the air and the big jet was banking toward the east. All four of the team members sank into their seats and drifted off to sleep.

Noah and the team woke several hours later, and the flight attendant served them a rather delicious meal. The plane landed at London's Heathrow Airport an hour later, at just after one AM local time, and they made their way down the steps. An airport employee was putting chocks under the wheels, and looked up as they stepped onto the tarmac.

"Morning, mate," the man said, and Noah nodded in response. He started to speak, but he heard footsteps behind him and turned to see a familiar face.

"Mister Colson," Catherine Potts said with a smile. "I was surprised when I was notified that you'd be coming back in tonight. I was told to get a car ready for you; I hope a Land Rover will be right."

Noah put on a smile. "It's good to see you again, Catherine," he said. "I take it you weren't left with any problems after our last visit?"

She laughed. "Oh, there might have been a wee fuss amongst the locals, trying to figure out who snatched up one of our favorite sources of information, but I was able to steer some of the investigators in the wrong direction. Speaking of Mister Pendergrast, I understand he arrived home today, with one arm in a sling. I appreciate you leaving him relatively intact, he really is valuable at times."

"My pleasure," Noah said. "He was rather useful to me, and he probably will be again. I'll be paying him a visit in just a little while. Am I going to run into any problems at his place, do you think?"

Catherine's brow furrowed slightly. "It's possible," she said. "I know that both NSA and MI6 are keeping pretty close tabs on him, right now." She chewed her bottom lip for a moment. "Are you going after him right away?"

Noah nodded his head. "Yes, I don't want to take a chance on him either getting away or finding out that I'm here. Any suggestions on how I should go about it?"

It was Catherine's turn to nod. "Actually, yes. It will take you 'round half an hour to get there, and I'll put the time to good use. I'll use a chatter channel I have that doesn't trace back to me, by which I can send out an urgent alert claiming that two suspects on our major terrorist watch list have just arrived at Heathrow. That will draw our boys off, and the NSA will intercept the message so theirs will follow. I can't do anything about the Germans or Italians, they watch him too, but they won't interfere with you. Just do try not to get yourselves killed, that could be so embarrassing."

Noah let his smile get even wider. "You're just a grab bag of surprises, aren't you, Catherine? Okay, I appreciate it." He accepted the keys to the Land Rover that Catherine held out to him, and instantly passed them to Sarah. Catherine turned and walked away without another word, and Noah slid into the front passenger seat, while Neil and Moose took the back.

The Land Rover had built-in GPS, and Sarah punched in the address for Pendergrast's flat. Twenty seconds later she put the car in gear and they were on the way. Traffic was light at that hour, and they had no trouble getting to the place. As Catherine had predicted, they arrived on the block where Pendergrast lived almost exactly 30 minutes later.

All four of them looked around as they cruised down the street, but saw no sign of anyone watching his apartment. At Noah's instruction, Sarah parked directly in front of the building and Neil got into the front seat as Noah and Moose got out.

Having arrived on a private flight, they had managed to bring weapons along, concealed in their bags. Moose had gotten their new special handguns out while they were on the way, and they were tucked neatly into their waistbands. Their light jackets covered the weapons, so that they were not readily visible as the two men approached the building.

This time, they didn't even attempt to pretend to have business in the building. Moose grabbed the door and yanked it twice, snapping loose the lock and pulling it open. Noah led the way inside and directly to Pendergrast's door.

Guns drawn, they burst into the flat immediately after Moose kicked the door open. Pendergrast could be heard somewhere further inside, and it sounded like he was in a panic. They hurried as quickly as they could through the apartment, and found the open door to his bedroom, where he was sitting up in his bed and staring toward the door. His eyes went wide as soon as he saw Noah and Moose, but rather than panic as Noah had expected, he flicked his eyes to the door that stood open.

Noah, who was the first to enter, instantly threw himself against the door. It crashed into someone standing behind it and there was a loud grunt and a thud. Noah snatched the door away and aimed his gun directly between the eyes of a tall, dark-haired man. The fellow raised his hands in surrender, and Moose snatched up the pistol he had dropped to the floor.

"Holy geez, am I glad to see you guys!" Pendergrast said. "He was about to kill me!"

Noah grabbed the stranger by his shirt and yanked him away from the wall, throwing him onto the foot of Pendergrast's bed. "Well, well," he said. "And just who might you be, my friend?"

The man simply sat on the bed, and did not respond. Pendergrast volunteered, "He's one of Nicolaich Andropov's people. Apparently, Nicolaich is a little pissed at you, and he's going to great lengths to try to track you down. This guy was sent to question me, and he wasn't happy about my lack of information regarding your whereabouts. I don't know how you managed to pick this moment to show up, but you couldn't have planned it any better if you'd tried." He threw off the covers and spun to put his feet on the floor, but Noah pointed at him and said, "Stop!"

"What the hell?" Pendergrast asked angrily. "You save my neck and then you get all pissy?"

"Saving your neck was an accident," Noah said, keeping his eyes on the stranger. "Tell me what you know about this guy."

Pendergrast gave a shrug and looked irritated. "I already did, he was sent here to try to get me to tell him how to find you. Just in case you didn't know it, that kid you killed in Kubinka was Vasily Andropov, as in son of Nicolaich Andropov. The old man didn't take kindly to you whacking his kid, and he wants your head on a platter."

Noah looked into the eyes of the Russian. "If you don't speak English, you're useless to me. If you're useless, I put a bullet in your head. Got anything to say?"

The man stared back at him for a moment, then shrugged his own shoulders. "You're going to kill me no matter what I say," he said. "At least I will die with the satisfaction of knowing that Nicolaich will make your death a long, slow and painful one."

"Don't be such a pessimist," Noah said. "If you're interested, I might be willing to bargain for your life."

The Russian rolled his eyes. "There can be no bargain," he said. "I have my orders, I am to either kill you or die in the attempt."

"And those orders came from Andropov?"

"They did, and I dare not disobey them." He narrowed his eyes. "I would very much like to know, however, how you knew that I was here. I know that I was not seen by those bunglers who sit outside in cars all day and night.

Would you tell me that, before I die?"

"I didn't have the slightest clue that you were here," Noah said, "but let's not end our conversation too quickly, *tovarisch*, okay? As it happens, I'm here because I'm looking for your boss just as hot as he's looking for me. You help me find him, and I might decide the world is better off with you in it. Care to deal?"

The Russian gave him a sad smile, and shook his head. "You are a madman," he said. "No one goes looking for Nicolaich, not if he wishes to live. As for me, I am not the average SVR operative; I am a former Officer with the 45th Guards Spetsnaz Brigade, forced into service with Nicolaich because he keeps my wife and daughters under his control. If I disobey or desert, they will die. He may kill them anyway, since I have failed in my mission."

Moose, who still had his gun pointed at Pendergrast, snorted. "Doesn't sound like you got much to lose, either way. You help us, maybe we get Nicolaich and your family could be free."

The man flicked his eyes to Moose, then turned back to Noah. "I wonder if you have any idea how many people have tried to get to Nicolaich? He is always guarded, always protected, and he never allows himself to be exposed in any way that can make him a target. He will not stand near windows, he will not walk out of any building into the open; if there is no garage structure that he can enter with his armored limousine, he simply will not go into any place. He is alive only because he never takes any chances. More than three-dozen have tried to kill him in the past few years, and not one has ever even seen his face. It is arrogant of you to think you might be the exception."

"But I am the exception. I killed his son, right? Do you think he'll be satisfied with just hearing that I've been killed? He wants to see me die, maybe even pull the trigger himself. I'm right, aren't I? Is he going to let someone else perform my execution?"

There was a brief flicker of brightness in the Russian's eyes, but it faded almost as quickly as it came. "I will tell you that it is true he demands that you be taken alive and held for his arrival, but if you think you might turn the tables on him, you are insane, as I have said. He will not come alone, but with enough of his killers that it would take a battalion to stop him. I do not think you have a battalion."

Noah winked at him. "I don't need one," he said. "Do you have any idea who I am?"

Another shrug. "You are an American killer. That is all anyone needs to know."

"Now, that's where you're wrong. I'm not just an American killer; I'm the number one, all-around-best, top-of-the-line American killer. It doesn't matter who I'm assigned to kill, I'm going to always carry out my mission, and I have the most capable support team in the world behind me. I'm going to give you one more chance. You can help me get Nicolaich, and I'll let you live, or I'll have no choice but to terminate you right now. Which way will it be?"

The Russian sat there and stared at him for a long moment, and Noah could see the wheels turning in his head. At last he spoke. "Your friend is correct, I don't have much to lose. As long as I am alive and do what Nicolaich wants, my family would be safe. If I die, however, then they will have no protection from him. I do not want them to suffer; my daughters are but children and my wife is young and beautiful." He stared into Noah's eyes for another ninety seconds, and then leaned forward. "My name is Dimitri Konstantinov, and if it is possible, I will assist you. I have only one request, however. If we succeed, will you help me seek asylum in America? It is for my children, not for myself. I do not think your country would welcome someone like me."

Noah watched his face as he spoke, and then lowered his gun. He tucked it back under his jacket and extended a hand to Dimitri. "I'll do the best I can," he said. "And you might be surprised about whether they let you in or not. I suspect you have a lot of information our side would like to hear."

"Hey! What gives here, guys?" Pendergrast was still sitting on the bed, his eyes wide and his face twisted in anger. "If you didn't come here to rescue me from this jackass, then why are you here? And for that matter, why are you kicking in my door?"

Noah turned to look at him. "Because, Jeremy old friend, you and I are going to have another little talk. I think maybe you knew more about what was going on with that girl than you admitted to me, and that kind of pisses me off."

Pendergrast's eyes went wide, and he began shaking his head from side to side. "Whoa, no way," he said. "Look, man, I figured out real quick that you are not a guy I want mad at me. There's no way I would've held anything back."

"Jeremy, you were bait. We were meant to find you, and find you quickly. I'm guessing that whoever was behind that harebrained scheme thought that we would simply come in, snatch the girl and everything would be over. What they didn't count on was the trail of bodies

I left behind. To be perfectly honest, I'm surprised they didn't kill you themselves. The fact that I left you alive, it seems to me, would make it pretty obvious that you were helpful to me. Don't you think?"

Pendergrast was still shaking his head, trying to appear innocent. "You shot me! I think they just figured I got lucky, and that's why I was still alive."

Noah started to answer, but Dimitri turned and looked at Pendergrast. "No one thought anything like that," he said. "Orders were given to allow you to return home to England, in order to leave you with a false sense of security. It was obvious that you were involved in the rescue, and I was specifically ordered to come here and do whatever was necessary to learn about this man."

Noah shrugged. "See? Jeremy, Jeremy, it looks to me like you're running out of friends in a hurry. Now, I can be a friend, or I can be an enemy. Which column would you like to put me in?"

Pendergrast let his head sag, and muttered something under his breath. When he looked up again, he said, "So what do you want to talk about this time? And can you do anything to keep me safe?"

"First, I want everything you can tell me about Vladimir Sokoloff. He and I need to have a little chat. Can you tell me where he lives?"

Pendergrast groaned. "Oh, come on, you know damn well that if I tell you that, it will get me killed for sure. If he finds out I gave him up, I'm dead."

"Well, you don't need to worry about that. He won't be going anywhere or telling anyone anything. I plan to get information out of him, and then I plan to kill him." Noah stepped closer to where Pendergrast was now sitting on the edge of his bed. "You can either tell me where to find him, or I can take you back to the farm for a little while."

"Okay, okay," Pendergrast said. "He has a large house on Palace Garden Mews, just a few blocks from the Russian Embassy. It's the last house on the left heading away from the Embassy, you can't miss it."

"Does he have security there?"

Pendergrast rolled his eyes. "Of course he does, he's a Russian! He hires local security, though; I think he's afraid the Russian guards would spy on him and report back to the Kremlin. At night, there are probably a half-dozen guards on duty. I spent a few nights there, and I never saw a lot of security guards wandering around."

"I know Sokoloff," Dimitri said suddenly. "If I asked him to come with me somewhere privately, he would do so. If this is part of your plan to reach Nicolaich, I will assist."

Noah gave him a grin. "That sounds like a plan," he said. He turned back to Pendergrast and said, "Jeremy, old buddy, I can't take a chance on you tipping Vladimir off. I'm afraid you're coming with us. If you don't give me any trouble, I'll let you put some clothes on. Otherwise, you're coming with us just the way you are."

SIXTEEN

Pendergrast stared at him for a moment, then shook his head and got up out of bed. Moose kept his gun trained on the man as he opened a closet and began putting on street clothes. Moments later, the four men walked out the front door together, and anyone observing would have thought they were all old friends.

Unfortunately, the Land Rover had bucket seats in the front, and wasn't big enough for all of them. Dimitri pointed to a sedan a hundred yards up the street. "That is my car," he said. "If I am going to bring Sokoloff out, I would do best to have only one of you with me. I realize that you do not trust me yet, so if one of you wishes to ride in the backseat where you can keep a weapon trained on me, I would understand."

Noah looked at him for a moment. "Do you anticipate any problems in bringing Sokoloff out of his house? Getting past the security?"

Dimitri shook his head. "No. Vladimir and I have done business many times, and it is not unusual for me to need his assistance even in the middle of the night. He will come with me, and if there is someone waiting in my car, he would think nothing of it. It would not be the first time."

"Neither of us speaks Russian," Noah said. "Is that going to be a problem?"

The Russian smiled and shook his head. "Not at all. No one there will speak to you unless I introduce you, which I will not do. You will not have any reason or opportunity to speak."

Noah turned to Moose. "You three take Jeremy on out to the farm. Blindfold him so he doesn't know the way, but you don't have to tie him up in the barn. I don't think he's stupid enough to try to run away, but keep half an eye on him anyway. I'll go with Dimitri and bring Vladimir as soon as we can."

Moose eyed Noah as if he wanted to argue, but turned and got into the Land Rover, ordering Neil into the front seat so that he and Pendergrast could sit in the back. Noah turned to Dimitri and motioned for him to lead the way.

The sedan was a Jaguar XE, and Noah chose to sit in the front with Dimitri. He didn't bother to draw a weapon, but Dimitri seemed to understand that Noah didn't particularly need one. As the car pulled away from the curb, Dimitri said, "May I ask what to call you?"

"Alex," Noah said. "Alex Colson."

Dimitri looked over at him for a second, then turned his eyes back to the road. "Colson? That is the name used in Kubinka, but I do not think it is your true name. No matter. You are Alex." He grinned. "I have a brother named Alex, or I did. He died during a mission to Syria."

"Dimitri, if I succeed in my mission to kill Nicolaich Andropov, what will happen to you if the SVR finds out you helped me?"

The other man shrugged. "Russia today is not as bad

as the old Soviet," he said. "In those days, my entire family and I would be executed, but today it would only be me. There are what you call death squads, and no matter where I went, they would hunt me down. If we can avoid letting my involvement become known, that would be good."

Noah nodded. "I'll do my best."

It took almost an hour to make their way across the city to the area where the embassies were clustered together. Dimitri drove straight to Sokoloff's house and turned into his gated driveway. A security guard stepped out of a guard shack and approached the driver-side window.

Dimitri spoke to the guard in Russian, while Noah attempted to look bored and uninterested. There was a brief moment when the guard seemed to pay a lot of attention to Noah, but Dimitri barked an order and he quickly returned his attention to the driver. Dimitri sounded angry, and a moment later the guard went back into the shack and picked up the telephone.

Dimitri turned to Noah. "He tried to tell me that Vladimir is sleeping and cannot be disturbed. I informed him that if he did not notify Vladimir that I wanted to see him, then he would be far more disturbed by the screams of the guard as I disemboweled him."

Noah grunted. "I'll have to try that technique sometime," he said.

The guard hung up the phone and returned to the car. He seemed thoroughly chastised and even subservient, and while Noah could not understand his words, it was obvious that he was telling Dimitri to go on into the compound. Dimitri didn't even bother to respond other than with a curt nod, putting the car in gear and driving away quickly enough to make the guard jump back a couple of steps.

"I told him to tell Vladimir that I was forced to kill someone and need to show him where I left the body. If it were true, then tomorrow morning he would send people out to clean up after me. That is part of his duties here in London."

"Have you done that with him before?" Noah asked.

"Yes, on two occasions. He knows that I do not trust anyone else here. Vladimir and I served together in the 45th Guard a few years ago, and became friends. We are not so much friends today, but I have always been able to trust him. For his part, he worries about repercussions from those above me if he does not cooperate with me when I ask it. In that, he is wise."

"I can imagine so," Noah said. "Okay, then I just sit here in the car, right?"

Dimitri nodded. "Yes, and when you see us coming, moved to the back seat. It is what he would expect."

They came to the circular parking area in front of the house, and Dimitri parked the car directly in front of the door. He looked at Noah. "There is something about you," he said, "something that makes me believe you are as deadly as you claim to be. I have just driven you directly into the mouth of the bear, but I sense no fear, no anxiety. I will do nothing to betray you here, but if Vladimir becomes suspicious, it will be necessary for you to control the situation. While he is not as dangerous as I, he is an accomplished killer. If he gets the upper hand for even a second, he will not hesitate to kill you or me."

"Understood," Noah said. "I just want to get out of this estate before I let him know what's going on. If he figures out that I'm not one of yours before we make it past that gate, things could get bad."

"I will cover you. If Vladimir speaks to you, I will interfere. I will say to you in Russian to keep your mouth shut, and tell him that you are with Nicolaich, sent to observe and learn from me. He knows that I detest training others, so he will probably laugh, but he will not be surprised that I want you to be quiet."

Dimitri got out of the car and walked up to the front door. It opened as he approached it, and he stepped directly inside past the armed guard who had opened it for him. As soon as he was inside, the door closed once again.

A pair of guards appeared from around the side of the house, and came to stand only a few feet from Noah's side of the car. They looked at him, but said nothing. Noah let his eyes rest on them for only a second, then leaned his head back and lowered his eyelids until they appeared to be closed. He heard one of the guards snicker, but resisted the temptation to look at them again.

Dimitri was inside the house for nearly half an hour, and Noah began to wonder if he was being betrayed, after all. He had paid close attention as they came up the drive, and had already planned out various scenarios in his head if he had to try to escape. Beneath his nearly closed eyelids, he kept the two outside guards in sight, ready to shoot both of them instantly if it became necessary.

The guards both turned suddenly, looking up at the door of the house. Noah opened his eyes and looked that way himself, to see Dimitri and another man step through the doorway and start down the stairs. Noah opened his door and stepped out, then immediately opened the back door and climbed back inside. Dimitri and his companion came straight to the car and got inside, with Dimitri behind the wheel again.

Neither of them spoke to Noah, but the car started up and began moving. Noah kept a bored expression on his face until they drove past the guard shack and out onto the street.

Dimitri and Vladimir had been talking in Russian, but Dimitri glanced at Noah in the rearview mirror and gave a slight nod, then said, "We will now speak in English."

Vladimir looked at him in surprise, and asked a question in Russian. Dimitri smiled and said, "Because my friend in the back seat is an American, who does not speak our language."

There was a split-second of confusion on Vladimir's face, but his eyes registered understanding as Noah's Glock suddenly pressed against the side of his neck. "Dimitri, what are you doing?" Vladimir asked, this time in English.

"I am taking the only chance I have to survive, and to free my family from the sword that hovers over their heads. This man is Colson, the American assassin. He is seeking Nicolaich Andropov, and you and I are going to help him."

Keeping one hand on the wheel, Dimitri reached over to Vladimir and removed the man's pistol from its shoulder holster. Without a word, he passed it back to Noah.

Vladimir slowly turned his head to look at Noah. "Do you have any idea who you have gone up against? Nicolaich Andropov is by far the most dangerous man alive today. He will never allow himself to be captured or killed by an American."

"Yeah, well, I don't share your opinion," Noah said. "Nor do a lot of other people, come to that. In fact, I know quite a few folks who think that title belongs to me, so I'm willing to take the risk. You and I are going to have a little chat, because I need to know everything I possibly can about how to draw him out. He wants me just as bad as I want him, maybe worse after I killed his son. He may want my head on a platter, but I don't think he could resist the temptation to take it for himself."

Vladimir looked over at Dimitri. "I can understand your desire to be free of Nicolaich," he said, "but do you honestly believe that this man has any chance of success? Western agents have tried many times just to identify Nicolaich, and none have ever gotten close."

Dimitri made a face that was a combination of an eye roll and a grimace. "Colson and one other man managed to take out five of our best Spetsnaz Security people when they took the girl. I have no doubt of his abilities. The only question that remains is how to get him within reach of the Boar. On that matter, I agree with his opinion that Nicolaich will want the pleasure of killing him personally."

Vladimir grunted. "And what is to keep this man from killing you as well, once he has used you?"

Dimitri looked at Noah in the rearview mirror again, and then smiled as he returned to watching the road ahead. "Because he will not need to kill me. I am his ally in this, because he will help me to get my family asylum in the United States. My children will grow up in freedom, with no fear of Nicolaich Andropov."

Both men fell silent. Noah directed Dimitri to the M4

highway, and they rode in silence the rest of the way to Twyford. Getting to the little village took less than an hour, with another twenty minutes to negotiate the back roads to the farm. Dimitri parked the Jaguar beside the Land Rover as Moose stepped out of the house with a short rifle in his hands.

"Okay, Vladimir," Noah said, "step out of the car gently. My buddy there is an expert marksman, and he won't hesitate to blow you away if you make any sudden moves."

Vladimir nodded, then slowly opened the car door and stepped out. Moose kept him covered as Noah and Dimitri also stepped out of the vehicle, and then Noah led the men inside the house. "Let's have a seat at the table," he said. "If we can continue to talk like gentlemen, then there will be no need for any of my less subtle tactics."

Vladimir glanced at him, then took a chair at the table as he was told. Dimitri joined him, and Noah sat down across from the two of them. He glanced up at Moose. "Where is our other guest?"

Moose grinned. "Hiding in a bedroom. I think he's shy."

"Bring him down. Let's have a little reunion, shall we?"

Moose nodded and turned toward the hallway. A couple of moments later, he reappeared with Jeremy Pendergrast. Pendergrast's face looked ashen when he saw Dimitri and Vladimir sitting at the table, but he didn't say a word. When Moose pulled out a chair for him, he simply sat down and looked resigned.

Vladimir sneered at him. "So they have you, too? Did you also volunteer for this suicidal mission?"

"Jeremy didn't get a choice in the matter, any more than you did. You're both here for the same reason. I want to know everything you can tell me about Nicolaich Andropov, and how I can flush him out. Where should we begin?"

Vladimir stared at Pendergrast, but then he gave a deep sigh. "Nicolaich is already looking for you," he said. "Every agent of Russia, no matter where they are in the world, has been told to watch for you. We have all been shown photographs that were taken by hidden security cameras when you took the girl, and instructed to report any sighting of you to the SVR. If you want him to find you, then you need only leave a trail for him to follow." He looked at Noah. "I do not, however, share your opinion that he will come for you himself. Nicolaich is no fool. Do you think he will not know that you're trying to trap him?"

"You can let me worry about that," Noah said. "The fact of the matter is, I'm not so much trying to trap him as inviting him to trap me. All I want from you is to know where I need to go to leave that trail of breadcrumbs for him to follow."

Vladimir shook his head. "It is not so simple, Mister Colson. Nicolaich is not a man who can be led about, he is always several steps ahead of you. You will think you are leading him on a merry chase, only to find that he is waiting for you at the end of your run."

Dimitri slapped the table in front of Vladimir. "Vladimir, old friend, stop this. Stop defending that monster. As long as Nicolaich Andropov lives, none of us are safe. This may be the only chance we ever have to free ourselves of his threats." He turned to Noah. "Nicolaich takes it personally whenever something happens to any of his top people. In his eyes, I am one of those people. If you will give me your word that you will get my family out of Russia, I will volunteer myself. Kill me, and leave my body where it can be found by Russian authorities. Nicolaich will know that it was you, and it will give him a place to start looking."

Vladimir started to speak but Noah cut him off. "I appreciate the offer, but I think you're more valuable to me alive." He turned to Vladimir. "What about you? Would Nicolaich get upset if something happened to you?"

Vladimir shrugged. "I don't think I'm that valuable to him," he said. "Men like me are easy to replace."

"He is correct," Dimitri said. "My suggestion is the best one, but if you don't like it then I have another."

Noah looked at him. "Let's hear it."

Dimitri nodded once, then flicked his eyes to Vladimir for just a second. "Let him go. He will immediately report to his superiors that you are looking for Nicolaich. That information will get to the Boar very quickly, and he will set all possible resources to locating you. Since Vladimir will also report that I am now working with you, Nicolaich will be enraged. He will want us both, and it will then become a matter of which of us is the hunter and which is the prey."

Noah studied him for a moment, and then turned to Vladimir. "I'm not sure I like that plan, but it might be my best option. You're not going to get off scot-free, though; your life comes with a price. I want you to give Nicolaich a particular message, will you do that?"

"If you give me a message for him, he would expect me to deliver it. As soon as word reaches him that you are looking for him and that I survived a meeting with you, he will undoubtedly contact me directly to find out how that is possible. If I tell him that you wanted me to deliver a special message, then he probably won't have me killed, and he will take the message very seriously. What is it?"

Noah smiled, a shark-toothed smile that sent a shiver down Vladimir's spine. "I want you to tell him that I killed Vasily as an afterthought, just because the kid was too damned cocky, and that I'm going to kill him for the same reason."

Dimitri suddenly laughed. "Oh, my goodness," he said. "That will be exactly the thing to say if you want an insanely enraged Boar on your trail.

Noah looked him in the eye. "That's exactly what I want," he said.

SEVENTEEN

"It's two o'clock in the morning," Noah said. "How long will it be before Vladimir is missed?"

"Probably," Vladimir answered for himself, "when I don't show up at my office in the morning. Because I left with Dimitri, none of my personal guard will think anything of it, and will expect me to go on to work or call in to say I will be late. If I do neither, our security will be alerted to begin searching for me."

"Good, I want them worried. Vladimir, you're going to be my guest until sometime tonight. Moose, is there a room we can put him in that he can't get out of?"

Moose grinned and nodded. "There is a room in the basement, solid concrete with a steel door. I guess it was a storm shelter of some kind—there are two sets of bunk beds down there and it even has a bathroom. The door can be locked from the outside, so he won't be going anywhere."

"That'll work. Take him down and lock him in, then we should all try to rest. In the morning, we can talk about our next moves." Moose stood and motioned with his gun for Vladimir to precede him down the stairs that led off the kitchen. Noah turned to Dimitri. "There are several bedrooms, find one that's empty and make yourself comfortable. I don't have to tell you what would happen if you suddenly decide to change sides on me again, do I?"

Dimitri gave him a half smile. "I am no fool, young man. At this point, I am a corpse that is still walking around, caught squarely in the crossfire between you and your archenemy. My only hope of seeing my family again is for you to succeed in your quest to kill Nicolaich. If you do not, then he will kill me for even considering this kind of betrayal. If I try to escape you, then there is no doubt in my mind that you will kill me."

"You're absolutely correct," Noah said. "Go get some sleep, and we'll talk in the morning." He looked at Pendergrast. "You might as well go back to bed, too, Jeremy. We'll talk more in the morning."

The two men looked at each other, and then rose and walked up the stairs. Noah sat there for another minute, thinking over all that had been said, and realized that something didn't feel right, but he couldn't put his finger on it. He finally shook his head and went up the stairs to the room he had shared with Sarah the week before, stripped out of his clothes and slid in beside her.

She rolled over to smile at him. "About time you got here," she said sleepily. "Hold me?"

"Sure," he said, and spooned up against her. He wrapped one arm around her and pulled her snugly into himself. "Something bothering you?"

"I'm just worried," she whispered. "This Nicolaich sounds like a pretty bad guy, and he already wants you dead. I'm scared, Noah, I'm scared he might be more than you can handle."

Noah held her close for a moment, then said, "In this

line of work, it's a safe bet that I'm going to meet the guy who's meaner than me sooner or later. I knew that when I signed on, we all did. If that time has come, then I have to think that's how it's supposed to be."

Sarah rolled back to face him, and he saw the tears in her eyes. "But that sucks," she said. "Damn it, Noah, why did I have to fall in love now? Why couldn't I have met some wonderful guy two years ago, someone who would have gotten me out of my dad's life and let me settle down? Noah, we can't ever have a life together, and I know that isn't what you want, anyway, but even if you did we couldn't have it. I want to love you, and I want you to love me, and I want to have babies with you and—but the best I can hope for is a few months or years of sleeping with you, and then one of us will probably be dead. It's just not fair." She looked at him for a moment longer, and then rolled away again.

Noah pulled her tighter against him. "Three months ago, I would have said that I wasn't capable of wanting a life like that," he said softly, "but that isn't completely true anymore. I enjoy the time we're together, even when we're just watching TV or cooking together, and if it could last for years, I'd want that. The truth is, though, that I don't know how to love anyone, so I think you'd get tired of me sooner or later, anyway." He moved his hand to caress her cheek. "I do want whatever time we can have, Sarah. Even if it's out here on a mission. And if I die, then I want you to be safe and go on, and find another way to have some happiness in your life."

She trembled in his arms. "I don't want you to die," she said through soft, gentle sobs. "I want every minute I can have with you, and I don't want anything to mess it up!"

He pulled her face back around, then leaned down and kissed her lips gently. "I'm not planning to die. Like I said, I figure you'll get tired of me sooner or later, but I want all of those minutes with you, too. That's a pretty good motivation not to let anything mess this up, don't you think?"

Sarah managed to grin through her tears. "Yeah, it is. I'm gonna hold you to that. You're not going to let anything go wrong, you got that?"

He kissed her again. "I've got it." He pulled her close again as she rolled back over, then lay down beside her. He was asleep within a minute, but Sarah lay awake for a while, just enjoying the feel of his arm around her.

Sunlight coming through the window woke Noah, and he carefully untangled himself so that Sarah could sleep. The bathroom in this house was at the end of the hall, so he dug his shaving kit and clean clothes out of his suitcase and padded down the carpeted hallway in his skin. He turned on the shower and got inside, closing the glass door behind himself.

Fifteen minutes later he stepped out and dried himself, shaved quickly and then got dressed. He went back to the bedroom to get socks and shoes, and was surprised to find Sarah gone from the bed. Normally, she would either sleep while he showered or come to join him. He sat down on the bed to put his socks on, slid his feet into the comfortable trainers he usually wore and headed for the stairs.

No one was in the kitchen, which struck him as odd. He looked out into the backyard, instantly noticing that the Jaguar was gone, but there was no sign of Sarah, so he made a quick search of the ground floor. When he didn't find her, Noah suddenly found himself feeling a rush of adrenaline.

He went back upstairs and looked in the bathroom, but it was empty. He instantly turned and threw open the first bedroom door across the hall from it, where he found Neil sleeping peacefully. He closed the door and turned to the next, opened it quickly and looked inside, then froze.

Jeremy Pendergrast lay on the bed, his eyes open and staring upward, but Noah knew instantly that he was seeing nothing. His face was pale with a bluish cast, and the pillow that had been under his head was lying beside him. Noah stepped into the room, carefully looking behind the door, then moved to stand beside the bed. A finger on Pendergrast's throat confirmed what he already knew; Jeremy Pendergrast was dead. He had obviously been suffocated with his own pillow, and the position of his arms told Noah that he had tried to put up a fight.

Noah turned away and hurried back to his room, snatched up his Glock and began searching the other rooms. They were all empty, as he had expected them to be. He hurried down the stairs and through the kitchen, then carefully made his way down the steps into the basement.

Moose was sitting on the floor, slumped over with his back against the wall beside the steel door to the storm shelter. The door was still locked, so Noah scanned the basement with his eyes and then called out to Moose.

The big man's eyes came open instantly, his head snapping up so quickly that he banged it on the wall behind him. "Noah?" Moose asked, his eyes locked on the gun in Noah's hand.

"Dimitri is gone, and I think he took Sarah with him.

Pendergrast is dead, but Neil is snoring like always." He pointed with his chin at the storm cellar. "Vladimir?"

Moose, his eyes wide, shook his head. "No one's been down here. He's still in there." He got to his feet and took a key from his pocket, using it to undo the padlock that secured the door. It creaked as it swung open, and Noah saw Vladimir's head rise up from the pillow on the cot where he lay.

"Dimitri is gone," Noah said. "He's taken one of my people with him. Where would he be going?"

Vladimir smiled. "I have no idea where he would go at this moment, but I can tell you where he will end up: somewhere in Russia. The man you call Dimitri has played you for a fool, and quite successfully. Who did he take?"

"My driver, a young woman. What will he do with her?"

Vladimir's eyes seemed to show realization. "This woman, she is important to you? To you personally, I mean?"

Noah nodded once. "She is. All of my team are important to me."

"But this one, she is possibly more important than the others," Vladimir said, a statement rather than a question. "She will be bait, at first. Nicolaich will use her to set a trap for you, and when you think you're going to get her back safely, then he will kill her. He will kill her just as you killed Vasily, so that you will know how it feels to lose someone you care for."

"Why would Dimitri take her to him? He wanted my help to be free of Nicolaich, why would he change his mind?"

Vladimir began to chuckle. "You truly are a fool.

When he came to me last night and told me his plans, I never believed he could deceive you so well, but obviously he has done so." He shook his head. "Mister Colson, you had your prey within your grasp, and never knew it. Dimitri does not exist; the man who has taken your woman is Nicolaich Andropov, himself."

"Holy crap," Moose muttered, but Noah only nodded once.

"I suspected as much this morning, when I saw that he killed Pendergrast and disappeared with Sarah. The whole thing, finding him at Pendergrast's flat, how easily I captured him, his willingness to make himself another target, despite the danger his family is in—it was all a setup, right?"

Vladimir nodded his head. "He knew you would be back, and would come for Jeremy again. He arrived in London a few days ago and immediately put people to watching the airport for you. You are easy to spot, coming in on your private jet. He had good photos of you from Kubinka, and expected you to come in on a private flight, so he had some of his own people working that area of the airport. One of them used an amplified microphone to eavesdrop on your conversation with the British woman, so he knew you were going after Jeremy at that time. Nicolaich was actually staying in another apartment in the same building, so it was easy for him to get into the flat and put on his act. He was certain that you would take him alive, as long as he gave you a reason to believe he could be turned into an ally." He chuckled again. "Obviously, he knows you very well, Mister Colson."

Noah looked at him for a moment, then nodded again. "Better than I know him, obviously. That doesn't do you any good, however, since he left you here for me to take it out on. I'm sure he would realize that if anything happens to Sarah, you'll never see the light of day again."

Vladimir shrugged. "I have been a dead man living on borrowed time for more than ten years," he said. "There is nothing you can do to me that I have not been expecting for some time. Nicolaich has already written me off, of that I can assure you. I am expendable."

"Maybe, maybe not," Noah said. "He managed to kill Pendergrast less than twenty feet away from me, but he made no attempt to kill me or any of the rest of us. If he can move so stealthily, he would have had no trouble taking out one of my other people, and that would've left him with weapons. That tells me that he doesn't want me dead yet, he wants me to suffer first. What should I be doing to get ready for what's coming?"

Vladimir suddenly laughed, a hearty laugh that echoed through the basement. "Oh, Mister Colson, you surely do not expect me to tell you that. Unlike your false Dimitri, my loyalty to Nicolaich is absolute. I will do absolutely nothing to help you. Feel free to kill me now, since you're going to do so anyway."

"Let me hang him up in the barn," Moose said. "He thinks he's tough, but he'll crack."

Noah shook his head. "Nicolaich and Sarah have been gone for at least twenty minutes. By now, he's called other agents and they'll be descending on us within the next half hour. We've got to get out of here, right now." He looked back at Vladimir. "Ironically, I'm not ready to kill you yet. Instead, I want you to give a message to Nicolaich when he finds out you're alive and contacts you. You tell him that I'm coming, and that I intend to kill everyone who stands between me and him. And you tell him that if anything happens to Sarah, I will not only kill him, but I will skin him alive, one square inch at a time so that it takes him a month to finally die."

Noah closed the door and reached out for the padlock, hooking it through the hasp without locking it. "Let's go," he said to Moose. "Get Neil up, and you guys get all your stuff into the Land Rover. I'll grab mine and Sarah's. I want to be on the road and off this property within fifteen minutes."

He turned and ran up the stairs two at a time, with Moose on his heels. They were both shouting for Neil as they entered the upstairs hallway, and Moose ran on to the boy's room as Noah entered his own.

He quickly snapped his own bag and Sarah's closed, then grabbed them and carried them down and out through the back door. He had found the keys to the Land Rover on the nightstand beside the bed, and had already loaded the bags into the back by the time Neil and Moose appeared with theirs. They tossed them in, and the three men got into the car.

"Now, will someone tell me what the hell is going on?" Neil asked. "What's the rush, and where is Sarah?"

"I got played," Noah said. "Dimitri, the guy I captured last night, the one who was supposed to help us catch Nicolaich, turned out to be Nicolaich himself in reality. He killed Pendergrast sometime during the night, then waited until I went to the shower this morning and took Sarah. He's planning to use her as bait to set a trap for me, and then kill her right in front of me when I show up."

"Oh, shit!" Neil said. "Boss, we can't—we gotta go get her! If Cinderella finds out…"

"It won't matter," Noah said. "Sarah and I had been in bed, sleeping. He took her while I was in the shower. She doesn't have her belt on, it's in her bag right now."

Moose groaned. "Oh, that's just great," said. "Without that belt, she could spill everything she knows about us, about E & E, everything."

Noah nodded. "She undoubtedly will; I'm certain Nicolaich is going to be quite skilled at getting information out of people. There's nothing we can do about that, but we can do everything possible to rescue her and kill him."

"Damn right," Moose said. "That son of a bitch just made a fatal mistake! Team Camelot takes care of our own!"

"We're going after her," Noah said, "and I want Nicolaich dead. He knows way too much, including what we look like, and he's about to know a lot more. We can't afford to have someone in his position knowing so much about us."

"What I can't believe," Moose said, "is how cool that bastard is. He actually sat there last night and suggested that you kill him in order to bait himself out. What if you had decided to take him up on it? I mean, I thought it was a pretty good idea myself, I figured you were going to go for it. I mean, knowing how you are, it wouldn't have been that big a deal to you."

Noah nodded. "I almost did go for it," he said. "On the other hand, it shows me that he doesn't know as much about me as he thinks he does. Somehow I don't think he would've made that offer if he had known that I have absolutely no conscience. The only thing that kept me from agreeing to it and killing him on the spot was that, logically, if he were who he said he was then he might be more valuable alive. He's expecting me to react like a human being, rather than a robot."

"Okay, I never thought I would say this, but suddenly I'm very glad that you are as messed up as you are," Neil said. "He's counting on you doing what most people in your situation would do, so logically, you want to do something completely different. Am I right?"

"Pretty much," Noah said. "I need to keep him in the dark about my lack of emotions and conscience, so I'll pretend to react normally at first. Then, when he thinks he has been where he wants me, I let the real me out of the box."

Moose, sitting in the front passenger seat, looked over at Noah. "Boss, if I didn't hate this son of a bitch so much, I might just start to feel sorry for him."

"Not me," Neil said, "this is one case where I'd love to be there and watch when you kill him. The question is, what do we do now?"

"We get to somewhere safe and hunker down for the moment," Noah said. "I'll check in with Catherine Potts, get her watching the chatter for any sign of Nicolaich, and you're going to get on your computer and do the same. Somewhere out there, there's got to be some sign of him on the Internet. You're going to find it, so that we can get a step or two ahead of him."

Neil reached back behind the seat and grabbed his laptop case. "I can get started on that right now," he said. "My computer can tap cell towers for a data connection, so I can start looking. Any idea what I should be looking for?"

"I've been thinking about that. He's not going to risk trying to go through one of the major airports, that would be too obvious. That means he's got another way to get out of the country. Could be a jet on a private airstrip, I suppose, or some smaller airport. I can't imagine he'd want to leave by water, but we might as well check ship departures, just to be safe."

"I'm thinking air," Neil said. "He may not know all about you, but he knows you're a deadly sucker. He's going to want to get out of the country fast, I think, not take a chance on you catching up with him. Let me see what I can find."

"So, where are we headed now?" Moose asked.

Noah glanced at him, and then looked back at the road ahead. "I'm going to London, we need a hotel." He pulled his cell phone out of his pocket and searched through his call log until he found the number he wanted. He hit the dial button and put the phone to his ear.

"Catherine? It's Alexander Colson. I've got a situation on my hands. I need a hotel room for three of us, all men, somewhere I can hole up and stay out of sight for a little while, something without my name attached to it." He listened for a moment, then nodded into the phone. "That sounds fine," he said. "Then I need you to do something else. Nicolaich Andropov was in London, and managed to convince me he was someone else. I thought I had captured and turned him, but this morning I found him gone, Jeremy Pendergrast dead in his bed, and my driver, Sarah, missing. Vladimir Sokoloff says Nicolaich has her, planning to use her as bait to set a trap for me. I need to know anything you hear about Nicolaich, two seconds after you hear it. I don't care how unrelated or mundane it sounds, I want to know everything you can find on the guy."

He ended the call and looked at Moose. "We're going

to the Wee John hotel, a dive place that doesn't ask for identification. She'll have a room waiting for us under the name William Bonner. We'll check in and wait until we have some idea of what to do next."

"Wee John?" Neil asked. "Let me guess, it has a really tiny bathroom, right?"

Noah shook his head. "No, from what she just said, the name of the hotel refers to a certain part of the anatomy of one of the former Kings."

"That would be John Lackland, most likely," Neil said. "He was the younger brother of Richard the First, and inherited the throne when Richard was killed in battle in 1199. He was considered a pretty naughty boy, taking the wives of some of the nobles of his court as his mistresses, and marrying his wife Isabella when she was only nine or ten years old."

"Ha!" Moose laughed sarcastically. "No wonder he got a naughty nickname."

EIGHTEEN

"Okay, I've got something," Neil said. The three of them had checked into their hotel room four hours earlier, and were sitting on a pair of beds. "There's a diplomatic plane from Georgia that took off twenty minutes ago from RAF Northolt, the British Air Force Base outside London. According to the tower there, only two passengers boarded, a man and a woman. The pilot filed a flight plan to Tbilisi, Georgia's capital, but radioed right after takeoff to change it to Moscow."

Noah nodded. "That's got to be them. How hard was it to get that information, about the flight plan change? Is that something he would expect us to be able to find?"

Neil looked at him. "I actually doubt it," he said. "I only got it because I tapped into the tower security video. The air traffic controllers didn't bother to log the flight plan change, I just overheard the conversation between the tower and the pilot."

Noah was leaning against the wall. "Good, then maybe we know something he doesn't. Have you got a flight number on that? Anything to positively identify that plane when it lands?"

"The plane is an Antonov An-148, registered as a diplomatic aircraft from Georgia. I don't see a flight number, but—just a moment—it looks like there are very few of these aircraft in the air, so it shouldn't be too hard to spot when it lands."

Noah took out his phone and dialed a number. It seemed to take almost two minutes to get an answer, but finally it went through and he put it on speaker.

"Hello?"

"Larry Carson? Good, I thought this was the right number. This is Alexander Colson, remember me?"

"Yes, Mister Colson. How are you doing?"

"Larry, is this line secure?" Noah asked.

"Yes, sir, it is. Go ahead."

"Larry, I need you to get someone at all of the local airports. You're looking for an Antonov An-148, a Georgian diplomatic plane. If I'm right, two passengers will disembark. One of them is Nicolaich Andropov, and the other is my driver. I need them to be kept under surveillance until I get there. I'll be leaving London within an hour, and I need to know as soon as possible where I should plan on landing."

"Andropov? Are you serious? Man, he's a ghost! I'm going to get cameras out there to all the airports, no one's ever even gotten a photo of this guy!"

"That's fine, but you may be too late. I have every intention of killing him as soon as I find him."

"No problem, I'll get on this right now. I'll call you as soon as we spot them. I take it you don't want my people to engage?"

"Absolutely not," Noah said. "It's a safe bet he'll have an awful lot of security around him, and I think you'd only end up with some dead operatives. This is my specialty, leave this guy to me. Just find a way to keep track of him without tipping him off, and let me know where he goes."

"You got it, Mister Colson. I'll have a car waiting for you. Do you need any other equipment? Weapons, backup, anything like that?"

"Yeah, give me the same bag of tricks as last time. They might come in handy. Call me as soon as you have the airport, so we can divert if we need to. This phone will work even in the air, so you can reach me."

Noah ended the call and then dialed another number. "This is Alexander Colson. I need my plane ready to go ASAP. Destination is Moscow, but I'm not sure which airport yet. Go with Sheremetyevo Airport, and if we have to divert to another one, we will."

Once again he ended the call and looked at Neil and Moose. "Let's get moving. The plane is already fueled and a flight crew will meet us there in thirty-five minutes."

It took them less than ten minutes to get everything loaded into the Land Rover, and twenty more to make it to Heathrow. Noah parked the car near the private boarding gate and tossed the keys under the seat. He had called Catherine Potts while they were on the way, and she'd assured him she had access to another set of keys and would retrieve the car later.

The flight crew had already arrived, and the boarding steps were open. The three of them hurried up into the plane, carrying their luggage along with them. The co-pilot took their bags and stowed them in the rear compartment as the flight attendant got them seated and brought them canned soft drinks.

"Are you gentlemen hungry? We have some lovely

dinners stocked on board, steak and Chinese vegetables."

"That sounds good," Noah said. "We might as well eat now, who knows when we'll get another chance?"

Neil and Moose agreed, but the food had to wait until they were in the air. It took the pilot about twenty minutes to get to cruising altitude, and then the flight attendant began heating the trays in a microwave oven. Within ten minutes, all three of the men were eating, with Moose and Neil telling the flight attendant how delicious the food was.

"Boss?" Neil asked when they finished eating. "Are you doing okay?"

Noah looked over at him in his seat on the other side of the plane. "Yes, of course," he said. "Why wouldn't I be?"

Neil rolled his eyes. "Oh, I don't know, let's see..." he said. "I just thought maybe since your girlfriend is in the clutches of a homicidal maniac, you might be just a little bit worried."

Noah stared at him. "I don't worry," he said. "If Nicolaich were to kill her before we get to him, there's nothing I can do about it. On the other hand, if she's still alive when we get there, I intend to do everything possible to keep her that way."

Neil made a face that suggested he didn't believe Noah. "Look, Boss, you and Sarah have been together since way back during training. Even you can't possibly be so cold that you're not worried. I mean, hell, if anything happened to Lacey like this, I'd be going nuts."

Moose, who was sitting directly in front of Neil and facing him, barked a laugh. "Lacey? Good grief, Neil, you only just met the girl a couple nights ago. I don't think it's quite the same thing."

"Hey, lug nuts, some of us aren't so emotionally stunted that we can't recognize love at first sight! I seem to recall you going head over heels for Elaine pretty quickly, yourself. Trust me, I feel just as strongly about Lacey as either of you does about your girlfriends." He looked over at Noah. "Okay, maybe more than one of you. The thing is, if it were Lacey or Elaine that Nicolaich had taken, you and I would be falling apart. Old Stoneface over here, he just acts like it's no big deal that Sarah could be dead already."

"Neil, you know how I am," Noah said. "It's not my choice, it's just the way things are. A big part of me wishes I could feel things the way you guys do, but right now I think Sarah's chances of surviving this are a lot better with me being just exactly who I am. If I had emotions to get in the way, I'd screw up and get us all killed. That wouldn't help Sarah or anyone else, now would it?"

Moose reached out with a foot and kicked Neil in the leg. "Noah is right," he said. "If this was you or me, we'd be thinking with our hearts, rather than our brains, and that would make us blow it. The reason he's the boss is because he doesn't make mistakes like that. If Sarah has any chance of coming out of this alive, he's it, and I'm going to do everything I can to help him accomplish it."

"Ouch! Asshole! Trust me, I want to help, too. Sarah calls me her kid brother, and I feel pretty much like she's a big sister I never had. Anything happens to her, I'm probably going to fall apart. Believe me, that's not something you want to see, it isn't pretty."

"I'm going to need both of you to help me," Noah said. "Neil, will your computer work up here?"

Neil grimaced, but nodded. "As long as we're in range

of a cell tower, it will. That should cover us for the most part, as long as we're over Europe, but once we get into Russian airspace there won't be nearly as many towers under us. What do you want me to look for?" He reached down beside the seat and grabbed the laptop case, which he always kept close at hand.

"We need a base of operations. Find a rental house somewhere close to Moscow. I'll call Larry Carson and have him arrange it for us."

Neil opened the case and began tapping the keys on the computer. He scowled for a moment, but then grinned as the computer found a tower to connect through. He was silent for almost five minutes, then looked up at Noah. "I've got one, a private estate about six miles north of Sheremetyevo Airport. On Google Earth, it looks a lot like a small fortress, but it's available for lease and by the week or month. It's open right now."

Noah took out his phone and called Larry Carson, the E & E station chief in Moscow. He briefly told Larry what he wanted, then passed the phone to Neil so that he could give Larry the information.

"If it's available, I'll get it for you," Larry said when Neil handed the phone back to Noah. "Call you back in an hour."

Noah leaned his head back to rest, and Moose and Neil followed suit a few minutes later. None of them actually went to sleep, but they had learned in training to always rest whenever they knew it was safe to do so. The flight attendant left them alone, and they were undisturbed until Noah's phone rang just over an hour later.

"Colson, it's Carson. I went through a local real estate company that we have connections with through the embassy, and arranged to get you the place for a week. If you need it longer, I can extend it, just let me know. I'll have all the relevant information in the car whenever I meet up with you. Oh, and incidentally, that plane you're looking for is coming into Sheremetyevo. It's scheduled to land in about fifty minutes. Shall I meet you there?"

"Yes, we're already set to land there. We'll be about an hour behind them."

"Good job," Carson said. "I'll see you then."

Noah leaned back again, but Moose and Neil were getting fidgety. With nothing else to do, they both sat and stared out the windows at the earth passing by below.

Ninety minutes later, the pilot announced that they were descending as they approached Sheremetyevo Airport. They all fastened their seat belts in preparation for landing, and the plane was on the ground slightly more than half an hour later. As soon as it stopped moving at the private flight gate, the three of them disembarked and headed into the terminal. Since their plane was not on the diplomatic roster, they expected to have to go through customs, but when they got to the customs green line, Larry Carson was waiting. A customs official was standing beside him as they approached, and the two of them were smiling like old friends.

"Alex!" Carson called out. "Alex, it's Larry." He waited until Noah smiled an acknowledgment and led the others toward him. "Sorry about having to rush you onto a private flight," he said with a chuckle, "I know how much you love the diplomatic planes. I really appreciate you coming so quickly, though. I got your embassy credentials right here." He passed an envelope to each of the three men, and they opened them to find embassy ID cards. Each was stamped "Diplomatic Immunity," and bore their photos and the names that matched their current IDs.

Carson turned to the customs man. "We all good, Boris?" The other man nodded with a big smile, and Carson motioned for Noah, Moose and Neil to follow him. They slid past the customs lines and Carson led the way out the door to the diplomatic parking area. Another man was waiting there for them, and handed them the keys to the same Land Rover they had driven before.

"Wasn't sure if you're going to have any problems with customs," Carson said, "so I decided at the last minute to have those IDs burned for you."

"Probably saved us a lot of trouble," Noah replied. "Moose and I are each carrying a pistol that I would hate to have to give up. I think I could have bluffed my way through, but you saved me the trouble."

"Glad I could be of help. Everything you wanted is in the car, including the location of your two little birdies. Nicolaich took the girl into a van filled with some of the baddest badasses I've ever seen, but we were able to tail it with drones. They're in an SVR safe house on Ul. Ramenki. The address is already programmed into the GPS in the car." He looked at Moose and Neil, then leaned close to Noah and spoke softly. "This particular safe house is incredibly well guarded, with two squads of their equivalent of Navy SEALs stationed there twenty-four seven. I've got a rough idea of who you are, but that isn't the place you want to tackle with just these two. If you can give me a little time, I can round up a few of our boys to help even the odds."

Noah shook his head. "No offense, Larry, but I've never heard of an embassy that was truly secure. There is at least a fair chance that Nicolaich already knows we've arrived, and if you start getting me backup forces, he'll probably find that out too. I don't have any intentions of storming his fortress, and I'm certain that isn't part of his game plan, either. He's out to set a trap for me, and I'm quite certain he will find me soon enough. For now, I just want to get to our base and see what we can do to start preparing."

Carson shrugged. "Okay, but I had to try. Best of luck, and let me know if you need anything else."

Noah and the others put their bags in the back of the Land Rover, and Noah slid behind the wheel. He had already programmed the address of the rented house into his phone's GPS, so he began following the directions to get there.

The drive took almost half an hour, mostly just getting out of the airport and the city. They found the place with no trouble, but got a surprise when they arrived and saw that it came with a full domestic staff. A butler met them at the door, and they were surprised once again to find that he spoke with a crisp British accent.

"Good evening, Sirs," he said, bowing his head for a brief second. "My name is Rothschild, and I am in charge of the staff, here. Some of the maids do not speak English very well, but they know to call for help in the event you ask one of them for something they do not understand."

Noah dipped his own head in greeting. "Thank you, Rothschild," he said. "To be perfectly frank, the main thing we require is to be left alone. Can you pass that word among the servants?"

Rothschild smiled. "Indeed I can, Sir. In addition, may I say that you remind me greatly of some other American gentlemen who have used these lodgings in times past. They were here on business, the sort of business that leaves the Politburo scrambling for information when it is over. This is one of the reasons I willingly employ people who are not fluent in any language but their own. The only ones you might want to be wary of are the cooks and the senior housekeeper. They understand English quite well, and at least one of the cooks and the senior housekeeper are related to Russian officials. Should I let them go, I would find SVR at my door within an hour, so I'm simply careful to warn my guests about them. Now, may I show you to your rooms?"

Noah nodded and returned the smile. "Please do, and thank you. Also, can you make certain that no one bothers our vehicle? We have some things inside that could be quite fragile, and shouldn't be disturbed."

"Indeed, Sir," Rothschild said as he led them into the house. They followed him up a flight of stairs, amazed at the beautiful woodwork and marble appointments. Rothschild stopped in front of a door that was made of mahogany, and turned to Noah. "This is the master suite," he said. "I would think that it should be yours for the time being. Your associates will be quite comfortable in the next two suites on the side of the hallway." He opened the door and stepped inside, and Moose whistled at the luxurious apartment they found inside.

Apartment was the appropriate word. There was a small kitchen, a sitting room with several chairs, two couches and a massive television, a bedroom, and a bathroom that was bigger than Noah's bedroom in his house. The plumbing fixtures were gold plated, and the tub had been carved from a single block of marble.

Noah went into the bedroom and tossed his bag on the bed. "This will be fine," he said. "Let's see where the guys will be."

The other two suites were not quite as large, but each boasted a kitchen, sitting room and bathroom. Neil took the first one, and Moose was happy to take the second.

"On each of the telephones, there is a button marked intercom. If you push that button, I will answer quickly. If anyone else answers, simply ask for me. The kitchens are provided for your convenience, should you choose to prepare a meal for yourself, and are fully stocked. However, the main kitchen is manned by a staff of cooks and helpers that can prepare absolutely anything you might desire. You can reach the kitchen by dialing one, or you can relay your request through me. As I mentioned, the cooks speak very good English, but your meals will be delivered by a maid who speaks none at all."

The Butler turned and left, and the three men returned to Noah's rooms. There was a desk in the living room, and Noah pointed at it. "Neil, get on your computer and look for anything that you think might give us any advantage on Nicolaich. Moose, I'm going to empty my bag. You take it down and stuff the weapons into it, bring them up here."

"No problem, Boss," Moose said. "Of course, the rifle is not going to fit in there. I should probably just leave it under the seat, don't you think?"

Noah nodded. "Of course. I doubt we'll need it here, anyway. We'll want it to be available when we figure out where the battleground will be."

Moose waited as Noah dumped his bag on the bed, then took it and walked out the door without another word. Neil had set his computer up on the desk, and was looking at something that appeared to be a computer game.

"What on earth are you doing?" Noah asked, and Neil turned to him with a grin.

"This place has some high-speed Wi-Fi," he said. "I'm scanning it to see if it has any bleeds. That's what I call it when someone else can watch your Internet activity." He turned back to the monitor and tapped a few keys. "Good thing I checked," he said. "The system is bugged. Every bit of data I send or receive over it will be copied to another location, probably the SVR."

"Do you have to use it?" Noah asked.

"No. There aren't any cell towers close enough to do me much good, but I can use my phone to go directly to a satellite, and it has a built-in, password-secured hot-spot. I can log on through that, and no one can see what I'm doing. We can run a cell phone through the Wi-Fi, just so they see some activity, but I doubt it will matter."

"Get on it, then. Find me anything you can that might lead us to Nicolaich or Sarah or both."

NINETEEN

Team Camelot, minus Sarah, had arrived at their luxurious base of operations at just after seven PM. Five hours later, at midnight, Neil was still searching for any sign of Nicolaich online.

"There's nothing," he said. "From the moment he got into that safe house, no one in any intelligence agency has made any reference to him. I've gotten into every intelligence network in this hemisphere, but there's absolutely nothing I can find. If he's making any kind of plans, he's keeping it pretty secret."

Noah, who was lying on a couch, nodded. "Okay, give it up for tonight. You guys get some sleep, and we'll talk again in the morning."

Moose had been sitting on the other couch, flipping channels on the TV. He turned it off and got to his feet as Neil shut down his computer for the night. The two of them walked out of Noah's room, mumbling goodnight as they did so.

Noah continued to lie on the couch. Calm on the outside, his mind was racing as he tried to formulate a plan that would speed the process of getting him in position to kill Nicolaich Andropov. Unfortunately, he had nothing to go on, and another part of his mind was occupied with something that the others might have considered to be worry. Noah didn't see it that way, but there was a part of him that was trying unsuccessfully to avoid any thought of what the future might be like without Sarah.

For as long as he could remember, Noah Wolf had never worried about anyone, not even himself. Whenever a situation that might have been dangerous arose, he simply examined it and took whatever action he deemed necessary, without any thought of the risk to himself. That wasn't to say that he didn't know how to take precautions, but only that he wouldn't let a lack of precaution stop them from doing what he felt he needed to do.

Suddenly, though, he found himself in a position he had never known before. Without realizing it, he had become so accustomed to Sarah and her attentions that he was taking them for granted. The thought that she might be gone, that he might not be able to save her and be with her again, was causing him to feel something akin to impatience. He wanted to move, wanted to take action, but he had no idea where to begin.

For the first time, Noah forced himself to consider whether he might be feeling an emotion. Certainly, he didn't want Sarah to die, and a large part of that was simply because she was a member of his team. One of the things he had incorporated into his own psyche while in the Army was the necessity of taking care of your own. In three tours of duty in combat zones, Noah had never willingly left anyone behind, earning three different medals for valor because of wounded compatriots he'd carried on his back.

Back then, it was simply logic. Soldiers were important to the military effort, so any soldier that was alive should be brought back for rehabilitation. He had served with other men who had been wounded in combat, brought back to health with medical treatment and then volunteered to return to the front.

This case was different. Sarah wasn't just a fellow soldier, she had become important to him on a personal level. That's what made it new; Noah had never needed anyone before. Even as a teenager, when his childhood friend Molly had become his lover, it had never bothered him when she was busy and unavailable, and when she finally moved away, he simply said goodbye and felt nothing. Now, however, the thought of never seeing Sarah again was enough to fuel something inside him that he didn't recognize.

Could it be anger? Was he actually experiencing anger over the danger that Sarah was in? Even worse, was it possible that he had actually grown emotionally attached to the girl? If there was one thing he knew, it was that emotional attachments caused people to make mistakes in judgment. Otherwise-sane men had been known to murder their wives over an erroneous belief that they were unfaithful, or to kill or injure friends who seemed to be paying too much attention to a wife or girlfriend. Noah forced himself to examine what was going on inside himself.

No, he concluded, he wasn't suffering from any kind of romantic attachment to her. That was obvious to him because of their swimming adventure a few days before. All three of the men had stripped naked in front of Sarah, and her wet underclothes had left her almost as exposed when they had climbed out of the water. Noah had felt nothing akin to jealousy, even though he knew both of the other guys had taken the opportunity to get an eyeful of her charms. He thought that he would surely have been jealous to some degree over that, if he was actually attached to her in such a way.

After a half hour of logical analysis, Noah concluded that his problem was dependence. He had come to be dependent on her, not only for sexual encounters, but also for the subtle touches of humanity that she allowed him to share in. Her own feelings for him were clear, she had made sure of that, but he couldn't find anything in himself that implied reciprocation. Noah wasn't in love, he just didn't want to do without her. Jealousy wasn't an issue, because nothing that had happened had affected that dependence.

Analyzing it this way allowed him to clear his mind of a lot of the turmoil, and he began to think more clearly. As he had told Neil, there was nothing he could do if Sarah were killed before he got a chance to try to rescue her, but he finally acknowledged to himself that he would feel some kind of emptiness if she were gone forever.

Logically, then, he knew that he needed to make every possible effort to ensure that she came back to him alive and safe. There was no doubt in his mind that he would do so, if only he could determine a course of action.

He let himself think about movies he had seen wherein a character was faced with a similar situation. Someone important to them was in danger, and the character had to go to the rescue. Unfortunately, in those stories, it was the character's anger that gave them the strength to overcome insurmountable odds, but Noah didn't know how to turn his anger on. The best he could do, as he had always done, would be to fake it.

He sat up suddenly. Maybe that was the answer. If he took actions that seemed to be emotionally driven, it might force Nicolaich's hand and cause him to expose whatever trap he was setting.

Noah quickly created some scenarios in his head, then got up and stripped. He lay back down on the couch and was asleep within moments.

The sitting room had no windows, but Noah had always awakened near the crack of dawn, and the habit served him well again. Even the changing time zones as he traveled around the world didn't seem to cause him any difficulty in knowing when the sun was coming up, so he rose from the couch, picked up his discarded clothing and went to the bedroom. He chose clothes to wear for the day and headed for the shower.

Twenty minutes later, he went down the hall and tapped on both Neil and Moose's doors, calling to them to meet him for breakfast in his room. Both of them grunted acknowledgment, and he returned to his room to order breakfast. He picked up the phone and punched the intercom button, and was surprised when the butler answered instantly.

"Good morning, Mister Colson," said the stiff upper lip. "I trust you slept well?"

"Like a baby," Noah said. "Rothschild, what's good for breakfast here?"

The Butler chuckled. "Absolutely anything you might desire," he said. "The cook on duty spent several years as a chef in one of London's finest hotels. However, I might suggest that he is excellent at preparing eggs and beef, what you might call steak and eggs. Might that suffice?"

"That will be fine, and make it times three. Eggs

over easy, steaks medium rare. Do they have any decent coffee down there?"

"Everything from Russia's own Zhokei, which I find delightful, to American brands like Folgers or Maxwell House."

"Good, send up a pot of the Russian variety. Better send along a big sugar bowl, that skinny kid with me can't seem to get enough of it."

Moose tapped on the door a moment later, and by the time Noah opened it for him, Neil was also staggering down the hall. They were both dressed, but while Moose looked fresh and alert, Neil's hair suggested that he had showered before he went to bed and hadn't bothered to use a towel.

"Steak and eggs on the way," Noah said. "I'm sure it will be a few minutes, so we can talk until he gets here. I've had an idea, and I think it might make Nicolaich tip his hand."

"We're listening," Moose said. "What are we going to do, Boss?"

"Remember we figured that Nicolaich expects me to act like a normal person? I was thinking about how normal people act in situations like this, going over some of the movies I've seen. Whenever the hero's wife or girlfriend or daughter is in danger or has been kidnapped, the hero gets angry. I need to let Nicolaich think he's driven me to a rage."

"Oh, dear God," Neil moaned. "Don't tell me you're going on a killing spree. Liam Neeson always goes on a killing spree in those movies."

Noah looked at him. "Pretty close," he said. "What I'm going to do is start snatching SVR people and demanding Nicolaich's whereabouts. I will kill a few of them, just to make it look like I'm out of control, but I have to let some of them live so that he'll hear about it. He'll think he's got me all torn up, not thinking clearly, and I suspect that's when he'll make his move."

Moose grinned. "I like it," he said. "We going after them soon as breakfast is over?"

"We aren't," Noah said. "I am. This is one time when I need to operate alone, so that it looks like I'm freaked out over Sarah being taken hostage. Don't worry, though, I've got things for each of you to do." He turned to Neil, who was staring at him open mouthed. "Neil, I want you to find a phone line going into that safe house, and listen to everything that goes through it. Any mention of Nicolaich, I want you to tell me. We'll be using those super communicators Wally gave us, so you can be in my ear all the time."

"Whoa, hold on," Neil said. "How the hell am I supposed to know what might be important and what isn't? I don't speak Russian!"

"Are you going to tell me you can't find some kind of an audio translation program? I'm sure there has to be one out there somewhere."

Neil blinked at him. "Well—well—yeah, I guess there is. Fine, I'll see what I can do. But not until I have some coffee, okay?"

"It's on the way." Noah turned to Moose. "Moose, I'm sending you on some special errands. I want you to take pot shots at the police. Don't kill anyone, and don't let yourself get trapped, just scare the crap out of them. Shoot close to them, but miss, or shoot their cars. I want the police in the city in a panic, so keep moving around. Think you can do that?"

Moose rolled his eyes. "Of course I can," he said. "I

thought you wanted me to do something difficult."

"All right, we all jump on it as soon as we eat. I'll drive you into the city, Moose, and have Carson get you some wheels. Wait, on second thought, you can have the Land Rover. There are a lot of flashy cars running around Moscow. I need something similar, something that will get attention . Within a couple of hours after I start, I want every SVR agent in the city to panic every time he sees anything similar to whatever I'm driving."

There was a tap on the door at that moment, and Noah opened it to find a maid pushing a serving cart. She smiled prettily, tittered once and then pushed the cart into the room. She put it in the small kitchen, then set three large covered plates, three silver mugs and a large silver coffeepot on the table. When she had finished, she turned and looked at Noah, tittered again and then hurried out the door.

The three men sat down to eat, and each of them was surprised when they took the covers off the plates. The steaks were porterhouse, and large enough to be the entrée of a dinner, and the eggs were very large. There was a serving of fried potatoes on each, as well, and a large, heavily buttered roll.

Finishing their meals took the better part of an hour, but they were all wide-awake and ready for the day by the time they got done. Neil filled his coffee cup for the third time, and carried it over to the desk. Within minutes, he was back online and trying to crack the Russian telephone system. It took him all of ten minutes to find the numbers assigned to the safe house, and ten more before he could listen in and record everything that went through them.

Noah went to his bedroom and retrieved his Glock;

Moose had already brought his along. Noah handed Neil one of the paired Bluetooth-style earpieces and put the other on his own ear. "Remember, you get anything interesting, you just pipe up and tell me. No one else will be able to hear what you say, but we can talk back and forth through these things as we need to."

Noah turned to Moose. "Ready?"

"Hell, yes," the big guy said. "Let's go make some mayhem."

The two of them left the room, and ran into Roths-child as they came down the stairs. Noah told him that they were going into the city to take care of some "busi-ness," and the butler wished them luck. They walked out the door into the morning sunshine, but the air was rather cool.

"I don't think it ever gets actually hot here," Moose said. "This time of summer, you'd think it would be pretty warm. I don't think it's over sixty degrees, right now."

"Don't complain," Noah said. "Remember how hot it was in Mauritania? At least we're in a decent climate."

They got into the Land Rover and Noah retraced the route to Moscow. Along the way, he decided to take a look at the safe house, and activated the car's built-in GPS system. He followed the directions, and an hour later they were on the street in front of the place.

It looked more like a fortress than a house, and it was easy to spot the guards patrolling the grounds.

Moose let out a low whistle. "Larry boy was right," he said. "I don't think we'd ever get in there. Those guys look like they mean business and know what they're doing."

"No doubt about that," Noah said. "Going in there

would be suicidal, anyway. If Nicolaich has any idea I know where he is, he's probably hoping I'll try. We're going to let him keep hoping, at least until he finds out what I'm going to do to his organization."

Noah called Carson and told him they needed another vehicle, something flashy that would draw attention.

"I've got just the thing," he said. "The CIA has a Marussia B2, the only real Russian sports car ever built. This one's been tuned to over five hundred horsepower, and can hit two hundred miles per hour. The sound alone is enough to make sure you get attention. There are a few of them around the city, and a lot of other cars that people mistake for one of these." He gave Noah an address and told him the car would be waiting when he arrived.

The car was incredible. Low and sleek, it looked like a combination of a McLaren and the Bugatti Veyron, and both men were extremely impressed. A British agent went over the controls with Noah, showing him how to shift from automatic to manual mode, and then handed him the keys.

"Okay," he said to Moose, "time to put this plan into action. You keep the police busy, because I'm going to be driving them crazy." He climbed into the spectacular automobile and fired it up, then drove away quickly.

Moose got back into the Land Rover and headed for some of the busier parts of the city. He found an alley and ducked inside long enough to get the sniper rifle out from under the seat, then got back in with it leaning against his leg. Moments later, he spotted a police cruiser and followed it until its lights came on to pull over a driver ahead. Moose cruised slowly by and found another alley, turned into it and stopped just at the entrance. He raised the rifle and aimed it carefully at the patrol car.

The sound suppressor on the big gun couldn't silence it completely, but the report was not nearly as loud as even a handgun. Moose shot off the driver side mirror, then put a couple of rounds into the windshield. As soon as the first bullet struck, the policeman hit the ground. Moose stowed the gun in the floorboard again, then took off through the alley.

He continued to cruise the city, and every time he saw a policeman or a patrol car, he found a concealed position and squeezed off two or three shots. No one was injured, but there were suddenly a lot more patrol cars running around the streets of the city. It became difficult for Moose to find stations to shoot from, but now and then he would get another opportunity. Some of them were close enough that he simply used the Glock, but most of the time he employed the rifle. Luckily, he had a large box of ammunition on the floor under his legs. Over the next few hours, the Moscow police began to think they were under attack, and were concentrating all of their forces into the area of the city he had chosen for his campaign.

TWENTY

Noah wasn't being much more discreet. Another call to Carson had gotten him the names and locations of several SVR agents who were known to have ties with Nicolaich Andropov. He started by scouting them, cruising past the houses and offices where they could be found. The car he was driving was getting a lot of attention, with almost everyone he passed stopping to stare and sometimes point.

His first opportunity to strike came after almost 40 minutes, when he spotted one of the agents he was looking for coming out of his house. Carson had sent him photos by SMS, so he knew he had the right man. He watched the fellow make his way to a car, and then suddenly slid his own vehicle to a stop beside him and leaped out of the car. He grabbed the man by his throat and slammed him against the side of his own car, as he pointed the Glock at his face.

"Sergey Chegin?" he asked. The surprise man stared into his eyes, but refused to answer. Noah pressed the gun against his left cheek and asked again. This time the man nodded once. "Where can I find Nicolaich Andropov? Answer me, and you might live through this."

"Nicolaich? I don't know, I don't even know who you

mean."

"Wrong answer," Noah said. He removed the Glock from the man's cheek, pressed it against his left shoulder and squeezed the trigger once. The forty-caliber slug almost tore his arm off, and the man screamed. "Let's try this again. Where can I find Nicolaich Andropov?"

"I don't know, I swear I don't know! I don't even think he's in the city, the last I knew he was on his way to the UK."

Noah quickly patted the man down, removing a pistol from a holster on the back of his waist. He let go of Chegin and spun back to his car, getting in and driving quickly away. In the rearview mirror, he could see Chegin fumbling with what looked like a cell phone.

Fifteen minutes later, he found another target. Nikolai Ukhov was standing on a sidewalk in front of the building where he had an office. As far as the locals knew, Ukhov was a financial analyst, but his real duties involved funneling laundered money into black operations accounts. Noah pulled up and parked just beside where he stood talking to another man, lowered the passenger side window and leaned over so that he could speak to them.

"Nikolai? Is that you?" Noah asked.

Ukhov and his companion both looked down at Noah. "Yes? Do I know you?"

"Not really, I just wanted to ask where I can find Nicolaich Andropov."

Ukhov suddenly looked wary, and his companion turned white. Both of them began to shake their heads, but Noah raised his pistol and fired once, blowing the top of Ukhov's head completely away. The other man spun and ran, but Noah let him go.

Over the next three hours, Noah struck six times. Two of his victims were left alive, wounded but not mortally. The rest died instantly, immediately after they were heard by bystanders to deny any knowledge of Nicolaich Andropov or his location.

Noah was cruising, looking for another victim, when an armored police car suddenly appeared behind him. The lights came on, and Noah slapped the car into manual mode and floored it. He was on Ul. Ostozhenka, a main thoroughfare, and was doing more than a hundred miles per hour in less than eight seconds. Fortunately, the traffic was fairly light, but he knew that the police car would radio ahead. He saw an intersection approaching just after he passed a couple of large trucks, and he managed to slow the car to about sixty before he had to cut the wheel and drift around the corner. The turn cost him speed, but then he spotted an alley in the middle of the block. He downshifted again and managed to slide the car into the alley without hitting the buildings on either side. He pressed on the brake pedal to slow the car even more, and then took a left turn onto the next street it met.

He continued to zig and zag for several minutes, until he was certain that he had lost the police car. Driving sedately again, he continued to cruise for several minutes more, but then he heard Neil's voice in his ear.

"Hey, Boss? I think I got something. I just heard Nicolaich's name mentioned on the call, and I'm running it through a translator right now. Give me a couple of seconds to listen."

"Go ahead, Neil," Noah said. He waited patiently for almost a minute, and then Neil's voice returned.

"You've got some people pretty shook up," he said. "Whoever just called that safe house was screaming that people are getting killed. He claims that a dozen of their best agents have been blown away by somebody in a super car who keeps asking where to find Nicolaich. Whoever answered in the safe house told him to calm down, and to repeat what he was saying more slowly. The next voice to come on the line sounded different, deeper, and apparently it was Nicolaich himself. He seemed pretty pissed off, and said it was, and I quote, that crazy American doing it."

"Good," Noah said. "It means I've got his attention. Now let's see what he's going to do about it. Call Moose and tell him to get back to base. I'm headed there right now."

"You got it," Neil said, and then Noah could hear him talking to Moose on the phone.

Noah pointed the car toward the outskirts of the city, intending to circle around and avoid running into more police, but his phone rang. He looked at the caller ID display and saw that it was blank, so he tapped a button and held it up to his ear.

"Colson," he said.

"Noah?" It was Sarah's voice that came through the phone, and she sounded shaken. "I'm sorry, Noah, they just kept at me and kept at me and I—I told him who you are. Noah, I'm so sorry..."

"So you are not Mister Colson," Noah heard, in the voice he had known as Dimitri. "Your lady friend was surprisingly strong, and it took quite a lot of persuasion to make her give up your name, Mister Noah Wolf."

"Hey, what can I say?" Noah asked. "You use a fake name, I use a fake name. That's just part of our business, isn't it?"

"Of course it is. However, it is not your use of a false name that I'm interested in, as you well know. I could care less about your Elimination and Eradication Agency. Every nation has such an organization, I don't begrudge them anything. You, on the other hand, you have personally offended me. Vasily was my youngest child, still only a boy. How dare you kill him?"

"Oh, go screw yourself, asshole. If you wanted your kid safe, you should have kept him out of the family business. He was involved in international blackmail, and my orders were to terminate anyone I found mixed up in it. It was just business, nothing personal about it."

"Really?" Nicolaich asked. "And will it be personal to you, when I cut the throat of this pretty young girl?"

Noah suddenly felt impatience rising up in him again, and forced it down. "She's not the one you want, it's me. You know that and so do I. Why don't we cut the bullshit and just meet face-to-face? Only one of us walks away, how about that?"

Nicolaich laughed. "Now you are beginning to understand," he said. "We will most definitely meet face-to-face, and very soon. I want to look into your eyes as I kill this girl, I want to see the anguish in them as she bleeds to death in front of you, and then I want to watch the life go out of them as I kill you, Mister Wolf."

"Then say when and where," Noah said. "Let's get this show on the road. Just remember, only one of us will walk out alive, and I plan on it being me, with Sarah alive right beside me."

The laugh got even louder. "Oh, Mister Wolf, you are such an optimist. Very well, let us meet. There is a liquor establishment called Krysha Lindow. It opened an hour ago. My men are already stationed there, so that you will not have a chance to pull any tricks. They will wait outside, to make certain you bring no weapons in. Go into the club and get us a table. The young lady and I will join you shortly. We will sit together at a table and talk about things, and perhaps you will persuade me not to take her life. Perhaps you will persuade me to let both of you go free. We shall see what the conversation brings."

The phone went dead. Noah looked at it for a moment, then shoved it back into his shirt pocket. "Neil? Did you catch all that?"

"Holy shit," Neil said, "I sure did. Smart move, holding the phone up to the Bluetooth thingy. I could hear both of you almost crystal-clear. Want me to get Moose in position at that club?"

Noah thought for a second. "Call him and tell him to find high ground, a sniper position. Tell him whatever he does, do not fire unless he sees me walk out the door with Sarah. Then I want him to take out everyone who even looks like one of Nicolaich's people, just as fast as he can. I have to go in unarmed, but I'll do my best to come out alive and bring her with me."

"I'm on it!" Noah heard him calling Moose again, and relaying the orders.

Noah punched up the club on GPS and pointed the car toward it. He would be there in less than twenty minutes, probably before Moose could get into position. That didn't worry him, because he was certain that Nicolaich's agents would let him enter the club. It was getting out again that was uncertain. By that time, Moose would be somewhere on top of a building in the area, ready to cover them as they made their escape.

He pulled into the parking lot of the club, and three

men with obvious and poorly concealed weapons approached his car. Noah slid the Glock up under his seat, then stepped out and locked the car. The three men advanced cautiously, but Noah smiled and raised his hands.

"I'm not going to give you any trouble," he said. "Nicolaich told me to go inside unarmed, and I'm doing exactly what he wants. Feel free to pat me down, I have no weapons on me."

One of the men stepped forward and ran his hands roughly over Noah's body, unashamedly groping him everywhere. A moment later he nodded at the others, and they waved Noah inside. He stepped through the door that one of the men held open, and then stopped to let his eyes adjust to the dim light. Music was playing in the back of the room, but Noah ignored it as he moved toward an empty table. It was in a corner, and Noah took the chair that was protected on two sides.

A barmaid came over and switched to English when she realized that he didn't speak Russian. "What would you have to drink?"

"You know how to make a vodka Collins?" Noah asked, and the girl nodded. "That's what it'll be, then."

The barmaid walked away and Noah sat quietly, just watching the room and the other patrons. Most of the people he saw were younger, couples who enjoyed getting out on the dance floor. The scene reminded him of dancing with Sarah only a few nights earlier, and he wondered if they would ever get to do so again.

"Boss?" Neil said in his ear. "Moose is in position. He says there are six SVR around the building, but two of them are where he can't get a shot. You'll have to watch for them when you come out."

"Understood," Noah said. "Keep him on the phone with you, and you keep listening to what happens here. Don't talk to me, I can't afford distractions."

"Got it, Boss," Neil said, and then he fell silent.

His drink arrived, and he sipped at it slowly. He had been there for almost 20 minutes when the door opened, letting light in, and he looked over to see Sarah and Nicolaich walk into the room. As Noah had done, Nicolaich stopped and let his eyes adjust. A moment later, they began walking toward the table where Noah sat alone.

Nicolaich put Sarah in a seat that placed her between him and Noah, on his left and Noah's right. The table was small, so they were all pretty close together. The barmaid hurried back over, and Nicolaich spoke to her in Russian. She nodded and left, and then Nicolaich looked at Noah.

"So," he said. "There have been rumors in the intelligence community that the Americans had an organization of assassins, and that they had recently acquired a new one who was particularly well skilled. I understand that this is you. Is it true that you have no emotions? This young lady seems to believe it."

"It's true," Noah said. "Something got screwed up in my brain when I was a kid, and I don't have any feelings. No conscience, either, so if you're expecting an apology for blowing your kid's head off, you can kiss my ass."

Nicolaich grinned from ear to ear. "My goodness, but you do have a sense of humor. Let us sit here and wait until our drinks arrive, shall we? We don't want to be interrupted. Then we can talk."

Noah looked at Sarah, and could see that her face was badly bruised. He slowly raised a hand and reached out to touch her cheek, watching Nicolaich for any sign that he would object. He didn't, and Sarah leaned her face against his palm. There were tears on her cheeks, and Noah brushed one away with his thumb.

"Noah, I'm so sorry," she whispered, but he shushed her.

"It's okay, Sarah," he said. "I'm here now, and I'm going to do my best to get us out of this."

"Ah, the American spirit. I never tire of the optimism your people display. I have killed dozens of you, and I have yet to see one that didn't hold out hope until the very last second."

"I don't have any dealings with hope," Noah said. "Did you ever see *Star Trek*? Well, an old friend of mine got me started watching it when I was a kid, because she said I was just like Mister Spock. The more I watched him, the more I knew she was correct. I deal in logic, Nicolaich, and my logic tells me that your success in killing me is not a foregone conclusion."

The Russian continued to smile. "And that may be true," he said. "We will know, before this day is over. However, let me explain to you that I tend to be very good at what I do."

"So do I, Nicolaich. So do I." Noah let his eyes bore into Nicolaich's own, a game of stare down between two men who knew nothing of fear. Neither of them looked away, and neither blinked, until the barmaid returned with a pair of glasses. She set one in front of Sarah, and gave the other to Nicolaich.

As she walked away, the Russian raised his glass. "I propose a toast," he said. "To the survivor. May the best of us be the one to end this day alive."

Noah looked at him for a second, then raised his own

glass and touched it to the other. Both men were surprised when Sarah clinked her own against theirs, but she proposed a toast of her own.

"To me," she said, "as I piss on your corpse." She pulled her glass back and took a drink, then set it on the table.

Nicolaich looked at Noah, then shrugged and drank. Noah took a sip of his own drink, then set his glass down on the table as well.

"So where do we go from here?" Noah asked.

Nicolaich grinned, leaning his elbows on the table. "What makes you think that we will be leaving? If one of us dies here this day, he would not be the first to lose his life in this place. I've left two of my victims sitting in chairs right here. No one is truly surprised when a body turns up dead in this club."

Noah returned the grin. "I was speaking metaphorically," he said. "I was asking what you want to discuss, and how we're going to determine which of us lives through the evening."

"Ah! I see, more American idiom. I have made a great study of your language, but there are so many things about it that I simply do not understand. Sometimes an American says something that I take as a joke, only to find that he is deadly serious. Other times, I take them seriously and literally when he is only being rhetorical. Your language is hard to grasp in its entirety." He took another drink from his glass, then looked back at Noah. "We shall have a little contest here, with this girl as the prize. If I win, she will die. If you win, she will live, at least as long as you do. Once we have concluded that little game, you can get down to the serious matters."

Noah raised his eyebrows slightly. "And what are the

rules of this game?"

"But I have just told you. Oh, you mean how to play. That is easy. At some point, as we sit here, I will strike to kill her. If you can stop me, you win. Simple, isn't it?"

Noah could see Sarah's face in his peripheral vision and knew that she was terrified, but he didn't take his eyes off of Nicolaich for even a second. "I'd rather play a game where you and I go into a dark alley, and see which one of us comes out alive. Wouldn't that be more satisfying for you? If you win, you killed the man who killed your son."

"Ah, but that would be the second part of the game. First, we must conclude the beginning. You're doing quite well, by the way. Most people would have turned to look at the girl, but you have watched me without fail." He sighed deeply. "You may have a small chance of winning, but I doubt it." He looked over at Sarah, and she cringed back into her chair. "How does it feel, little girl, to know that you may be within minutes of your death?"

"Don't let him get to you, Sarah," Noah said without taking his eyes off Nicolaich's face. "He's trying to make you more afraid; he thinks that will make me look away from him at you. If I do, that's when he'll strike, and I probably wouldn't see it in time to stop it."

"I'm okay," she said, but he could hear the tremor in her voice. "I just want you to kill the son of a bitch."

"I'm sure he intends to," Nicolaich said. "The only question is whether you will be alive to see which of us survives."

Noah continued to watch the Russian, keeping his eyes focused on the man's face. Many years before, his martial arts instructor had taught him that every move a man's body might make can be seen in his face just before it happens. Noah had never forgotten that lesson, and had spent the years since then studying every possible expression and micro expression the human face could make. He could spot them in a split second, even the ones that most people never saw at all. It made it difficult to deceive him with a lie, but it also gave him the ability to predict what an opponent would do.

Nicolaich, on the other hand, had a face that was constantly in motion. He was constantly moving from a smile to a frown to an expression of curiosity, or surprise, or even one of mock fear. Noah didn't dare take his attention from the man for the smallest fraction of a second, because he might miss the tiny twitch of facial muscles that telegraphed his next move.

"Drink up," Nicolaich said. "This place serves the finest liquor in Russia—we should not let it go to waste." He picked up his glass and took another drink, then looked at it as he set it down. He seemed to be contemplating what he would say next, but Noah never relaxed his attention.

TWENTY-ONE

And then it happened. Nicolaich's left cheek twitched slightly, and his eyes moved the barest fraction of an inch toward Sarah. In his peripheral vision, Noah saw the Russian's left shoulder tense, and knew the strike was going to come from his left hand, which was resting on his leg under the table. Noah had put both his hands under the table, gambling that Nicolaich planned to strike low, and now he knew that he had made the right bet. He shot his right hand out toward Sarah just as he saw Nicolaich's left arm move toward her. Something struck Noah's hand and an intense pain shot up his arm, but he closed his fist around the object and yanked.

Something clattered to the floor. Nicolaich's eyes went wide, and suddenly he slammed his left hand on the table. It was empty, but then Noah brought his own hand up.

The broken-off blade of a knife, a six-inch stiletto switchblade, had pierced through his palm and was sticking out the back of his hand. Sarah squealed when she saw it, but Noah simply grabbed the thicker end in his left hand and pulled it out, letting it drop to the floor. Blood gushed from the wound, and Sarah grabbed several napkins that the barmaid had left on the table and used them to cover both sides of Noah's injured hand.

Noah kept his eyes on Nicolaich throughout the whole incident, and now he put a smile on his face. "Looks like I win round one," he said, and Nicolaich raised his eyes from Noah's hand to his face.

A moment later, a grin spread across his own. "I must say, Mister Wolf, you did surprise me. No one has ever beaten me at that game before." He looked at Sarah, and his face was more sober. "Ms. Child," he said. "You have been won. You are safe, at least as long as the rest of this game will last. If I win, however, then you will be mine as spoils. Perhaps I will keep you alive, and use you for other pleasures. There's really no point in killing you, once Mister Wolf is dead."

"I would kill myself before I let you touch me," Sarah said. "You can just get that out of your mind right now, you perverted old bastard."

"Round two," Noah said suddenly. "How do we play it? I want this over with."

Nicolaich nodded and smiled again. "I am certain you do," he said. "I'm also certain that your injured hand would give me an advantage, should I face you without weapons. I have two strong healthy hands, and you have only one. Perhaps that dark alley might be satisfying, after all."

Noah reached up with his left hand and brushed beads of sweat off of his forehead. He pulled his hand away and looked at it, then felt his hair for just a moment. He grinned at Nicolaich. "Now, look what you've done, you messed up my hair." Still with his left hand, he reached into his shirt pocket and pulled out a comb, then raised it and began running it through his hair.

Nicolaich continued to smile as he watched, but then suddenly, Noah pressed one end of the comb against his head and twisted the other. There was a nearly silent *click*, and then Noah smashed his hand down and jammed the comb's now-exposed blade into the Russian's right hand, pinning it to the table.

The Russian let out a shriek as the knife pierced his hand, and Sarah instantly let go of Noah's injured palm and grabbed her glass. She swung it as hard as she could into the side of Nicolaich's face, ignoring the cuts to her own hand as it shattered. Nicolaich screamed again, as blood began pouring from numerous cuts on his temple and cheek, and Noah saw that a sliver of glass had pierced his left eye.

Noah snatched the comb back, pulling the blade free, and Nicolaich yanked his hand to his chest. He stumbled to his feet, knocking his chair over backward as he struggled to get his left hand under the jacket that he wore. He was going for a gun, Noah realized, but he was having problems because the gun was holstered for his right hand, and he was trying to grab it with his left.

Noah grabbed the edge of the table and pushed, tipping it toward the Russian. Once again, Nicolaich fell back, this time tripping over his fallen chair. He rolled, surprisingly quickly, and came up on his feet. He spun and ran for the door, just as several of the patrons came toward them to see what was going on.

"Neil!" Noah shouted. "Nicolaich is leaving the building, tell Moose!"

The Russian made it to the door, and slammed his way through it as a group of people were trying to come in. Suddenly, people were screaming just outside, and Noah knew that Moose was doing his job. He and Sarah were both on their feet, and he grabbed her injured hand in his good one and led her quickly toward the door.

He paused at the doorway, looking out to see what was happening. The group of people who had been trying to come in were scattered all over the parking lot, running in different directions. Noah saw two of the three men who had frisked him lying on the ground, pistols beside them as blood seeped out of their heads onto the concrete. There was no sign of the third man, nor of the other three that Moose had said were out there.

There was also no sign of Nicolaich Andropov.

Noah turned to Sarah and whispered, "Stay low," then pulled her through the doorway. He rushed to where the first of the SVR men lay dead on the concrete and snatched up their pistol in his injured hand, ignoring the pain as he wrapped his rapidly swelling hand around the grip and put a finger on the trigger. His car was only thirty yards away, and he pulled Sarah along as he hurried toward it.

A bullet struck the concrete just in front of his foot, and he spun in time to see another agent preparing to fire again. He thrust the pistol toward the man, squeezing the trigger three times in rapid succession. Two of the bullets struck the man in the chest, but the third took him between the eyes. Most of his face seemed to collapse in on itself, and he dropped onto his back like a sack of wet clothing.

Another shot rang out from the opposite direction, and Noah felt an impact in his left thigh. He stumbled, but managed to stay upright as he tried to turn toward this new shooter. Just as he got his eyes on the man, the shooter's head exploded. Moose had seen what was going on, and had them covered. Noah continued toward the car, but his leg was weak and couldn't support his weight. Sarah ducked under his arm and wrapped her arms around his chest, holding him up as he hobbled along. They made it to the car, and Noah had to switch the gun to his other hand as he fumbled in his pocket for the keys. He hit the button on the fob and yanked open the passenger door, shoving Sarah inside.

He slammed the door and leaned on the car as he hurried around to the driver's side. Sarah had leaned across and opened the door for him, so he let himself fall into the seat and then used his hand to drag his wounded leg inside.

Another SVR agent appeared from around the side of the building and took aim at the car. Noah grabbed Sarah's head and pushed her down, just as a bullet blasted a hole through the glass just in front of where she had been sitting. Noah got the key into the ignition and turned it, then yanked the shifter into reverse. He shoved his foot to the floor on the throttle, and the car roared backward, making the agent's next shot go wild.

The car hit the street and Noah spun the wheel, causing it to spin completely around. He slammed it into drive and the car rocketed forward, the last sounds of gunshots falling away behind them.

"Neil, I'm hit," Noah said. "I'm going to the embassy, they've got a clinic there and Sarah and I both need medical attention. Tell Moose to fall back to base and wait to hear from me. Meanwhile, you keep looking for any sign of Nicolaich. The son of a bitch got away, and I'm not going to let that happen."

"Okay, Boss, okay," Neil said. "Don't you die on me,

you big asshole! We had that conversation, remember? Don't you dare die on me!"

"I won't, unless you talk me to death. Just get Moose back there, and you guys lay low until you hear from me."

"Noah," Sarah said beside him. "You're bleeding pretty bad. How far is it to the embassy?"

"I don't have a clue. Get my phone out of my pocket, look in the contacts and call Larry Carson. We may have to meet him somewhere, I can feel shock starting to set in."

Sarah got the phone from his pocket and found Carson's number, then pushed the button and held it to her ear. When he answered, she almost shouted. "Larry, this is Team Camelot! Camelot has been shot, he's bleeding badly. We need medical attention, and quickly!"

"We're getting reports about gunfire involving SVR, is that you guys?"

"Yes! Yes, that's us! Camelot seems to be going into shock, can you get someone to us?"

"Look around, tell me what you see. I need to know where you are."

"Um, I don't know, I can't read any of these stupid— wait a minute, there's a Starbucks ahead on the right. And we're just passing a KFC!"

"Okay, that tells me where you are! Pull into that Starbucks and wait, I'll have an ambulance there in five minutes."

The phone went dead. "Pull into Starbucks up there," Sarah said to Noah. "He's sending an ambulance, he says it will be there in five minutes."

Noah nodded, but didn't speak. A moment later he

pulled into the Starbucks parking lot, put the shifter in park and turned off the engine. Sarah wrapped her arms around him and pulled him close to her. "Noah? Noah, talk to me. Oh, God, Noah hold on! Help is coming, Noah, you have to hold on for me, Baby!"

"'m here..." Noah muttered, but then his eyes rolled up into his head and he slumped against her. Sarah began to cry, interspersing her sobs with kisses she was planting on his face. Noah wasn't responding, and she began feeling for a pulse on his throat, but didn't find one.

People were coming out of Starbucks and gathering around the car, staring at the bullet-riddled windshield and the sobbing girl inside. Some of them were pointing, and a few were taking pictures with cell phones, but Sarah ignored them. She thought she could detect faint breaths, but that was the only sign of life Noah displayed, and she wasn't sure that she wasn't imagining it.

An ambulance suddenly appeared, its siren shrieking. It pulled into the parking lot beside the car, and then another car slid to a stop just behind it. Paramedics rushed to the car and yanked opened the driver's door, reaching in to carefully pull Noah out and put him on a stretcher. Sarah climbed out of her side of the car and ran around to stay near Noah, but the paramedics pushed her back.

She started to scream at them, but then someone took hold of her arm and she spun around. Larry Carson stood there, and after a moment she realized that he was trying to talk to her. She shook her head and looked at him again, and then realized what he was saying.

"...Come with me, we'll follow the ambulance.

They're taking him to the embassy, we have a fully staffed clinic there, it's like a small hospital. It's a big secret, but I think you have enough clearance to know about it. Come on, let's get into my car. Someone will come to take care of this one later."

Sarah let him lead her to his car, watching over her shoulder as the paramedics worked on Noah. She realized that he must be alive, because they were starting an IV right there on the spot. Once they had it flowing, and had wrapped something around his bleeding leg and hand, they lifted the stretcher up and pushed it into the ambulance. The doors closed, and it roared away.

Carson opened the door for her, and she got into the seat. A second later he was behind the wheel, and they were following the ambulance. The ride seemed to take hours, but later she would realize that it had lasted only a matter of minutes before they pulled into the embassy and drove into its underground garage. The ambulance was already there, and the paramedics were wheeling Noah through a pair of glass doors.

Sarah opened her door, and followed Carson through the same doors the paramedics had taken Noah through. He led her down a hallway, then turned left to enter the clinic. A nurse looked up at them, and Carson pointed at Sarah. "She's with the guy they just brought in," he said. "She's also bleeding, her hand."

The nurse hurried over and looked at Sarah's hand, then looked at her face. "Dear Lord," she said, "this girl's been beaten! Come on, honey, you come with me." She led Sarah into the same room that Noah was in, and had her lie down on a bed that was only a few feet away from him.

"Is he gonna make it?" Sarah asked, and one of the

paramedics looked around at her.

"This guy?" The man's accent was thick, but he smiled at her. "This guy is tough, he's very strong. He would be up in no time, except he gets Doctor Novotny. Doctor Novotny, he is good, but he don't let nobody go until he thinks he has tortured them all he can. But you don't worry, your man, he is strong. Heartbeat good, breathing good. We give him some blood and sew him up, he will be good as new."

Sarah began to cry again, this time from relief. She looked at the nurse who was trying desperately to take her blood pressure. "He's not lying to me, is he? Noah's going to be okay, right?"

The nurse glanced over her shoulder for just a second. "That's Pavel," she said. "He's probably the best paramedic in all of Russia, at least for my money. If he says your guy is going to be okay, then he's going to be okay. Heck, if you ask me, Pavel is better than most of the doctors we get here. You're pretty lucky that he was on duty when the call came in."

Sarah gasped in relief, and then exhaustion hit her. She fell back on the bed and relaxed as the nurse started looking at her own injuries.

"Well, honey, what did you do to your hand?"

"You see these bruises? Well, I busted a glass into the face of the bastard who did this to me."

The nurse's eyes got wide. "Good for you, Sweetie! Too bad you didn't aim a little lower, you might have saved another whole generation from people like him." She cleaned and bandaged Sarah's hand, then began going over the rest of her body. Sarah winced several times, and the nurse clucked each time it happened. "Well, you've got a couple of cracked ribs, and I suspect you've got a couple of minor fractures in your left ulna—that's the long bone in your forearm, right here. Other than that, I don't see any signs of serious internal injuries. I'm going to draw some blood samples, and as soon as you can I need you to pee in a cup for me. That will tell us even more."

Sarah nodded, but she was rapidly succumbing to exhaustion. It suddenly dawned on her that she had not been to sleep since she had been taken from the farmhouse in England the day before, and she couldn't stop yawning. The nurse smiled down at her. "All that stuff can wait, Sweetie. You look like you need some rest, so go ahead and take a nap."

Sarah started to nod, but sleep closed over her.

Back at their base, Moose and Neil were getting worried. Neither of them had Carson's phone number, but Neil found the number for the embassy online, and used it as a foundation to start looking for other numbers. He finally stumbled across an office number for Carson, and dialed that.

A secretary answered, and Neil tried to explain to her that he was looking for information about his friend, Alexander Colson. The woman didn't seem to have a clue what he was talking about, so finally he just demanded to speak to Carson.

"I'm sorry, but Mister Carson isn't in right now. If you leave your name and number..."

"I do not have time to wait for a call back, you stupid bitch! I don't care where Carson is, you get him on this phone right now! Trust me, if he finds out that I called and you didn't, you'll be looking for a new job before the day is over!"

The woman put him on hold without saying a word,

and he listened to some ridiculous music for almost two minutes. He was just about to hang up and call again when the music stopped.

"This is Larry Carson," a voice said. "Who are you, and why are you shouting at my secretary?"

Neil rolled his eyes. "Well it's about freaking time," he said. "Do you know what I'm talking about if I say Team Camelot?"

Carson's voice lost all of its anger instantly. "I do," he said. "Are you affiliated with that organization?"

"You're damned right, I am, I'm Camelot four, the computer whiz. I'm trying to find out what happened to Camelot, can you tell me?"

"Yes, he's downstairs in our clinic right now. He was in pretty bad shape when we brought him in, but the doctors assure me he's going to be fine. It's just gonna take a few days before he's up and about. If you need to come and see him, I can arrange it, but I'm sure he's going to be out cold for at least the next twelve hours or so. He's in surgery at the moment, to remove a bullet from his thigh. Luckily, it didn't hit any major blood vessels, but he did bleed a lot."

Neil was suddenly overwhelmed with relief, and felt tears streaming down his cheeks. He couldn't talk for a moment, so Moose reached over and took the phone from him.

"Mister Carson, this is Camelot two. My buddy here is crying and can't talk, can you fill me in?"

Carson repeated what he had told Neil, adding the additional details about Sarah, and Moose suddenly understood the tears on the boy's face. He wasn't the type to cry, himself, but he knew that Neil was extremely emotional. The relief at learning that Noah was going to be okay had overwhelmed the kid, and Moose could understand that. He thanked Carson, and said he would call the next day to see about visiting Noah. He hung up the phone and looked at Neil.

"He's gonna be okay, little buddy. He's gonna be okay. Sarah is all right, too. She got beat up pretty bad and has a few minor fractures, and her hand is cut up, but other than that she's okay. We'll go see them tomorrow, okay? Tonight we just need to crash here and try to relax."

Neil tried twice to get words to come out, but failed. On his third try, he managed to say thanks, then suggested they call down to the kitchen to get something for dinner. Moose thought that was a great idea, and it got even better when the cook said that making them a large supreme pizza would be no problem at all.

TWENTY-TWO

The doctor kept Noah sedated through the night, but canceled the order for sedation the next morning. Noah finally woke up at around 10 AM, and was surprised to find the whole team gathered around him. Sarah had bandages on her own hand, and she had obviously had a bath. Neil and Moose were sitting on chairs across the room, and Larry Carson was chatting with the two of them. When they realized that Noah was awake, they all hurried over to his bedside.

Neil was the first to speak. "I'm going to explain the situation to you, Boss, and I want you to listen to me real closely. I want to make sure you get it the first time, because I like to repeat myself." He leaned down close to Noah's face. "You are not authorized to get shot! Do you understand me, Mister? No more getting shot, not ever!"

Noah stared into his face for a moment, trying to figure out exactly what the kid meant, then concluded that he was being sarcastic. "I didn't exactly volunteer for it," he said, and all of them laughed.

"Boss, you're getting a whole lot better at making jokes, lately," Moose said. "That one almost sounded like you knew what you were saying."

Sarah pushed both of the men out of the way, and leaned down to kiss Noah full on the lips. Moose whistled, Neil groaned, and Larry Carson said, "If that's what you get for getting shot, I need to go find me a gunfight." Another round of laughter made its way through them, but then things settled back to normal.

Sarah had already told Moose and Neil what had transpired in the nightclub, and Moose had told her about climbing up onto a nearby building to play sniper. He went over it again for Noah, and then Larry Carson took his place beside the bed.

"You might not have managed to kill Nicolaich," he said, "but you did something almost as good. The fact that you took out so many of his operatives really pissed off his bosses at SVR. He ran an illegal operation for personal reasons using SVR assets, everything from people to equipment and favors from other governments. He was completely renegade on this, and has been officially disavowed by the Russian government as of this morning. There's a half-million-dollar bounty on his head, so he's not going to be showing himself anytime soon. His entire operation is under investigation, and is almost certain to be shut down. Under current Russian law, the government is not permitted to operate death squads the way the KGB used to do, so a few more heads besides his are going to roll before it's all over. I talked with our boss lady right after that news came out, and she said I'm supposed to put you on your plane and send you home the minute the doctor says you can travel. I got him to admit that you're stable earlier this morning, and he says you can probably fly home sometime tomorrow. He was a little worried about letting you get on a plane at first, because there's some risk of blood clots after surgery, but when he looked at everything they did, he said you shouldn't be in any real danger."

"Then tell him I'm ready to go on today," Noah said. "If all I'm gonna do is lie around, I can do that in my own house. Besides, I think I've earned a vacation." Noah suddenly looked over at Sarah, and then turned back to Carson. "On second thought, scratch that. Call the Dragon Lady and tell her that I need to be here for at least three or four more days, then convince the doctor to go ahead and release me tomorrow. I think all four of us deserve a vacation, and we should take it right here in Moscow."

Larry grimaced. "Actually, I don't think that's a very good idea. You really did kill off a lot of their people, and a few of them were important enough that they would have survived this shit storm. The government here wants Alexander Colson and Company out of the country as soon as possible. Nothing but the diplomatic immunity I got you when you arrived has kept them from demanding we turn you over right now."

Noah shrugged, but doing so tugged on muscles all the way down to his leg, so he winced. "Fine, then send me on home, and when I get well enough to walk I'll take the whole team to Disney World."

"Disney World?" Neil asked. "Can I hold you to that, Boss? I've always wanted to go to Disney World, and never had the chance."

Noah looked at the kid who idolized him as a big brother. "You bet you can," he said. "Like Sarah said, the team is like a family. We can take a family vacation, and you guys can even invite Elaine and Lacey to come along, if you want."

Neil suddenly looked like he was going to panic.

"Lacey? Um, don't you think I ought to get to know her a little better before I ask her to go to Disney World?"

Moose wrapped an arm around Neil's neck. "Kid," he said in a loud stage whisper, "you and me have really got to have a talk about women."

The team stayed with him the rest of the day, and the embassy kitchen fed them all lunch and then dinner. Doctor Novotny came in late in the afternoon and pronounced Noah fit to leave his care, and then suggested that Moose, Neil and Sarah should go and get some rest, so that Noah could do the same. Sarah took fifteen minutes to kiss Noah goodbye, but finally Moose managed to drag her out. The three of them headed back to the base house, to get everything packed up for the trip home.

Larry Carson came in to see Noah one more time that evening, and handed him a box. "We had to send the car to the repair shop, and we're lucky that our mechanic is an honest one. He found this up under the driver's seat, and I'm pretty sure it belongs to you."

Noah opened the box to find his Glock, and he grinned. "I hope he didn't take it out back and try to get a little target practice in," he said. Carson looked at him strangely, but Noah declined to elaborate.

Morning came, and the doctor stopped in just long enough to sign Noah's release order. The rest of the team came in a half hour later, with everything packed and ready for the flight home. Noah was loaded into a wheelchair and pushed out to the parking garage, where the ambulance was waiting for him once again.

"What's that for? I don't need an ambulance, the doctor released me."

"That's to help you make it out of the country alive,"

Carson said. "Diplomatic immunity only goes so far in Russia. After the things that happened the day before yesterday, there are agents of the government here that would ignore it if they got a chance to blow you away. If you ever decide to come back to Russia, change your hair color and make sure you have a different name. Now, get into the ambulance, all of you, so that we can get you to the airport alive.

Noah shook his head, but did as he was told. Moose and Neil brought all of their bags over from the Land Rover, and then they climbed in. Sarah had already gotten in and was sitting beside Noah on the padded stretcher, leaving the guys to sit in the tiny jump seats that folded down from the side.

The ambulance took a circuitous route, so they finally got to the airport about an hour and a half later. The paramedics, who were actually CIA agents in paramedic uniforms, helped Noah up into the plane while the rest of them waited on the ground. When the agents stepped down once again, Sarah was the first one up the steps, followed by Moose and Neil.

Sarah had just gotten into the plane when a car suddenly came screaming through the gate, and gunfire erupted. One of the CIA agents went down instantly, and the other produced a pistol and began firing at the car. There were three men in the vehicle, and the two on the passenger side were firing automatic weapons.

A few bullets hit the plane, and then Neil screamed and fell to the tarmac as a bullet ripped through his lower leg. Moose spun on the stairs and jumped down, scooping Neil up in his arms and then turning to run back up the stairs. He made it to the hatch, but had to turn sideways to get Neil through, and that's when a bullet struck him in the back. He fell into the plane, landing on top of Neil, and Sarah grabbed hold of them to help them crawl further inside.

Down on the tarmac, the remaining agent rolled out from behind the ambulance he was using for cover and fired several shots in quick succession. The car sped away, and the shooting stopped. The agent turned to his partner, but there was nothing he could do. The man had taken a bullet through his throat, and had already bled to death.

Sarah appeared in the hatch of the plane, screaming for help. "They've been shot, two of our guys have been shot! We need help, we need it now!"

Noah had slid off his seat on the floor, and was keeping pressure on Neil's leg. The bullet had passed all the way through the boy's thin calf muscle, and the bleeding was already beginning to slow. Sarah was trying to help Moose, her unbandaged hand pressing on the hole in his back.

Several people had come running from the terminal, trying to see what was going on. One of them announced that he was a doctor, and the agent ordered him into the plane, then jumped into the ambulance and grabbed one of the paramedic emergency boxes. He ran up the steps of the plane with it and passed it to the doctor, who was bending over Moose.

The doctor snatched the box and opened it, found a pair of scissors and quickly cut Moose's shirt away. The bullet hole was a little lower than halfway down his back, and two inches left of his spine. The doctor examined the wound, and muttered in Russian that Moose was a very lucky man. The bullet had passed into him away from his heart, and just below his left lung, slightly above his kidney. He was in no immediate danger, but surgery would be required to repair damage to his intestines. The doctor called to the CIA agent, still thinking he was a paramedic, to bring up a stretcher.

The agent spoke to the doctor in Russian, and the conversation went on for several minutes. Finally, the doctor reached into the emergency kit and began applying bandages. When he was finished, the agent helped him get Moose into one of the seats, and then the doctor inserted an IV line, connecting it to a bag that he found in the ambulance. Working through the agent as an interpreter, he explained that Moose was in shock from the wound, and that the solution in the IV would help his body to endure it. The IV should last long enough for the plane to make it to London, they said, and then the doctor turned to wrapping Neil's leg. Neil would not need an IV, the doctor said, but he gave him an injection of morphine for the pain and to let him sleep on the flight to London.

"We're diverting to London, then?" Noah asked.

"I'm afraid so," the agent said. "Under the circumstances, we can't take you back off the plane, none of you. Since the doctor says both men are likely to survive, the only thing we can do is get you to the nearest friendly hospital. I'll see to it that arrangements are made for an ambulance to meet the plane at Heathrow, and get them the treatment they need. I'm afraid that's the best solution, and I know it sucks."

"No, I understand," Noah said. "Let's get the flight crew on board, and get this plane in the air as soon as we can."

The flight crew had been in the terminal when the shooting occurred, and were among the people who had come rushing out afterward. The copilot gathered up the team's luggage and carried it to the storage compartment, while the flight attendant worked to rig up something to hold the IV bag high enough for gravity to make it work.

Fifteen minutes later, they were in the air. Both Moose and Neil were out cold from medication, leaving Noah and Sarah awake.

Sarah looked over at Noah. "It just occurred to me," she said, "but I haven't thanked you for coming after me. Thank you, Noah. Thank you from the bottom of my heart."

Noah looked her in the eye. "I had to," he said simply.

Sarah grinned at him. "I know, I know, don't tell me. It was the *logical* thing to do, right? Take care of your team, and all that?"

Noah tilted his head in a half shrug. "Yeah, it was the logical thing to do. That was part of the reason I did it."

Sarah's eyebrows rose. "Part of the reason?"

Noah nodded his head. "Yeah. Part of the reason."

Sarah stared at him for a moment, and it dawned on him that her breathing was getting rapid. "What was the rest of it?"

Noah looked at her for almost a full minute, then smiled. "The rest of it is because it dawned on me that I don't want to live in this world without you."

Sarah's eyes were wide and her mouth was hanging open. "Noah..."

"Don't ask me to explain it," he said, "because I can't. I wish I could tell you that I feel something, emotionally, but I still don't. The truth is plain and simple; I simply didn't want to go on living in this world if you had died. Therefore, the only thing I could do was see to it that you didn't die. I know that's not what you want to hear, and I wish I could say those words to you, but this is all I can offer. Something inside me has decided that I need you in my life. I want to be with you for as long as you can stand to have me around, however long that may turn out to be. I don't want to be apart from you anymore than I absolutely have to be—and if it ever happens that we could actually be together, like really together, then I would be more than willing to have children with you. Sarah, if that's not enough, or if I'm going about this the wrong way, I'll understand, but..."

Sarah unbuckled her seatbelt and all but threw herself across the narrow aisle. She dropped to her knees beside him and reached up to take his face in her hands, then kissed him as passionately as she could.

"It's enough," she said, with tears of happiness streaming from her eyes. "It's enough, Noah. Just don't expect me to keep my own feelings quiet. I love you, Noah Wolf, I really do."

She sat on the floor beside him throughout most of the flight, only getting back into her seat when the flight attendant told her they were getting ready to land. The two of them had talked over many different things, and while Noah's emotionless condition hadn't changed, he had come to recognize some part of his own humanity in acknowledging his need for her. To Sarah, that was close enough to those three little words, but she couldn't help believing that he would finally say them to her someday. Until then, she would wait and love him enough for both of them.

The ambulance was waiting at Heathrow as promised, and all four of them were taken to the London

Bridge Hospital, reportedly one of the finest hospitals in all of England. Moose was rushed into surgery, but Neil was admitted and placed in a room. A doctor named Billingham cleaned and redressed his wound, complaining the entire time about the incompetence of Russian doctors. When he saw Noah and heard what had happened to him, he insisted on admitting him as well and ordered x-rays and blood tests to be sure "those Russian idiots didn't stitch up their own fingers inside you!"

Since Sarah didn't need to be admitted, even after the doctor checked her own injuries and redressed them, and since she told the doctors that she was Noah's fiancée, at which he only smiled, a spare bed was wheeled into his room for her. Moose would have to be there for a couple of days, at least, and Doctor Billingham saw absolutely no reason to release any of the others any sooner. Noah started to complain, but Sarah hushed him with a kiss.

"Hey, you want a vacation, right?" Sarah asked him, so Noah stopped complaining. The two of them lay in his room all that day, watching British television programs.

Moose came through surgery with no problems, and it turned out that the bullet had only damaged a small part of his pancreas and intestines. The pancreatic damage was negligible, once it had been cleaned, and repairing his intestines had only required the removal of a four-inch section. Other than that, he simply needed rest and time to heal. He would be sore, the doctor said, for a couple of months, but he should be able to return to work within four to five weeks.

Neil had finally awakened, and nearly panicked at

finding himself in the hospital. Sarah heard him yelling, since he was in the next room, and went to calm him down. He finally chilled out when he was allowed to get into a wheelchair and visit Noah and Moose.

When Moose awakened, Noah, Sarah and Neil were all in the room. He looked at Noah and Neil in their wheelchairs and raised his eyebrows. He started to speak, but found his throat was sore.

"The doctor said you'd have a sore throat for a day or so," Sarah told him as she raised the head of the bed so that he could see them more comfortably. "They stuck a tube down your throat to make sure you could breathe during surgery, that's why. You're going to be fine, there's no permanent damage that will cause you any trouble. The doctor will be in to explain it to you himself when he gets time."

Neil wheeled himself up close to the bed and looked up at Moose. "Hey, lug nuts," he said. "Remind me to do something special for your next birthday, okay?"

Moose narrowed his eyes and looked at him. "Why?" His voice came out as a croak, but it wasn't too hard to understand what he was saying.

Neil rolled his eyes. "Oh, as if you didn't know. You only saved my life! When the bullets started flying and I got hit, you came back down the stairs to get me. You picked me up and carried me up the stairs, even while they were shooting at you, that's how you got a bullet in the back. Yeah, I'm thinking I need to do something really special for you."

Moose managed a small smile. "Gotta take care of the little brother, right?"

Neil suddenly fell into sobs, and reached up to grab Moose by the hand. He tried to say something, but words just wouldn't come out.

"I think he's trying to say he loves his big brother," said a voice from the doorway, and they all turned to look. Allison Peterson stood there, her arms crossed, leaning against the doorjamb. She looked at Noah. "Camelot, I don't know how you did it, but you took this team and turned it into a real family. I got your after-action report from our station chief in Moscow, and I've got to tell you, you did a helluva job over there." She looked at Sarah. "Sarah, I know you might not believe this, but I'm awfully glad he brought you back alive. Camelot is my favorite team, but don't tell any of the other teams I said that or I'll call you all liars."

Sarah smiled at her. "You know what, Dragon Lady? You're not half as ferocious as you have everybody thinking you are." She walked over and opened her arms, and the men were astonished when Allison spread her own and embraced the girl in a hug.

"Well," she said afterward, "this is a first. I've never had an entire team get shot up and beat up in a single mission. Usually it's one or two who get hurt, and then a few missions later one of the others. But Team Camelot does everything in a big way, I guess. Can I hope that you've gotten your quota of injuries out of the way for a while?"

"Yes!" Neil and Sarah said together.

Allison nodded her approval. "Good. I'm putting you all on recuperation leave for the next six weeks. The doctors say you'll all be fine in a month, but I want you all to be working out and back in shape before I send you back into the field. When you're released here, we'll fly you all home so that you can start getting yourselves back into operational condition. Everyone is now convinced that you are our best team, and there are some things happening in the world that will be needing your attention sometime soon. I had to come over here on some other business anyway, so I moved it up on my calendar just enough to let me come and visit you in the hospital. And incidentally, that's something else you don't tell anyone. This is the first time I've ever gone to visit any of our people when they were laid up. We don't want anyone thinking I'm playing favorites, now do we?"

"No, Ma'am," Neil said. "But since you're here, can I ask a favor?"

Allison's eyebrows shot up her forehead. "Depends. What is it?"

"Well, I know we're not supposed to use our operational cell phones for personal use, but there's this girl back home who really wants me to call her…"

Read on for a sneak peak of In Sheep's Clothing (Noah Wolf book 3), or buy your copy now:
davidarcherbooks.com/in-sheeps-clothing

Be the first to receive Noah Wolf updates. Sign up here:
davidarcherbooks.com/noah-updates

DAVID ARCHER

IN SHEEP'S CLOTHING

A
NOAH WOLF
THRILLER

RIGHT HOUSE

ONE

Noah Wolf walked into the conference room with Sarah Child, his transportation officer and apparent girlfriend, beside him. Neil Blessing, his computer and intelligence specialist, was already there. Allison Peterson, the director of E & E, and Donald Jefferson, her Chief of Staff, shook hands with them and pointed to the coffee and doughnuts that were always present in these meetings. Moose Conway, who was Noah's backup muscle, arrived only a few moments later and the briefing got underway.

"You've had almost four months to take it easy since you all got yourselves torn up on the last mission, so we've got an easy one for you, this time," Jefferson said. "No international travel this time; you're going to be working right here at home. The DEA has identified high-ranking members of the Angelos Michoacan drug cartel operating from a base in the Midwest, and has requested our services to eliminate them. There are five primary targets in all, and it's necessary that they're eliminated in such a way that it sends a message back to the cartel."

"I've got a question," Neil said. "If they know who

they are, why don't they just go and arrest them? Why send us in?"

"That's a valid question," Allison said, "so I'll give you a straight answer. DEA and FBI have been tracking them for a few months now, but these people are smart. They don't allow anything to happen that could provide evidence to back up a warrant or lead to an arrest. DEA has picked up dozens of their dealers and mules, but none of them are allowed to know enough to give us any valid intelligence. This is a case where the best way to put a stop to their enterprise is to simply cut off the head."

Neil was shaking his head. "Wait a minute, wait a minute, let me get this straight," he said. "They don't have enough evidence to arrest these guys, but they have enough to say let's just kill them and get it over with? Correct me if I'm wrong, but I thought we were still in America."

Allison smiled her famous dragon-lady smile at him. "We have detailed intelligence from before these people came to the United States, positively identifying them as major players in the cartel. The DEA can prove that many of the dealers and mules they've arrested have had regular contact with them, but nothing that adds up to sufficient evidence to get a warrant. Since those dealers are distributing some pretty high-grade heroin and cocaine with all the chemical signatures to prove it's coming from the Angelos cartel, I didn't have any problem authorizing the sanctions."

Neil shrugged but settled back into his chair without any further comments. Allison nodded to Jefferson, and he went on.

"As I said, the idea is to make a statement with their termination," he said. "We want the cartel to think long and hard before they send any more people or product into our country. How you go about it is entirely up to you, Camelot, but the messier you can make it, the better. The Angelos Cartel is one of the most brutal in the world, and the FBI credits this particular group with at least three-dozen murders here on our soil. Some of those murders were execution-style, and rumor has it that they were ordered because of a few dollars missing from the daily take. The worst of it is that when the Angelos decide to take you out, they don't just stop with you. They take out your entire family as well, eliminating, as they put it, 'you and your seed from the gene pool' completely."

"I want to say something before we finish up here," Allison said. "Noah, I want you to make it look like the evil they've been dishing out came back to haunt them. Each of the cartel members in Columbia has a family with them. I'd personally like to see you give them back exactly what they've been handing out."

Sarah gasped. "You want him to kill their families?"

Allison didn't even blink. "Yes," she said, looking Noah in the eye. "If it's feasible and can be done without significantly putting you or the team at risk, that's exactly what I want, and before you go all moral on me, Sarah, listen up. The higher-ranking members of any drug cartel tend to operate like a family business. As long as any member of the family is still around, business goes on as usual. Besides that, the cartels use terror tactics to try to keep people in line, which means that a lot of people who never intended to get involved in the drug trade are too frightened to try to get out. Feeding them the same slop they dish out might throw a bit of a worry into their leadership, but it's also almost certain to strengthen the spines of the people they run roughshod over. Maybe we can get those people to rise up against the cartels and help to shut them down for good."

She paused for a moment, as if thinking. "That being said, I should point something out. Alejandra Gomez, one of the members in Columbia, has a two-year-old daughter and a three-year-old son. No matter how I feel about their tactics, I can't sanction the murder of children, so leave them alone. Other than that, the next youngest is Eduardo Menendez's sixteen-year-old son, Manuel, but he's a soldier in his father's operation with a half-dozen kills to his credit already. The rest of the family members are brothers and sisters and aunts and uncles. They tend to take the whole clan with them when they go somewhere."

Jefferson had stopped talking and let her hold the floor, but then he nodded. "As terrible as it sounds, this really is the best way to handle the situation."

Noah never broke eye contact with Allison. "I'll do it," he said. "And I'm glad you clarified that about the kids. I'll make sure they're not around before I strike."

There was an uncomfortable silence for a few seconds, but then Jefferson cleared his throat and said, "I've got your ID kits ready, along with the dossier on your targets, so you can leave whenever you're ready. Columbia is a college town, so it has a ready-made drug market. We believe the cartel chose it as their central distribution point because of its location, and because transportation to just about anywhere else in the country is readily available there. There is an airport, but I'm going to suggest that you drive in, rather than fly."

"You'll want to swing by the Armory," Allison said,

"and pick up any weapons you might want to take along, and I've already told Wally to expect you. You'll get your vehicles there, and I'm sure he's got some other toys that might come in useful on this mission."

Packets were passed to each of the men, and Sarah received a leather purse. Inside, they found wallets and the special, ultra-secure cell phones used during missions, and Noah also received a thick file folder that contained information on all of the targets. They all glanced at their IDs and scanned through the wallets and such to learn more about who they were supposed to be for this mission.

Noah would be Wyatt Wilson. His wallet contained a driver's license, several credit cards and a few hundred dollars in cash, along with several photos. Some of them showed Noah with an older couple, others had him posing with Sarah or another woman, and one showed him with a couple of young boys. There were also numerous worn-out business cards, a few scribbled notes and a long-compressed condom. The data sheet that came with the wallet explained that the people in the digitally constructed photos were his parents, an older sister, a girlfriend (Sarah) and two nephews.

Moose's new name was Jimmy McCormick, while Neil became Leonard Kincaid. That left only Sarah, who found that she was now known as Rosemary Wingo. Her data sheet told her that she was Wyatt Wilson's fiancé, and Sarah's eyes grew wide when she saw a modest but lovely engagement ring in a plastic bag attached to it.

She took it out and slipped it onto her finger, then glanced up at Allison and caught the woman grinning at her. Sarah blushed as she grinned back, but the men seemed not to notice.

Jefferson cleared his throat to get their attention. "Since this is your first time running a mission domestically, I want to point out one thing you need to know. On each of your driver's licenses is a magnetic strip. If you happen to be arrested for anything connected to the mission, tell them that you are a federal agent working undercover and insist that the officers run that strip through a reader. It will instruct them to contact the US State Department, and arrangements will be made immediately for your release."

Noah looked at Allison. "What kind of timetable do we have on this?"

"If it takes more than a week," Allison replied, "I might begin to wonder if you're slipping. It's not about getting it done quickly, though, it's about making sure there's no doubt that they were taken out deliberately and as a result of their activities. To the rest of the world, it can look like a drug war, but I want the cartel back in Mexico to know exactly what it is: Uncle Sam got pissed and had them whacked. Taking out their whole families, especially in an obviously orchestrated way, would be beyond the capability of any of our local drug gangs. They'll get the message."

"I'll play it by ear," Noah said. "What kind of techniques does the cartel use in executions?"

"The usual," Allison said. "Bullet to the head, decapitation, evisceration, bombings. It depends on just how strong a message they're trying to send. You'll need to think the way they do."

Noah nodded. "I can handle it," he said. He rose from his seat at the table and collected the rest of the team by eye. They shook hands all around and followed him out of the room. A moment later, three vehicles left the underground parking garage. Neil and Moose headed home, while Noah took Sarah along in his Corvette to begin choosing equipment.

Noah flashed his ID at the guard shack that marked the entrance to the restricted area of the gigantic compound. Taking up almost half of the fifteen-square-mile region, this was where the top-secret aspects of E & E could be found, and the local residents simply thought it was some sort of military complex. Noah drove along the twisting, mile-long roadway and emerged into a cluster of large concrete buildings.

He pulled up in front of the R & D building and was greeted at the entrance by one of their security officers. Once again he showed his ID, and Sarah produced her own. The guard studied them intently for several seconds, comparing the photographs to the faces in front of him before he handed them back and allowed them to pass into the main hallway.

Wally Lawson stepped out of one of the rooms off that hallway, saw Noah and broke into a big grin.

"Camelot!" Wally shouted, and then he reached out and grabbed Noah's hand, pumping it vigorously. "It's good to see you. Man, oh man, have I got some goodies to show you today!"

Noah's eyebrows rose slightly. "We got a mission," he said. "I was told to come to you for vehicles and to see what else you might have."

Wally's eyes went wide and his face lit up in a gigantic smile. "Oh, great! What kind of mission? Where at? You do know that I'm cleared for all that information, right?"

"Yes," Noah said, "I've been told that. It's a domestic

mission, the elimination of some high-ranking cartel members and their families. They've set up an operation in Columbia, Missouri, and I gather their drugs are flooding the streets throughout the Midwest, maybe even a lot further."

Wally began chewing on his bottom lip, his eyes darting all around as he thought about what Noah had told him. "Okay, okay," he mumbled. "Okay, I've got just the thing for you! Come on, you're gonna love this!"

Wally took off down the hall without even waiting to see if Noah and Sarah followed, and they fell in behind. He led them to one of the development rooms further down the hall and motioned for them to follow him inside.

Within the room were two technicians, a man and a woman. They looked up, curious, and Wally introduced them to Noah. "Jazz, Lenny," Wally said, addressing the woman first, "this is Camelot! Camelot, meet Jasmine and Lenny. These two are a pair of the brightest and most diabolical minds you'll ever find anywhere, and we were lucky to get them."

Noah shook hands with both of the technicians and introduced Sarah, as well. When all of the introductions and handshakes were over, Wally spoke up again. "Okay, kids, show 'em what you've got."

Jasmine smiled. "I'm guessing you're familiar with plastic explosives, right? Well, Lenny and I have come up with a whole new formula that is half again as powerful when it explodes, but a dozen times more stable. As a result, we're able to do things with it that no one has ever done before. Take a look over here."

She pointed to where Lenny was standing beside a workbench that held what appeared to be a very large suitcase. He opened the lid and raised it, and a metal framework expanded upward until it made a cube that measured about thirty inches on a side. There were a number of components inside the framework and a lot of circuitry on the outside.

Tucked inside the lid of the case was what appeared to be one large plastic tank and several smaller ones. The big one contained a thick, white liquid, while the others contained thinner liquids in various colors.

A slot near the bottom of the case opened up, and something slid out. A second later, it opened to become the keyboard and monitor of a computer.

"This is a high-speed 3-D printer," Lenny said, "but instead of using plastics, it uses our formula of plastic explosive. The explosive itself is a neutral color, sort of an off white, but this printer can inject color into each cubic millimeter of the plastic, so you can make an object that is intricately detailed. It can blend colors to give you exactly the shade you need, anything from dull plastic to shiny metallic. Let me show you what it can do."

Lenny turned toward the small computer that was attached to the case. He tapped the keys for a moment, calling up a file in a CAD program, and it displayed a three-dimensional image of an intricately painted figurine of a clown. He used a trackball to rotate the image on the screen, then pointed at some parts on the upright supports of the printer.

"Another difference between this printer and others is that this one is also a 3-D scanner. You simply set an object on the print bed and tell it to scan through the computer, and it does the rest. Those lasers will get an absolutely accurate measurement of the shape and size of the object you're scanning." He pointed at the screen in front of them again. "Now, I scanned this figurine in a couple of months ago, as we were first testing the printer. Notice how it has almost a dozen different colors, counting the clown's face and costume, right? Now, watch this." He tapped another key and the printer's nozzle began moving over the print bed at the bottom of the machine.

"That's going a lot faster than the ones I see on TV," Noah said.

Jasmine, who was standing beside him, smiled. "It's called a Rep Rap, which means Replicating Rapid Prototyper. That clown is about nine inches tall, and a normal 3-D printer would take up to four hours or more to complete it. This one can do it in about eight minutes."

Lenny grinned at them. "That's because of our formula," he said. "Most 3-D printers use a solid string of plastic, melting it a little at a time to put it where it belongs. Ours is liquid, and the hot print head actually causes it to solidify where we want it."

"Look," Sarah said, "I can see its feet already. How do you make them so shiny? That almost looks like real ceramic."

"Well, in a way, it is ceramic," Lenny said. "Along with the color, we add a glazing agent that crystallizes quickly. As it's pushed through the hot nozzle, the glazing agent melts and gives it that shiny-wet look. Without special analytical equipment, you'd never be able to tell it isn't a real ceramic figurine."

Suddenly, the print head rose away from the work it was doing, and a mechanical arm swung down from the top of the machine. A small cylindrical object, about an inch long and a quarter-inch in diameter, was placed inside one of the hollow legs that stood there. The arm then moved away, and the print head resumed its work, securing the little device in place.

"Before you ask, I'll just tell you what that was," Lenny said. "That was the detonator. It has a small charge of its own, a super small battery and a micro-circuit receiver that can be activated manually, or set to go off at a certain time or after X number of minutes. Give it a few more moments, it's almost done, and then we can show you what it's capable of."

It took about four more minutes to complete the figurine, and then Lenny invited Noah to remove it from the printer. He picked it up and felt its weight, then ran his fingers over the surface.

"You're right," he said. "If I hadn't watched you print it out, I'd never know this wasn't real. I'm assuming it's pretty stable? What would happen if I dropped it right now?"

Jasmine grinned. "Not a thing," she said. "This stuff is so well bonded together that it wouldn't even break. Go ahead, try it if you want to."

Sarah's eyes went wide, and she shook her head at Noah. "That's okay," he said, "I'll take your word for it. What about impact, or fire? I know that C4 won't explode unless it's got a detonator, but it will burn."

Lenny took the figurine from his hand and set it on a workbench, then picked up a propane torch and aimed the flame at its head. After several seconds, it was obvious that the flame was having no effect, so he turned it off and picked up what looked like an eight ball from a pool table.

"I made this the other day," he said, "but I don't really need it." He set it on the workbench and then picked up a small, heavy hammer. He grinned at Sarah and then brought the hammer down as hard as he could onto the ball. It shattered into several pieces, and they saw that it had been hollow. Inside was one of the small detonators, stuck to the inner wall of one of the pieces.

"You could shoot holes through it, and it wouldn't explode. It takes a special detonator that uses Triaminotrinitrobenzene and Diaminodinitroethene in combination to produce enough heat and shock to set it off, but boy, when it does! Come on, we'll show you."

Lenny walked into what appeared to be a steel box with a window in it, and they could see through a square, obviously thick window as he placed the clown figurine onto a heavy iron block. He stepped back out into the room and closed the door of the box, which they could see looked a lot like the door on a major bank vault. Lenny spun the wheel on the outside of the door to secure it and then stepped over beside Noah and Sarah as they looked in the window. Jasmine and Wally stood right behind them.

Lenny reached over to pick up a small black box from the workbench and handed it to Noah, who looked it over. There was a small numerical keypad and a single-line display on the front, a red button that sat in a depression on the side, and an open round socket on the top. "That's the detonator remote," he said. "Just push the red button whenever you're ready, but keep your eyes on the clown."

Noah glanced at Sarah, who looked very nervous, then grinned at her. He turned his eyes back to the clown that he could see through the window and brought his thumb down on the button.

A muffled *boom* reverberated around the room, and

Sarah grabbed onto Noah's arm to keep from falling as vibrations shook the solid concrete floor beneath her feet. Her eyes were wider than before and she looked at Noah as if in shock.

"Holy cow," she said.

Noah's own eyebrows were pretty high, as he leaned close to the window to try to see inside. When the clown had exploded, the window had been filled with flames that were bright red and yellow, but that had lasted only a couple of seconds. He could see no visible residue, other than the obvious burn marks on the walls and on the block.

"That's pretty impressive," he said. "And I can see a lot of uses for it." He pointed at the printer. "How much does it weigh?"

"About sixty pounds," Jasmine said, "but that's with all its tanks loaded. You can also carry extra material and inks. The compound is extremely stable, and can't explode without a detonator."

"Does it take a separate detonator and remote for each piece you make?"

Lenny pointed at the remote that was still in Noah's hand. "You need a separate detonator for each one, but that remote will handle them all. All you have to do is insert a detonator into the hole on top and you'll see the numbers zero through nine appear on the display. One through nine are the channels available and you simply press the number of the channel you want that particular detonator to respond to. That programs it, then you just put it into the grip on the detonator placement arm. The computer will decide the best place to put it inside whatever you make. Then, when you want to set it off, you just press the channel button and then the red button. Or, if you choose zero, it goes into timer mode. You'll see a 1 and a 2. If you choose 1, it will let you put in a time based on a twenty-four-hour clock, and then it will ask for a date. That sets the detonator to go off at a particular time on a particular day. If you choose 2, on the other hand, it asks you for the number of minutes you wanted to wait before detonating, and you can go up to 525,600 minutes. That's the number of minutes in a year. It's that easy."

"What frequency does it work on? What's the chance that a stray signal might set it off?"

"There's no chance, none at all. The signal is encrypted, a string of numbers so long that you couldn't fake it in a million years. You can have a thousand devices transmitting on the same frequency, and none of them could ever set these off."

"So, if I want to detonate manually, I can have up to nine devices ready to go and set them off in whatever order I want, right?" Noah asked.

Lenny nodded. "Yes, or you can have more than one device on a single channel. As long as you're in range of all of them, they all go off at once. The detonator has a range of about three-quarters of a mile."

Noah said. "How many of those clowns could it make on a single fill-up?"

"Probably about thirty," Jasmine said. "Making figurines and such, you just make it hollow. The outside is about a quarter-inch thick, but that gives you plenty of explosive power, as you saw. If that explosion had been set off in an average house, it probably would have taken out about half of it. Walls, ceiling, roof, you name it."

Noah looked at her for a moment, then asked, "So a smaller object that was solid, not hollow, would have just as much effect?"

"Or more. The compound tends to reverberate, actually build on its own shock wave. The denser the item you make, the more explosive pressure you get from its detonation. The clown was nine inches tall, but hollow. A three-inch clown that was solid, molded around a detonator, would deliver about half again as much power as the hollow one."

"Okay, one more question. How do I get the things I want to make into the computer?"

Lenny grinned. "There are two options. Number one, just use the built-in scanner if the object is small enough to fit inside. Number two, we've adapted the 3-Sweep software that can make a 3-D model from a single photograph, so you can just take a few pictures of something, extract them into 3-D, and then print it out. Or number three, if you know how to use CAD, you can literally just design something and then print it out. The software in the computer already has about fifteen thousand 3-D images stored in it."

Noah stood and looked at the printer for several seconds, then turned to Wally. "I want one, and give me a couple of refills on the explosives and inks. I'll need a few dozen of the detonators, too."

Wally grinned from ear to ear. "I had a feeling you might like that," he said. "Would it be safe to assume that your cartel people might be receiving some presents in the near future?"

"Yeah," Noah said. "They're likely to think I'm Santa Claus."

TWO

Wally led them through several other sections of this facility, but Noah didn't choose any other devices. He ended the tour by leading them out into a parking area behind the building. There were numerous vehicles there, ranging from beat-up old pickup trucks to new luxury cars. Two security guards sat in a small air-conditioned office, and they waved at Wally.

"We'll need two cars," Noah said. "Anything special about these?"

Wally grinned again. "Nothing like James Bond's cars," he said, "but don't let their looks deceive you." He pointed to a line of cars and pickup trucks. "Every vehicle in that line has a lot more power than you would expect. We're talking the eight hundred horsepower range, so don't let it get away from you."

"Eight hundred horsepower?" Sarah asked, incredulously. "That's pretty serious."

Noah looked at her, and one side of his mouth lifted in what she thought was almost a grin. "Pick the one you want," he said, and then pointed at a small utility van. "We'll take that one, besides whatever Sarah wants.

How long would it take to get a florist's logo on the side?"

"About an hour," Wally said. "We've got about ten thousand logos already made up, it's just a matter of printing it out and sticking it on. No addresses, no phone numbers; people don't pay much attention to those, anyway. I'll get that started right now." He took a walkie-talkie out of one of his pockets and spoke into it for a minute. "Okay, I was wrong," he said as he looked at Noah again. "Our camouflage division has a flower shop sign ready to go. They'll be out to put it on in just a few minutes."

"Sounds good," Noah said. "What about license plates, registration, insurance cards?"

"We can put any state tag on it you want, and create registration and insurance cards to match. The van's registration, for instance, will come back to a flower company with its headquarters here. Incidentally, any of these vehicles are disposable. If you need to ditch one, just go ahead. The registrations trace back to a dummy outfit, a dead end. If you crash one or have to leave it behind for some reason, don't worry about it."

Sarah walked around the lot for a few moments, then pointed at a silver Chrysler 300 sedan. "My father always said that was one of the best-handling machines he'd ever driven," she said. "If I'm going to have that much horsepower, I want something that can cope with it."

"You're going to love that one," Wally said. "Incidentally, it's all-wheel drive, with some very special tires that grip the road like nothing you've ever seen. That sucker will take a corner at seventy miles an hour if you really want to, but that's just the beginning. Let me show you some of the special features of this car." He went to the guardhouse and got the keys to both of the vehicles they had chosen, tossed the van keys to Noah and then walked directly to the Chrysler. Sarah followed him and slid behind the wheel at his invitation.

"Okay, you're gonna love this. This car is one of several that we designed specifically to help you teams escape when things go bad, or duck the local police as necessary. In order to accomplish that, we've added some things you're sure to like." He pointed at a spot on the dashboard and told her to press it. A panel opened up and she saw a dozen buttons arranged in rows of four. "The top row of buttons changes the license plate. There are four different sets installed, and each one is registered to a car identical to this one. Pretty cool, right?"

Sarah was grinning at him. "That's slick," she said.

Wally held up a finger. "But you haven't seen the best part. The next two rows of buttons do something even more special. Push the second button, and you'll see."

Sarah looked at him suspiciously. "It's not gonna, like, throw me out of the car, is it?"

"No, no," Wally laughed. "Trust me, just push it."

Sarah eyed him for another couple of seconds, then reached over and pushed the button. She was watching the dashboard as if expecting something to happen there, when Wally said, "See what I mean?"

She looked up, and that's when she realized that the silver hood of the car had suddenly become a dark green. Her eyes went wide. "Did this car just change color?"

Noah was standing stock still, his head cocked to one side as he kept his eyes on the car. "It did," he said. "One second it was silver and the next it was green."

Wally laughed and did a little dance. "Isn't that awesome? It's called electroluminescence; it uses varying amperage of electrical current to cause prismatic crystals within the paint to slightly alter their shape and size, which results in reflecting a different color for the eye to see. Try another button, I never get tired of watching this stuff work."

Sarah pushed another button and the car suddenly became bright yellow. Another button turned it to a deep blue, and yet another made it red. "Okay, this is just absolutely incredible. How do I get a paint job like this on my car?"

"Oh, you can get it, but it won't be quite as good as this. We just happened to have the resources to take the technology to a whole new level. The stuff that's available commercially isn't quite as good as this, but it does work."

Two men came out a moment later and applied a genuine-looking florist's logo to the van. Noah and Sarah drove both of the vehicles around to the front of the building, where a man met them with a handcart carrying the printer and several other boxes. He loaded everything into the back of the van, and Noah followed Sarah back to his house. The Corvette would be safe in Wally's care until they returned.

The next stop was the Armory. Sarah followed Noah inside and waited while he selected a couple of assault rifles and a pair of Interdynamic MP9 machine pistols, then loaded several cases of ammunition with them into the van.

Moose's car was parked by Neil's trailer, which sat on Noah's land. Moose and Neil were sitting at a table on his deck, with an umbrella over them to block the sun's bright rays. They waved as Sarah and Noah pulled in, then got up and began walking over toward the bigger house.

"Hey, Boss," Moose called out as he pointed at the van. "We going into the flower business?"

"Yep," Noah said. "Neil, you know how to use CAD software?"

Neil sneered at him. "I knew how to use that when I was in kindergarten," he said. "Why?"

"Wait just a minute," Sarah said, "you guys have got to see this!" She spent the next five minutes showing off the Chrysler's special abilities, and both Moose and Neil were fascinated.

Finally, Noah called a halt to the show. He opened the back of the van and told Moose to grab the big suitcase, bring it inside and set it on the table, and a few moments later Neil's eyes grew wide as the 3-D printer rose from within the concealing suitcase. He did a double take when the computer slid out of the base.

"Holy crap," he said. "Is that what it looks like?"

"Yes and no," Noah said. "It's a 3-D printer, and very fast, but you don't want to be making toys with it." He pointed at the big tank. "It turns that liquid into solid objects which just happen to be extremely explosive. The stuff is very stable, and can't go off without a special detonator. See that little arm off to the side? That thing puts the detonator inside whatever you're making, and there's a way to program it so that we can make it go off when we want it to."

Noah and Sarah spent the next half hour explaining it all to Neil, while he played with the CAD and 3-Sweep programs on the computer and made himself familiar with them. To the surprise of no one, both he and Moose wanted to see the explosive in action, so Noah gave the okay. There were thousands of 3-D images already available in the software, so Neil chose a mouse figurine that was about three inches tall. It would print out the figurine, leaving it hollow.

Noah picked up one of the detonators and plugged it into the remote, then programmed it to channel 1. He set the detonator in the arm's grip, and then nodded at Neil.

The printer began working and the mouse was finished in about three minutes. Noah reached in and picked it up, flipping it casually in the air as he walked out his front door. Sarah followed right behind him, but Moose and Neil were watching closely as he tossed it from hand to hand.

"Hey, Boss, don't you want to be a little more careful with that?" Moose asked.

"Relax, Moose," Sarah said. "Like he told you, it's very stable. It won't go off until he tells it to."

Noah led the way out into the yard and walked directly to a dead tree. The tree was hollow, and he put the little mouse inside a hole near its roots. "I've been meaning to take this tree out, anyway," he said. "Let's see how well this stuff really works."

They backed off about a hundred feet and then Noah turned on the remote. He pressed 1, then immediately put his thumb on the red button and pushed.

The explosion sounded a lot like a shotgun going off, and the base of the tree suddenly seemed to disintegrate into a cloud of dust and dirt. As far away as they were, specks of dirt and tiny splinters of wood managed to hit them, though without any real force. The tree itself stood for a couple of seconds, and then slowly leaned to one side and fell.

"Tim-berrrrr!" Neil yelled, his face covered in a massive grin. "Boss man," he said, "that stuff is awesome!"

Moose had gone by his house and packed up some clothes for the mission, also picking up the special Glock automatic that was the twin of one that Noah carried. It was another of Wally's team's creations, matched wirelessly with a ring that Moose wore on his right hand, and would not fire at all unless the hand holding it was wearing that ring.

Should anyone try to fire the gun without it, a high-voltage charge would be delivered through the grip, more powerful than a commercial stun gun. That person would be completely incapacitated for several minutes. They had not yet run into a situation where it was helpful, but both Noah and Moose agreed that it was a great tool for people in their line of work.

It was almost lunchtime, so Noah suggested they all go out for a bite to eat. They piled into the Chrysler, and Sarah took the wheel.

"Sagebrush?" she asked, and everyone agreed. She wheeled the sedan gently out of the driveway and then floored it. The car leaped forward, pressing everyone back into their seats.

"Good Lord, girl," Moose said from the backseat. "Lead foot, much?"

"Hey, I have to get familiar with this machine. You never know, I may have to pick you two up out of a bad situation. You wouldn't want me to be learning how to drive it in the middle of a firefight, now, would you?"

The in-dash GPS showed a scrolling view of the road, with a bright blue triangle representing the car. The curves in the road seemed a lot sharper on the little video display, and the rapidly moving triangle made it seem like they were going even faster than they probably really were. It seemed like only seconds before they came to the end of the country lane, and then they were on Temple Lake Road. It was just a few miles to the Sagebrush Saloon, but they were very curvy miles. Sarah put the car through its paces, and commented that the all-wheel drive and traction-grip tires made it seem like they were running on rails.

"I don't think so," Neil yelled. "The freaking tires are screaming around these curves, I don't think anything on rails would do that. Would you please slow down? We have enough chances to get killed when we're out on a mission, we don't need to risk it running around here at home!"

"Oh, poor baby," Sarah said, "am I scaring you?" She dropped her speed back down to the limit and drove sedately the rest of the way. When they got out of the car in the Saloon's parking lot, she actually patted it on the roof. "I could get used to driving something like this all the time."

Moose and Neil shook their heads and just walked past her into the restaurant. Noah stood at the front of the car and waited for a moment, then the two of them walked in together.

Elaine Jefferson, Moose's girlfriend, was working that afternoon and happily led them to one of her tables. She knew them all quite well and went to fetch their usual drinks while they thought about what to order for lunch. They had just gotten their orders in when Neil's cell phone rang.

He glanced at the caller ID display and broke into a huge smile, then got up and left the table while he answered the call.

"Must be Lacey," Sarah said. Lacey Jackson, who happened to be the daughter of their physical fitness instructor and was almost as tall and thin as the six-foot-five Neil, had introduced herself to him in the Saloon a few weeks before and they had become quite involved. It wasn't uncommon to see Lacey's car parked over at the trailer in the mornings. "She's been pretty good for him. Notice he's growing up a little bit, lately?"

"Neil? Growing up?" Moose asked, then looked over at Noah. "What kind of dope is she smoking lately? That kid ain't never gonna grow up."

Noah shrugged. "Actually, I think he's been a lot better lately. He doesn't whine nearly as much as he used to."

"Yes, he does," Moose said. "It just seems like it's not as much because he isn't constantly complaining about not having a girlfriend. Now he spends all his time complaining about not getting to spend enough time with his girlfriend."

"Which proves my point," Sarah said.

Moose shook his head. "Yeah, yeah, you keep on believing whatever you want to. Trust me, he's still a whiner."

"Yeah, maybe so, but you love him. You proved that when you took a bullet dragging him out of the line of fire, remember?"

"I never said I didn't," Moose said with a grin. "He's like the annoying little brother I never had. I always wanted one, just so I could pick on him, but Mom and Dad wouldn't cooperate. Now I got Neil, I'm making up for lost time."

Neil came back to the table just then, still smiling.

"You guys don't mind if Lacey comes out to join us, do you? She went by the trailer and I wasn't home, so she called to see where I was."

"Oh-oh," Moose said. "When a girl gets to the point she's checking up to see where you are when you're not home, things must be getting pretty serious. Next thing you know, you'll have to ask for her permission to go on a mission with us." He put on an effeminate grin and tried to imitate Lacey's voice. "Okay, honey, you can go. Here's your balls, just make sure you get them back to me when you get home."

Neil gave him a sneer and stuck out his tongue. "Lacey isn't like that," he said. "She really cares about me, that's all."

Sarah watched the exchange with her eyes wide, then looked at Moose. "You're right, I take it back."

"Take what back?" Neil demanded.

"She just got through trying to tell me you had grown up since you started dating Lacey," Moose said. "I said you hadn't, and sticking your tongue out at me just proved my point."

Moose caught Elaine's attention and waved her over. "Honey, Lacey's gonna be joining us. Can we get another chair over here?"

Lacey arrived a little more than ten minutes later and took her seat beside Neil. She leaned over to give him a kiss and Neil blushed. "Hey, sweetie," she said, and then she looked at the rest of them. "Hope I'm not intruding."

"You're not," Sarah said, "and now that you're here, I don't feel quite as surrounded by testosterone as I did a minute ago. Thanks for coming."

"De nada, Chica," Lacey said. "Thanks for letting me barge in."

Elaine showed up only a few seconds later carrying a large tray and a folding stand. She flipped the stand open and set the tray on top, then begin passing out their orders. "Lacey, almost every time you come in here with Neil, you order the same thing he does. I hope it's okay, I went ahead and gave you an Italian beef like his."

Lacey smiled at her, delighted. "That's perfect," she said. "Thank you."

They dug in to eat, talking about inconsequential things. While Lacey and Elaine were privy to the type of work the team did, both of them being the daughters of top E & E people, most of the customers of the Saloon were simply local folk who knew nothing. As a result, mission work was rarely discussed there, and only when they were certain they could not be overheard.

Noah had already told his team that he was planning for them to leave for Missouri the following morning, so they decided to just hang out and relax for a while at the Saloon. It was nearly four o'clock by the time they finally left, and Neil rode home with Lacey rather than get back into the Chrysler with Sarah driving. Sarah kept the car under control, however, and her lead foot as well. Lacey stayed right behind her all the way, and they all ended up at Noah's house.

When they turned onto the county lane, Sarah quickly reached down and pushed one of the color buttons while Lacey was out of sight. When they pulled up at the house and got out, she barely managed to keep from laughing when she saw Lacey staring at the now-red car.

Neil hurried Lacey inside to see the printer, but Noah refused to allow another demonstration of what it could do. Despite a short and mostly friendly argument, he refused to budge, so Neil took her out to see the remains of the tree.

Sarah looked at Noah. "You okay?"

"Yeah," he said. "It's just interesting, watching Neil trying to grow up. I'm seeing things in his behavior that I've never noticed before in other people."

"That's because," Sarah said with a chuckle, "you've never had to deal with an insecure teenager before. Neil has been lonely and scared most of his life, I think, partly because of how tall he is. People expect a tall guy like that to be athletic, but Neil never quite made it. It's probably made him self-conscious."

Noah nodded his head. "Yeah, that's what I'm seeing. It's interesting."

Lacey hung around with them for a couple of hours, but then Noah suggested it was time for her to head home. He had come up with a mission plan and it was time for him to go over it with the team. Neil walked her out and kissed her goodbye, then came back in with a long face and took his seat at the table.

"Okay, here's what I'm planning," Noah said. "We're going to spend a few days playing flower delivery. Neil, your job is going to be making sure we have accurate location intel on each of the targets, then using the printer to turn out flowerpots and vases. We'll want a lot of different designs, don't want them all to be exactly the same or that might arouse suspicion."

Neil nodded. "Okay, I'll try to learn everything I can about the targets, so that I can sort of gear the designs toward what they might like."

"Smart thinking," Noah said. He turned to Moose. "Moose, you will be on flower duty. I'll send you out to other cities in the area, like Jefferson City or Springfield, to buy flowers and plants and potting soil, stuff like that."

"Got it," Moose said.

"Sarah, you and I will be scouting. I want to get an eyeball on every target, and particularly on those two little kids. I've got to figure out a way to get them out of the line of fire and I'm not sure how to go about that just yet."

"Okay," Sarah said.

"Now, I don't want the van to be seen around the hotel, so we need to find someplace to use as a base of operations. Neil, see what you can come up with. If you can arrange for us to have a building somewhere by the time we get there, that would be great."

"Shouldn't be a problem," Neil said. He took out his phone and began poking at it. "Just scanning over Craigslist for that area, I can see quite a few possibilities. There's an old warehouse building in an industrial park. The rent isn't too bad, not that we really care about that. Privately owned—want me to call them now?"

Noah nodded. "Yes, go ahead. It would be good if we could have it ready to go into tomorrow night, when we get there."

Buy In Sheep's Clothing now:
davidarcherbooks.com/in-sheeps-clothing

Be the first to receive Noah Wolf updates. Sign up here:
davidarcherbooks.com/noah-updates

ALSO BY DAVID ARCHER

Not all books have been made into paperbacks yet, but I'm working on getting them all formatted and available as soon as possible.
Up to date paperbacks can be found on my website: davidarcherbooks.com/pb

ALEX MASON THRILLER
Odin (Book 1)
Ice Cold Spy (Book 2)
Mason's Law (Book 3)
Assets and Liabilities (Book 4)

NOAH WOLF THRILLERS
Code Name Camelot (Book 1)
Lone Wolf (Book 2)
In Sheep's Clothing (Book 3)
Hit for Hire (Book 4)
The Wolf's Bite (Book 5)
Black Sheep (Book 6)
Balance of Power (Book 7)
Time to Hunt (Book 8)
Red Square (Book 9)
Highest Order (Book 10)
Edge of Anarchy (Book 11)
Unknown Evil (Book 12)
Black Harvest (Book 13)

World Order (Book 14)
Caged Animal (Book 15)
Deep Allegiance (Book 16)
Pack Leader (Book 17)
High Treason (Book 18)
A Wolf Among Men (Book 19)
Rogue Intelligence (Book 20)

SAM PRICHARD MYSTERIES
The Grave Man (Book 1)
Death Sung Softly (Book 2)
Love and War (Book 3)
Framed (Book 4)
The Kill List (Book 5)
Drifter: Part One (Book 6)
Drifter: Part Two (Book 7)
Drifter: Part Three (Book 8)
The Last Song (Book 9)
Ghost (Book 10)
Hidden Agenda (Book 11)

SAM AND INDIE MYSTERIES
Aces and Eights (Book 1)
Fact or Fiction (Book 2)
Close to Home (Book 3)
Brave New World (Book 4)
Innocent Conspiracy (Book 5)
Unfinished Business (Book 6)
Live Bait (Book 7)
Alter Ego (Book 8)
More Than It Seems (Book 9)
Moving On (Book 10)
Worst Nightmare (Book 11)
Chasing Ghosts (Book 12)

Made in United States
North Haven, CT
14 April 2023

35442267R00176